About the author

Kevin Parr has written for many years as Angling Correspondent to *The Idler*, for *Countryfile Magazine* and the Caught by the River website. He lives in Dorset with his wife. *The Twitch* is his first novel.

The Twitch

The Twitch

Kevin Parr

unbound

The limited edition published in 2013
The trade edition published in 2014

Unbound
4–7 Manchester Street, Marylebone, London, W1U 2AE
www.unbound.co.uk

Typeset by Lorna Morris
Cover design by Mecob

A CIP record for this book is available from the British Library

ISBN 978-1-908717-98-6 (Trade)
ISBN 978-1-908717-97-9 (Ebook)
ISBN 978-1-908717-99-3 (Limited Edition)

Printed in England by Clays Ltd, Bungay, Suffolk

To Sue-Sue – thank you for being you.

JANUARY

I'm not certain whose head I can see the top of, bobbing rhythmically into view above the low brick wall by the potting shed. There's a little plume of steam billowing up into the cold air: up and down, up and down. The hair colour's hard to discern in the moonlight, as both Mick and our landlady share differing shades of grey-flecked mousy mess.

Ah. It's stopped – and presuming whatever form of sexual encounter I was privy to has now reached its conclusion, Mick will soon be padding through the bedroom door full of drunken guilt – possibly crying, but certainly in need of his bed.

Tomorrow, of course, the bravado will be back and Mick will be bragging that he could have had the barmaid, or the girl in the petrol station or any one of the females we met throughout the day, but instead *chose* to shag the less-than-attractive, middle-aged landlady of this little Cornish B&B because nothing could quite compare with the experience; a lady with no inhibition who knew just what she wanted and just how to please a man.

No, Mick, I quite agree. If I were in your position, there's no way I would have blown out a chance with that ridiculously cute little barmaid in favour of a muddy roll in the garden with dear Mrs Bellchambers as her husband sleeps upstairs. And as for *her* experience, well, surely your encounter two years ago was enough to keep you out of Cornwall, leave alone the same bloody guesthouse.

Here he comes – will he speak? Cry …? No. Straight into bed, not a word, duvet pulled tight over his head.

If I sound slightly bitter, it's because I am. Today we were supposed to grip a gyr falcon: not just a near mega-tick on the first day of the year, but a lifer for me. I fear, however, that there never was a gyr. Instead I've been convinced to charge down to Cornwall, hungover, on New Year's Day, for the sake of Mick's libido – and his pride. His sudden decision to leave the party last night two hours before midnight seemed to neatly coincide with an apparent rebuff from the girl with the brown bob – Jackie's cousin, I believe. Mick would never admit to it, not with his ego, but he isn't the man he was twenty years ago; the hair is thinner and much greyer, the eyes are tired and the belly's hard to hide even under the baggiest of shirts.

At twenty-four, though, Mick had the looks and the jabber to back them up. He worked his way through most of the girls in Surrey, had an eighteen-month shagfest in Bristol, and then returned to marry Kerrie Bowers, the hottest girl in Guildford. The fact that Kerrie was in the kitchen last night as Mick leered all over the girl with the brown bob – accompanied by her sister-in-law to boot – was further proof of his utter delusion. Successfully pull and then what? Sneak her upstairs and hope no one noticed? Because if Kerrie got wind of anything untoward and her brothers found out, then, by God, I would not want to be in Mick's shoes.

Fortunately for Mick, though, the girl with the brown bob was quick to dash his efforts with a sneer of disgust, and I was probably the only one to notice his humiliation – and certainly the only person slightly suspicious of his announcement minutes later that he was going home, to bed, in order to be up before dawn. A probable American golden plover had just been sighted at the London Wetland Centre in Barnes, his pager had buzzed to tell him. At half nine on New Year's Eve? Did he think everyone was daft? Someone was calling an American golden in the pitch black at a wetland centre that closed at *five*?

Still, I was gullible enough to buy his gyr story this morning.

'What about the American golden?' I asked.

Mick paused.

'False ID,' he muttered, 'but the gyr is a definite.'

'But I've been paged bugger all ...' I reached for my pager. The message box was still empty, though I couldn't help noticing the time. 'Mick, it's not even seven. Who the fuck is down at Land's End calling a gyr on New Year's Day when the bloody sun hasn't even come up?'

'Tom. Picked it up yesterday afternoon. Sent me a text, which I didn't get until this morning. He wants to hush it for his bird race today.'

Cornish Tom was a regular Cornwall tip-off and a reliable caller, reporting both the white-billed and pacific divers at Hale in October before anyone else had a sniff and finding the gyr last March on three consecutive days; a bird I'd dipped on three consecutive days.

This news gave Mick's phone call a little more credence. The Cornish New Year's Day bird race was one of the biggies, so it would be natural for Tom to keep schtum on a gyr; it could give him the edge.

'Okay, I'll come. But not for a couple of hours – I need to have a stern word with Nicola this morning. She didn't roll in until five.'

'Gave some lad a very Happy New Year, no doubt, lucky sod.'

'She's fifteen, Mick …'

'And regularly plucked, Ted. I'll pick you up at eleven.'

He was right, no doubt. My second daughter certainly acts as though she's sexually active. But I did *not* appreciate my best mate making lurid reference to her, his bloody goddaughter, in fact. Sick. And, with hindsight, it was Mick's lecherous behaviour – and the subsequent explosive confrontation between Nicola, Abi and myself – that had distracted me enough not to question Mick's contentment to not leave until eleven. With at least four and a half hours on the road, we would have less than an hour of daylight, at best, to find the gyr. Futile, surely? Normally, Mick would be champing at the bit; outside, tooting the horn, within minutes. 'It'll fly, it'll fly!' he would panic, before breaking every speed limit en route. Today, though, he seemed happy to plod along at seventy, even on the dual carriageway, and I might have read more into that had I not been so damned tired and so confused about Abi's indifference this morning to her daughter's behaviour; she'd all but condoned it, in fact.

'What was his name?' she'd whispered as I left the room post-rant, referring to the eighteen-year-old pervert who had been knobbing our daughter while the rest of the country had been cheering in 2007. 'Was', she had asked, *was* – past tense – not 'is', not 'what-*is*-the-name-of-this-boy-you-admit-to-sleeping-with-and-who-therefore-must-be-a-long-term-boyfriend-because-otherwise-you-wouldn't-dare-consider-dropping-your-knickers-until-you-had-spent-months-getting-to-know-him-and-earning-his-respect'. No. My wife said 'was'. To my little girl who's still six months from sexual legality, my wife enquired, 'what was the name of your one-night-stand?'

Half two already. I've gone beyond tired. I may as well sit up and wait for Mick to stir in that early morning burst of sobriety that wakes you so rudely after a night on the sauce. He'll want to leave immediately – desperate to avoid Mrs Bellchambers, despite her award-winning breakfast. If I stay awake now, I can sleep all the way home. At least that way I can avoid the steady torrent of self-proclaimed sexual prowess dribbling out of Mick's mouth, the showboating becoming ever more vociferous as we near home and he tries to suppress his guilt and fear.

At the moment, though, Mick is snoring like a trooper – honking out a stench of stale booze (and I don't want to think what else) with every rasping breath. He put an awful lot of Mermaid's Revenge away in the relatively short time that we were in the pub.

Naturally, there had been no gyr falcon, and no sign of Cornish Tom. Mick didn't seem at all surprised and remained unperturbed that the only room we could get was back at the Porthcove Guest House; the very same room that we shared two years ago on my first ever twitch. I say shared, but Mick spent that night next door in Mrs Bellchambers's bedchamber, tending to her needs while her husband was away tending to his ailing mother.

This time the husband's home but was fizzing when we arrived, an empty keg of scrumpy already under the table. Mick insisted that he came to the pub with us and got the poor old bugger straight on the single malts. Within an hour he was on the floor and the landlord was driving him home to bed. Another half an hour and Mick suddenly announced he needed his bed, just after that text ...

I just checked his phone. **He's asleep** reads the last text received: the stupid sod's given her his number this time. A long way to come to get over his shun from the girl with the brown bob. And one hell of a guaranteed lay! Mrs Bellchambers ... well, she's certainly all woman.

I may as well tot up my first day total: 59 species. Dreadful. It's not a sprint, I know, but that's a pitiful effort, not least because there's *nothing* special there – I suppose the barn owl can be a mildly tricky tick, but the rest I could have picked up in a lunchtime stroll to the Barleymow. Mick's list will already be 150-odd. It's cheating, really, but he ticks all the 'dead certs' first thing on January 1st every year.

'The race is twelve months long, Ted,' he argues, 'and I will, without doubt, see all of these ticks by the end of December. This way I don't miss anything stupid off.'

He has a point. In 1999, Scott Mitchings, whose list was always completed chronologically, missed out on the title by one species only to notice a month too late that he had forgotten to include woodlark. Woodlark! A schoolboy error, and it was too late; his final list had already been accepted. Today, of course, everyone ticks a box for fear of 'doing a Mitchings', but Mick's own special method isn't foolproof. He admitted to me this evening that he couldn't recall having actually seen a little owl all year – and yet he had ticked the box, probably on January 1st, and submitted the list. Perhaps I should expose him to the board. Harsh, but fair – and he would most likely face a lifetime expulsion ...

I've just checked his list for 2007 and little owl is unticked. For the moment, at least, the board will remain uninformed.

I must admit that I came very close to shelving it this year. My heart's simply not been in it for much of this month.

Work hasn't helped. I got dragged into Whitcombe's office on the first day back after Christmas to discuss my sickness record. Apparently, I seem to have had a worrying number of single and half-days off sick in the last year, and obviously any ongoing health problems are of great concern to the Service. I muttered something about recurring migraines, and Whitcombe nodded impassively. I'd be a bit more open with a decent boss – I mean, let's be honest, if a brown shrike turns up at Box Hill, I'm hardly going to be fretting about Mrs Chakrabati's deputising allowance, or Terry's sick note for his angina – but I should be aware, Whitcombe lectures, of my duty to those on my desk – *my team* – and should most certainly be seeking medical advice for an ongoing affliction that may cause long-term issues for my managerial capacity.

Blah, blah – I let it wash over me. Though I'll have to be a bit more careful this year; I've already warned Abi that she might have to take the girls away without me in November if my holiday quota's spent. I've since toed the line at work, though, and Whitcombe has stopped passing my desk every morning these last few days, so he should be satisfied for a little while at least. He was happy enough to let me sneak off an hour early this afternoon for the awards ceremony, though until lunchtime I had been pondering my own attendance. Then Mick emerged from his near month-long incommunicado, hallooing down the phone with his usual gusto.

'You've got to go, Ted – you can't let the crowd down.'

'I suppose not …'

'Of *course* not – Rook of the Year! Come on, mate – you can only win it once. My mate Chip, Rook of the Year … and I haven't seen you for weeks. I'll drive, mate, I will happily drive.'

That made the event more tempting. The venue was some pub near Reading, so the prospect of a few pre-award ales was a pleasant one. Plus, the Focus was back at Ford for its 60k service and the thought of turning up in Abi's Ka just didn't wash. Anyway, I was, after all, Rook of the Year for 2006 – with a total only one away from the all-time record for a rookie. I had to go.

So I did. And the lauding and plaudits from my competitors stirred up the passion again, though I was cagey with my efforts this year, brushing off the inevitable questions with indifference when in truth I had all but stopped ticking already.

My own reception was nothing compared to that of Rod 'Emu' Smyth: overall champion for the second consecutive year, an achievement marked by the scope guard of honour, lenses pointing skyward as he left the podium. They raised the roof for him, helped on by the beer, and I decided there and then that I wanted a piece of it. Nigh on two hundred people on their feet, cheering and applauding. I knew many of the faces, and recognised some that had been casting doubts on some of Rod's ticks through the previous twelve months. Not tonight, though. Tonight they loved him. Tonight he was invincible. Tonight he was a god.

'He'll get laid tonight, no question,' Mick chattered on the way home, 'Rod – I mean Emu. They were all over him.'

'There weren't exactly many women there though, Mick.' I was mindful of Mick's driving. He'd had more than his two-pint limit, and was back to his pacy old self. 'I should slow down a bit, Mick – not worth losing your licence.'

'I'm fine, Ted, fine. And if we get pulled over we just show 'em our trophies! They'll probably want an autograph and let us on our way.'

Mick had also left the event with silverware: a small shield recognising his fifth consecutive top twenty finish. A nice touch, but very much a Best Costume Oscar compared to my Best

Actor. Rook of the Year was the second-to-last award of the evening – second most prestigious in other words – and was an award that had eluded Mick. He was trying to be gracious, but I knew deep down that he would be oozing with jealousy, particularly as he'd had such an influence on my achievement. I thanked him in my speech, of course, and bigged him up a little, pointing out that despite so many shared journeys, he had still beaten me by five ticks (including the phantom little owl, which I didn't mention) which was a country mile at this level of birding. Mick didn't much appreciate my little dig at the New Year trip, however, in which I suggested that, though he'd dipped out on a gyr falcon, he'd dipped into a bit of Cornish pasty.

'What if that gets back to Kerrie?' he scolded me afterwards.

'It won't,' I assured him, 'everyone thought I was having a poke at your belly.'

Mick visibly breathed in.

'It's just a little pot,' he pleaded, 'a sign of good living.'

Cornish Tom was among those quick to shake my hand afterwards, and quick to mention our Cornish debacle.

'Who sent you off to my patch for a gyr, then?'

'Er, you did, Tom. Apparently.'

I'd turned to Mick for clarification, but he had slipped away, well aware that the final thread of his wild gyr chase was unravelling. I was quick to mention it on the way home, however, though Mick was ready for it.

'Ah, you know Tom,' he reasoned, 'getting a bit forgetful in his old age. Or keeping his cards close to his chest. Either way, he was pretty bloody pissed by the time we left – propping the bar up with Emu, he was.' Mick was gabbling again. 'Spoke to Emu when we arrived – he reckons the board might be extended to a dozen. They're due to discuss it at tomorrow's AGM. Imagine that, Chip – it could be me and you. Just think …'

Both of our awards now give us select eligibility to join the board as and when a vacancy arises, and I'd certainly love a seat, despite the fact that half the members are jumped up little pricks. No one outside of that elite panel of ten has won the individual trophy for seventeen years, mainly because being on the board carries both perks and prestige. If two members are both witness to a mega-sighting, photographic evidence isn't required for acceptance, no matter how mega the mega. And being on the board means you aren't going to miss a trick, either. Most people, especially the less serious birders, get so excited at a mega-sighting that they submit the details there and then. The board have a code of conduct where they share tip-offs, and bingo, it's not unheard of for all ten board members to be on site within a few hours of a bird's discovery.

For the time being, though, my thoughts are very much fixed on this year's campaign. I'm not aiming top twenty, or top ten. I want top spot. And though I've wasted much of January fretting over errant family and friends and being far too work-conscientious for my own good, it's been a pretty unspectacular month for everyone. I missed a few biggies, though nothing that shouldn't reappear later in the year. Now I just need to focus and get a game plan together.

'I'm thinking of Sheppey tomorrow, Mick – do you fancy it?' I asked on the way home tonight.

'Damn right. I'll drive. But it's the last Saturday of the month, Ted, isn't that yours and Abi's special evening in – *sans* kids but avec erection?'

Bugger. It was, too – just when my twitching fire had re-ignited, the flames were going to be dampened by the prospect of cosy marital sex.

'I'll think of something, Mick – we've got to get to Sheppey while the rough-leggeds are about.'

Rough-legged buzzard, marsh harrier, Jack snipe, bittern, smew, bearded tit – the list could go on, but suffice to say a weekend in Sheppey has very much kick-started this year's campaign. I'm still over twenty species short on January of last year, but from here on in my planning will be meticulous.

I knew Sheppey could tick a lot of boxes just as long as I kept calm, kept to the schedule and didn't fart-arse about. No time for admiring: the only bird I would pause over would be one requiring a photograph, and none did. Job very well done.

I nearly didn't make it, though. Mick dropped me off on Friday evening without leaving his new mobile number (he had officially 'lost' his old mobile phone, though in reality it lay at the bottom of the Basingstoke canal, probably still gurgling with endless texts from Mrs Bellchambers). I'd told Mick not to call round unless I texted to confirm I'd got the all-clear – otherwise, I would train it down to Sittingbourne and meet him at the station.

First up was Abi, though, and a subject that would be tricky to tackle. With a few beers inside me, however, I tried my luck as soon as I got home from the awards.

'Sorry darling, I know we only have one evening a month alone together, but –'

'No need to explain, Ed,' Abi had interrupted, 'I spoke to Kerrie this evening – you should have told me. No need to be embarrassed. Just don't share a tent next time.'

I had absolutely no idea what my wife was talking about, but happily went with it. A weekend pass was seemingly secured, and if she had spoken to Kerrie it was obviously because of a story Mick had hatched.

Mick! I couldn't call him – and a check on the train times revealed engineering works were closing off most of Kent for the weekend. And I couldn't use the Ka; Abi was taking Lucy into town to get their hair done, reward for success in her A-level mocks. Fortunately, my phone bleeped – an unknown number, but it had to be Mick. **If Abi mentions little friends go with it. Will explain. Pick u up @0500.** The gist was nonsensical, but all I needed to hear was the final part. Sheppey was on, and Mick could elaborate the cryptics en route.

'Sorry about that, Ted – I didn't realise Kerrie would phone Abi while we were out.'

Mick had been seriously grumpy when he picked me up, and half an hour into the journey was only just starting to communicate, now that the carbs and caffeine from our Maccy D breakfast were kicking in.

'You see, Joyce – er, Mrs Bellchambers – gave me some … *friends* to remember her by. And I promptly passed them on to Kerrie. I had to think on my feet.'

'Crabs?' I was slow on the uptake.

'Yeah, lice – Kerrie was fuming at first – who'd I caught them off? Rah! Rah!

So I sold her a story. Said that you and I had both got them – caught them off Cornish Tom.'

'Why the fuck would we catch crabs off Cornish Tom?'

'I told her we'd shared a tent, the three of us, and Cornish must have been riddled because we were scratching all the way home and had to torch the tent in a lay-by.'

'Torch the tent? Mick, what bloody tent? And why would we be in a tent in the middle of winter?'

'I know, I know, it sounded dodgy as I said it, but Kerrie bought every word. And I told her that you had struggled with the itchiness so I had lent you the rest of my cream …'

'Touching, Mick – thanks – but now my wife thinks that I've got bloody *lice*!'

'Erm, not anymore, she doesn't. But, er, she does think that you have no pubes. The cream is a moisturiser, or something. Kerrie gave it to me after I shaved mine off – she uses it on her legs. Stops the irritation when the hairs start growing back.'

I was speechless. Momentarily.

'You utter bastard, Mick. You nail some aging old crone who gives you lice, and it's me, an innocent bystander, who ends up with no bloody integrity!'

'And no pubes.'

'Eh?'

'You mustn't forget – Abi thinks you've shaved 'em off. I brought a razor for you; thought we could duck into Clackett Lane. Sooner the better.'

Again, I was struggling for words. Mick was suggesting a stop at the motorway services so that I could use the toilets to shave myself – *down there* – in order to continue the charade he had created to cover his own infidelity.

'Mick … I just don't know what to say …'

'A "thank you" would be a start, Ted. It's a Mach 3 razor, you know. Not cheap, and I'm not going to use it again. Oh, and another benefit – no pubes equals bigger cock. Or, at least, it looks that way. Even your chipolata will look like *eine grosse Bratwurst* in half an hour or so!'

That final sentiment had an element of truth to it, as I shortly discovered, but I hadn't felt so self-conscious of my nether regions since my vasectomy, and I made little other than small talk from the moment we left Clackett Lane until mid-afternoon. It was only then, and with the sudden appearance of a rough-legged buzzard, that my paranoia eased and I finally accepted that my fly wasn't undone – the draught I felt was for an altogether different reason. The rough-legged was a big moment, though, and perked me up no end. I even laughed once or twice in the pub that evening and slept like a stone in the B&B, waking early on Sunday with an urge to get straight back out there. I woke Mick at six.

'Time to get up, Mick – we ditch breakfast, go bag a beardie and bittern, quick pub lunch and home for the football. The Blues kick off at four.'

'Bloody hell, Ted – can I at least have a bleedin' muck out?'

The morning went like clockwork: utter proof of the value

of planning. We knew after three weekends on Sheppey last year exactly where the birds would be and, sure enough, a pre-planned route had us ticking all the boxes. The only downside was seeing John 'Peregrine' Perry's Volvo pulled up on the verge just outside Eastchurch.

'What's Perry the Prick found there, then?' Mick's question was rhetorical, though I was equally curious.

No one calls him Peregrine – at least, no one who knows him well does. Peregrine was a self-given nickname, and far too grand a nickname for such a snivelling little sod as Perry. He is on the board, mind you, and a very successful birder, winning the title back in 1997, and doesn't he like to remind you. That's the problem with Perry. He's one of those guys who give twitchers a bad name: arrogant, ignorant and with zero respect for his peers and the general public.

The American robin in Grimsby was a prime example. It was skulking in a private garden with a whopping six-foot fence keeping it out of sight from the two hundred-plus birders crowded around the cul-de-sac. Then Perry turned up, and he wanted his tick. He couldn't climb the fence, so he kicked it down, and then bagged the robin (along with everyone else) as it fled in terror. The owner was out in a second, and Perry just squared up to him.

'Try it,' he threatened, motioning to the crowd behind him, 'and we'll burn your fuckin' house down.' The owner legged it, poor old bloke, not realising that if he *had* laid one on Perry, the crowd behind would have cheered.

For Mick and me, though, seeing that Volvo reminded us that for all we were bagging over the weekend, one of our main competitors had also ticked, and now he was parked off the beaten track, perhaps bagging something spectacular. We both reached for our pagers – nothing showing – but wouldn't you know it, three hours later as we pulled in the Medway Arms on the way off Sheppey, the same black Volvo was tucked into the car park. Mick couldn't help himself.

'What did you bag then, Perry? By Eastchurch. Saw you parked up there.'

We hadn't even reached the bar.

'That'd be telling, Michael,' Perry smirked, 'but I'll post it this evening, once the whole of the board are aware.' He turned to me. 'Good weekend, Rookie? Down for the rough-legs, I suppose. You'll need a few biggies this year, though, now you're mixing it with the big boys.'

Knob, I thought, and turned to Mick.

'Let's get going – the ale's rubbish in here.'

'I need a crap first.' Mick seemed happy enough to miss out on a pub lunch. 'I'll see you outside.'

I nodded vaguely in Perry's direction and left, suddenly aware in the cold air that I would need a pee before going much further. A pile of old pallets at the end of the car park made a handy shield and I steamed out a steady dribble whilst visualising Perry's head squashed beneath the wooden slats. A nail hung limply from the broken bottom pallet, and having failed to work it loose with my piss, I hatched another idea. Perry might be leaving Sheppey with a mega, but he would also be leaving with a puncture. I propped the nail under the inside edge of the off-side front tyre – unavoidable for Perry as he had to reverse on that angle in order to get out of that space – and was waiting for Mick as he wandered out of the pub door.

'Where shall we eat then, Mick?' I called.

'Clackett Lane, I guess, Ted – let's hope the toilets aren't blocked with your short and curlies.'

The toilets weren't blocked, and our lunch was swift and functional – I was still eager to get back for the football. Chelsea could be going top that day. I needn't have hurried, though, as we pulled back out onto the M25 and all three lanes were empty.

'Must have been a smash,' Mick commented. 'At least Perry won't be getting back home too early.'

'No, he won't,' I said, smiling.

FEBRUARY

The pager's been relatively quiet over the last week or so. There's plenty of good stuff knocking about, but mostly long-stayers, and I can tie them in with my weekend routing. High pressure has dominated the weather, meaning little wind and little likelihood of anything unexpected showing up and frazzling the pager network.

With this in mind, this weekend's route was easy to plan, and Abi was more than happy for me to have an overnighter as long as I was happy for her to get her hair done on Saturday. After sitting with Lucy last Saturday while her respectable shoulder-length bob was hacked into a weird floppy-fringed mess, Abi decided she wanted something similar, and as it turns out, she's had an identical cut.

I'm not impressed. She's thirty-seven, not seventeen, and should keep herself looking a little more respectable. How will I be taken seriously at work functions when my wife's floppy fringe means she can't even look someone in the eye? I'm a *manager*, for God's sake. And the way she's spent this evening flicking her head in order to keep both eyes on the telly – she looks like she's got a facial tic.

'Well, you have a nice new trendy cut,' she argued, during the adverts.

'I have a respectable, modern style,' I affirmed, 'suitable for the office, but identifiable by my younger subordinates.'

'It's messy.'

'It's tousled. There's a difference.'

I opted for an early start on Saturday and headed down to south Dorset, the only downside being that I would have to drive. It was Kerrie's birthday weekend, and Mick didn't dare miss it. Her family were big on birthdays, and they would all have been round on Saturday; Kerrie always likes an old-fashioned tea party. Fancy cakes and little crust-free sandwiches. Her brothers would have been drinking beer, but everyone else would stick with the Tetley – squash for the kids – and Mick doesn't dare drink at all, for fear of his loosened tongue getting him in trouble. He lives in utter fear of his brothers-in-law, and rightly so: the three Bowers Boys may all now be in their forties, but they're just as menacing, and wouldn't think twice about pummelling Mick into dust if he stepped out of line with their baby sister.

It does work both ways, though. Mick used to get into many a scrape when we were in our late teens and early twenties. He'd either get pissed and mouth off or get pissed and shag someone's girlfriend – either way, he'd have a fat lip on a Saturday morning. That all changed when he started seeing Kerrie, though. Obviously he wasn't still out shagging, but he would still get verbal after a few – only now, the whisper would go round, 'that's Kerrie Bowers's boyfriend', and anyone with any sense in Woking would back off.

Of course, Mick being Mick, he didn't see this new invincibility as a temporary and misplaced privilege. Instead he fancied himself as a bit of a boy, and abused his newfound status at every opportunity, pushing in at the bar and generally getting louder and cockier than ever before. People would leave him to it, but you could see the resentment building. One day, down at the George with two of Kerrie's brothers – I can't remember which – Mick overstepped the mark.

He fancied a game of pool, and strode over to the chalkboard, scrubbed it clean, and wrote his name at the top. Immediately, a couple of the kids in the pool room took offence.

'Oi, mate – you can't do that!'

'Yes I fucking can,' Mick snapped – ever the diplomat.

One of the guys playing at the time followed Mick out into the bar, pool-cue in hand, calling him back, only to stop in his tracks when he saw who Mick was drinking with. But, with Mick grinning as smugly as only he can, his brothers-in-law calmly went over, had a whispered conversation with the chap, took the pool cue, and then wandered straight out of the pub.

I wish I'd seen it (Roddy, the barman, saw it all), but Mick's face must have been a picture. The pool player strode over, plonked a fist straight onto Mick's nose, and went back through to the pool room. The Bowers Boys then wandered back in, gave the cue back and returned to their pints, muttering to Mick something along the lines of, 'if you can't back it up, don't dish it out'. Mick was blubbing by this point and stumbled home with a bloody nose and a lesson learnt.

And the chap with the pool cue got taught a lesson, too. The boys followed him outside as he left and gave him a ten-second pasting, explaining to Roddy afterwards that, despite being a twat, Mick was still family.

Lodmoor, in Weymouth, was the first port of call, where I nailed a spoonbill within minutes of arriving. A user-friendly bird, the spoonbill: big, white, and both confident and unmistakable. Pintail (not sure how I missed that so far) and black-necked grebe soon followed and meant three new ticks by half eight.

I texted Mick the news of my grip-off, knowing it would wind him up, and got an abrupt reply: **Beware the killer gulls.**

A bit below the belt, that. He knows how much I dislike gulls, and it isn't a phobia; I have good reason. It did prompt me to have a quick scan of the birds on the marsh, though, and Mediterranean and yellow-legged gulls were ticked before I began to get a shiver. The rest of the gulls can wait, for now. I can wait for a Ross's or Sabine's Gull to appear and hope to tick a few others at the same time. Hopefully, Mick will be around at the time and will drive us, meaning I at least can have a sip or two of something to calm my nerves.

Another bleep. The pager this time, and one of those moments when the sun and planets must have momentarily aligned: a solitary sandpiper had been called at Radipole Lake. A mega – a lifer for me – was potentially a mile away, at the very place I was next headed. My head began to swim. Mick would know; he would have got the same alert, and, sure enough, my phone hummed with another text from him. **You at Radipole?** he asked. *I will be, Mick,* I thought. But I couldn't reply yet. My fingers were cold and unlocking the car was proving a pain in the arse.

To anyone not in the know, Lodmoor and Radipole are two sites in Weymouth almost within scoping vision of one another, and I reached the latter in a couple of minutes. I was surprised to see only a couple of cars parked, but figured that I must have been one of the first here, barring the spotter. On the plus side, one of the cars I recognised belonged to Mike 'Penguin' Phelps, member of the board and 2004 champion. This was exceptional news, not just because I had his mobile number and could now head straight to the spot, but also because his presence both added credence to the call and increased the likelihood that another board member might just appear and give all present a solid, certified tick.

Another text from Mick. Again I ignored it – for the moment, at least. I found Mike and four other birders, all with smiles the size of a spoonbill's bill, though Mike's expression quickly changed when he saw me.

'Edward,' he shook my hand solemnly, 'good to see you. Terrible news about poor old Peregrine.' I must have looked at him blankly, as he quickly continued. 'You haven't heard? John Perry passed away yesterday – he'd been in a coma since that awful crash on Sunday.'

'I didn't know,' I uttered. In fact, I hadn't even heard that he'd been in a prang, though that might explain why the M25 was so empty when we left the services last weekend.

'The board felt it best to keep tight-lipped on it this week – out of respect for his family …' The board. Yes, of course; with Perry dead, there would be a vacancy on the board. Blimey, if there really was a solitary sandpiper in the reed bed beyond those scopes, I would be sending Mick the biggest double whammy in texting history. '… the funeral is a week today – Bath crem,' Mike continued.

Funeral. Next Friday. I had to pinch myself to check I wasn't dreaming. Whitcombe would *have* to give me the day off for a close friend's funeral in Bath. Opportunity knocks. I could stay down on the Friday night, bag a couple of ticks on the Saturday morning, and be back home in plenty of time for a shit and a shower before mine and Abi's rearranged 'evening in'. Another two-day tickathon without anyone getting the arse!

'Sorry, Ted,' – Mike was talking again – 'must be a bit of a shock for you. Come on, this little fella will cheer you up.' He motioned in the direction of the one telescope not currently being gawped into by an excitable birder, and I happily accepted the invitation. And there it was – or rather, there *they* were. Two birds filled my view, both slightly tucked up as they dozed upright. Before I could embarrass myself by asking any unknowledgeable questions, Mike was explaining.

'The green sandpiper is on the right. Sorry, you'll have spotted that, but I thought it perfect to frame them together to show the subtleties. The eye-ring on the solitary is so well-defined.'

'Stunning,' I murmured, but my mind was already wandering. Mega-tick in the bag, and I hadn't even had breakfast. Hmm, brekkie … I was sorely hungry. 'Thanks, Mike – but I've got to dash. Feel a bit disrespectful, you know – gazing at a mega while poor old Perry is lying cold in a box.'

'Of course, Ted – you're right.' Mike was clearly feeling a pang or two of guilt. 'We really shouldn't be here at all at such a time.' He reached for his tripod and started breaking down the legs. I panicked: if Mike left before another board member arrived, we might not get ratification.

'I'm sure that Perry would be happy *you're* here, Mike,' I offered, 'in fact, perhaps we could dedicate this bird to his memory – maybe let the rest of the board know so they can come and see it in his honour … I've got to go, though, because … well, I think there are a couple of people I ought to bear the sad tidings to.'

Mike reset his scope.

'Lovely idea, Ted. Spot on – I'll get on the phone. And it would be desperately sad not to enjoy such a fabulous bird.'

Result. I nodded, as earnestly as I could, shook Mike's hand

and left, pacing quickly to the car park. *Breakfast first,* I thought, *then I'll text Mick, and then I'll head down to Portland.*

There's nothing quite like a full English after a few hours in the cold of a February morning. I wrote Mick an essay of a text, babbling really, between sips of tea, the smell of frying bacon getting my juices flowing a treat. He replied before I had a chance to butter my toast; a stunned, panicky text. He was painfully aware that this could be his best chance of bagging a solitary sandpiper all year, and the fact that I had, with seemingly assured ratification to boot, had obviously got him quite worked up. There was little he could do, though. It was already late morning and the in-laws would be arriving imminently, if they hadn't already, so taking a five-hour toilet break was out of the question.

I smiled to myself, losing a lump of black pudding to the floor in the process. Poor old Mick. Were it closer to home, he could probably have got away with a sneaky trip out, and if it were at the other end of the country, it would be so unfeasible that he wouldn't feel so torn. But Weymouth was within reach: he could maybe drive it in two hours, though it could of course fly while he was en route. Maybe it would be there tomorrow – maybe it would be a long stayer. Too many maybes.

I'm sure, had I not been in the company of Mike Phelps, that Mick would have asked me to give him an alibi – certify his presence here – and I'm glad that I can't be put in that predicament, because it would upset him when I refused. At the end of the day, travelling partner or not, he's a rival for the title, and it might just be this bird that gives me an edge.

Another text from Mick, and the rest of my message had obviously only just registered. **Shitting hell – Perry's dead?!**

I waited until I had laid down my cutlery before I replied. **Funeral Friday. Bath. Gt bustard on way back?**

That would have appeased him a little. The great bustard is one of those pain-in-the-arse species that you have to go to a specific site to see, in this case Salisbury Plain, but will pick up precious little else along with it. It's also not officially 'on the list', due to the fact that it's a reintroduced species. The board, though, are all but certain to include it the moment it successfully breeds and becomes self-sustaining, and that could happen this year.

While running through options last year, I had thought that a spring trip to the Plain could tie in Montagu's harrier and stone curlew as well as the bustard, but I had already ticked the first two by the time my scheduled trip arrived. In the end I wasted a whole day for one tick, which didn't even end up counting. I can't afford such inefficiency if I'm to succeed this year, which is why Perry's funeral is such a bonus.

I drained the last of my tea and headed for the car, but my pager had buzzed before I could start the engine.

-- CATTLE EGRET - WEYCROFT NEAR AXMINSTER --

I grabbed the road atlas. Axminster was only thirty-five miles or so away, and a cattle egret was a bigger tick than the long-eared owl that had been called at the Observatory yesterday. Perhaps I wouldn't be going to Portland after all.

It took about an hour to get to Axminster, and then at least another hour driving around the country lanes surrounding Weycroft before I found the egret. There was only one other person on site, a field I had already driven past at least twice, who grinned as I pulled up on the verge. I can't recall the chap's name, but he was local, and the person who reported the bird. I think he was a little bit excited to have a rarity on his patch, and was keen for me to look through his scope. I obliged, even though I could make out the egret with the naked eye, stalking (or should that be storking?) around the cows toward the top of the field, waiting, presumably, for a wayward hoof to squelch something tasty from the mud. By the time I had taken a cursory glance through the telescope, it had become apparent that I was in the company of an anorak.

'Here, look at my field sketches.' He was thumbing through a posh looking notepad. 'I took a few drawings here and then popped down to Axmouth to sketch the little egrets on the estuary – I think you'll find the comparisons quite fascinating.'

I won't, I thought. This guy should have been getting together with Phelps; the two of them could spend the afternoon marvelling over the variance of egret bill colourations before masturbating over one another's field art.

I don't get it. They're just birds. It's about *ticking* boxes, not studying them to the point of exhaustion. I've had regular arguments with Mick on the subject: yes, I can appreciate some birds more than others, of course I can. A sea eagle is a pretty damned impressive sight, and even the spoonbill at Lodmoor I took pleasure in seeing, but some people will spend all day looking at the *same bloody bird*. Mick has. I know birdwatching was his guilty pleasure as a child – a passion he quite wisely kept quiet until his latter teens when he wouldn't be quite so ridiculed – but on occasion he still lets himself get too involved.

The snowy owl in Cornwall two years ago, my first ever twitch, is a case in point. I'm still not quite sure how he persuaded me to go along, but after five hours in the car we found the bird quite easily; Mick simply looked for the huddle of people with binoculars and asked them to point it out. We could only see it through a telescope, and even then it was just a white blob, so Mick wanted to wait for a better view.

Two hours we stood there, and it didn't move.

'It's got to fly soon,' Mick kept saying, but I was cold and more interested in the local pub that Mick had raved about, with Doombar on draft and sexually frustrated local sirens serving it. To be honest, it was the pub that'd persuaded me to come at all.

Sure enough, when Mick had finally admitted defeat and we had thawed out back in the car, we had a belting night, complete with a lock-in. And we couldn't get locked out of the B&B because the landlady was enjoying the knees-up in the bar with us. She later got her knees up around Mick's ears back at the B&B, as I may have mentioned already – an act which prompted us to get up at silly o'clock on the Sunday morning and go back up to the moor to see the bloody owl again.

'It'll blow the cobwebs out,' Mick argued, in the face of my protestations, 'and it's one of my favourite birds – I really want to see it fly.'

I remember making a clever crack about Mick having already

blown out Mrs Bellchambers's cobwebs, which was not well received, but succumbed to Mick's wish. He was, after all, in a state of hyper-guilt, so prolonging the inevitable blubbing as we headed home was no bad thing. Surprise surprise, though, the snowy owl was still in exactly the same place, tucked up in the heather half a mile away. Mick unfolded his telescope and got himself comfy. I was already bored, and took to people watching instead.

Three chaps were hurrying up the hill towards us, all in camouflage coats and hats, stumbling through the undergrowth like drunken paratroopers. They soon reached us and asked Mick for the location of the snowy owl. Mick pointed it out; one by one they spied through his scope, called, 'Got it!' and, without even pausing for breath, were off again, back down the slope towards the road. I could hear them chattering as they went – they were off to Hale next, I think, for a scoter, and then the Lizard for the choughs and then to the pub for lunch.

That sounded more like it. Action packed, results driven – no wonder Mick had never actually won this bird race he entered. A year may be a long time for a race to be run, but he was wasting an awful lot of time looking at the same set of feathers and he would have sat there all day, had Mrs Bellchambers not put in her appearance. There were a dozen or so people there when she appeared, draping herself over Mick like a lovesick puppy. As he pushed her away her coat flapped open; she was naked beneath it, and it wasn't a sight for hungover eyes. I retched a little, but had no time to dwell on the image – Mick was charging off down the hill in terror.

'Bring my telescope, Ted!' he'd shouted over his shoulder.

In East Devon, another twitcher came to my aid, pulling up unwittingly alongside the most boring man in the world. I said nothing as the pair engaged, field sketches already on view, but slipped back into the car and headed back to the A35. The day couldn't have gone much better, and I was ready for a pint.

I had a lazy start this morning (Sunday), partly because I had a couple of pints too many last night, and partly because the weather front promised for this evening had arrived sooner than expected in the early hours. A peer out of the window during my early morning pee revealed a beautifully blanketed pub garden with snow still falling, but by the time I went down for breakfast at around ten, the snow had turned to sleety rain and anything on the ground had long since melted. Breakfast was a bit of a struggle – God knows how long it had all been sitting there, the egg was like rubber – and I kept burping up reminders of last night's whisky.

In truth, coming to the Adder Arms was a decision made with an ulterior motive. Yes, it presented a good birding location on the edge of the New Forest where not one but two great grey shrikes were currently in residence, but more importantly, when Mick and I stayed here last year, one of the girls behind the bar had caught my eye. I say girl; she was a woman, really. Early thirties at a guess. Her name was Donna, and she definitely seemed to like the look of me.

Mick noticed before I did.

'She wants you, Ted. She can't take her eyes off you.'

I wasn't quite so convinced at the time, but looking back she did seem to smile at me longer than anyone else in the bar, and she would linger for a second or two when giving me my change, making sure our fingers brushed. Nothing happened, of course, and perhaps it's no bad thing that she wasn't working last night, if she still works here at all. I did want her to see my new haircut, though, just to gauge her reaction. I'm referring to the hair on my head, incidentally, not the itch-fest that's regenerating in my boxer shorts. Christ, I've had to choose my underwear carefully over the last few days. Soft cotton acts like Velcro against freshly sprouting pubes.

I did drive into the forest, heading for Bishop's Dyke and those shrikes, but the snow was still quite thick across the open heath and the roads pretty dodgy so I diverted north when I reached Lyndhurst, back to the M3 and home. The shrikes would be there for a while yet, but would almost certainly be tucked up under a gorse bush this morning. Out of sight, and out of the cold.

A strange, strange week, though at least I've got the 150 up;
a little later than last year, but I'm making ground rapidly. My
marriage, however, may be a little trickier to patch up.

Mick found himself in Weymouth on Monday – it's always
handy working in sales, though I'm not sure how many clients he
actually has in south Dorset – and gripped the solitary sandpiper,
or so he says. Mike Phelps stayed with the bird until 3.57 on the
afternoon of Saturday 3rd, when he (and the sizable crowd that
had gathered) watched it fly south. At 4.04, a solitary sandpiper
was recorded just south of the observatory on Portland. Here
it was viewed (and photographed) for just over two minutes,
whereon it flew south, out of sight and out to sea. At no point
was the bird picked up at either location through the whole of
Sunday 4th – and there were an awful lot of people looking,
especially at Radipole.

There's a single report of the bird at Radipole at 9.37 on the
morning of Monday 5th from a certain M. Starr, though he had
no fellow witnesses and the bird hasn't been seen since. Naturally,
the initial rumblings this week have been fairly dismissive
of Mick's claim. The board convened briefly in an unofficial
meeting on Wednesday evening via Skype, primarily to discuss
the funeral service for Perry (and the scope guard of honour
outside the crematorium on Friday), but also to speak about the
solitary sandpiper. With the bird now officially being recognised
as a symbolic tribute to the late John Perry (the suggestion of
which has meant my balls are currently more golden than David
Beckham's), its significance is ever greater, and the lone sighting
made on Monday 5th February seems, therefore, destined to be

rejected at the next official meeting. Of course, Mick was up in arms and threatened his resignation on Thursday ('from what, exactly, Mick?' I had queried), only to calm down a bit on Friday when it dawned on him that Perry's seat on the board was now open and he was a viable candidate. Come the post-service chitchat on Friday afternoon (not a single birder actually made it to the wake, all instead spotting an opportunity for a tick or two, it being what Perry 'would have wanted'), Mick was fawning all over Claypole, the Guv'nor and all the rest of the remaining board members, withdrawing his sighting verbally ('it must have been a green,' he simpered, 'I just wanted to see it for Perry …') and kissing more arse than is healthy.

'Are you going to apply then, Ted?' Mick asked as we got into the car. His tone suggested that he was keen my answer should be in the negative.

'Maybe, Mick. I'm undecided yet. I need to focus on other things at the moment.' We had spent two and half hours in the car already that morning, and Mick hadn't once asked after me. How a man can talk solidly for that long about the validity of a sighting is quite astonishing.

'Just because it's called a solitary friggin' sandpiper,' he argued, 'doesn't automatically mean it was solitary.'

A fair point, I agreed, but most American birds that find themselves on British shores do so on their own, and as the solitary sandpiper was a migrant unusual in the fact that it did, normally, migrate alone – hence the name – which made the likelihood of two turning up in Weymouth, in February, and at the same time, well, a little slim.

'What's going on at home then, Ted?' Mick *almost* feigned genuine concern.

'Much the normal,' I answered. 'Nicola went round to a friend's house to do homework on Wednesday and didn't get back until gone midnight, stinking of fags.'

'Smoking won't kill her, Ted,' Mick was reaching for his own packet, 'but I hope she's at least taking precautions with all these lucky little pricks?'

'I hope so too, Mick.' I couldn't be bothered to get angry.

'Anyway, if you don't apply for Perry's seat, you can second me ... hello, what do the Old Bill want?'

Our slow crawl out of the crematorium was explained by the presence of two policemen near the entrance who appeared to be cross-checking registration plates with a list on their clipboards, and Mick's registration was apparently a match. I wound the window down as we drew near, a constable coming round to my side of the car in order to speak to me independently.

'Sorry to bother you on such a sad occasion, sir.' He sounded genuinely sincere. 'I am PC Nicholls, investigating the events leading up to the RTA in which Mr Perry lost his life.'

'Okay ...' I was trying not to sound uneasy, but it's never straightforward when you talk to a uniform.

'Were you present at the, er,' he glanced at his notepad, 'Medway Arms, near Sittingbourne, at lunchtime on Sunday 28th January?'

'I was, briefly, yes ...' I had to be a little careful now. I hadn't really considered the hand I might've played in Perry's death until this moment, and was suddenly aware that my face was reddening. I could feel myself shutting down. Clamming up.

'We just stopped for a pee,' I muttered, and I recall the quizzical look on the PC's face. *He's onto me,* I thought, and the next few moments were a blur. I remember being given a card with his name and number, but not the completion of the conversation. My head cleared as we pulled away, Mick pulling a wheelspin in a silly little display of defiance.

'Bloody pigs,' he started, 'why the fuck should we know what happened to Perry's car? Something flicked off it, they said, but they don't say what. It's just one of those things: something's hit another driver, he's panicked, clipped Perry, and the poor guy's dead – a million to one shot, just like your brother, Ted ...' I switched off at that point. There was really no need to bring my brother into the conversation. I reached for the road atlas instead, but Mick pre-empted me. 'It's alright, Ted, I know where I'm going. Time for a great bleedin' bustard. Let's hope it counts this year.'

We didn't hang around for long up on the Plain. Having

seen our bustard, Mick and I were soon heading south towards Ringwood and our overnight accommodation. I'd left Mick to book it and had expected us to be heading for the Adder Arms, so was taken aback when Mick pulled into a Travelodge car park.

'I can't have any temptation, Ted.' Mick had sensed my shock. 'I'm here for the birds, nothing else. The shrikes, that is, and maybe a hawfinch. If we get up early we can head to the roost site.'

'What about the Adder?' I argued. 'I expected us to be going there.' I'd hoped that Donna might have been working. Not that I would have done anything, of course. Mick turned to me and rolled his eyes.

'Truth is, Ted – and this goes no further – I stayed at the Adder back in the autumn. For work. And you remember that bargirl you had your eye on?'

'Donna …?' I knew what was coming.

'… yeah, Donna … well, she had a drink with me after closing … one thing led to another, and, well – it's probably best we don't go back.'

'Right.' I was speechless. And, to be honest, a bit jealous. She had definitely been giving me the eye last year, paying me attention.

'I tell you what, though, Ted,' Mick had lost his guilty edge again, 'she was something special. Hadn't had it from her old man for *five years*, she reckoned. Un-be-lievable … she didn't stop …'

I had stopped listening, and merely followed Mick into reception and down to our room while he banged on and on about banging.

I don't think Mick stopped talking until we arrived back in Woking yesterday afternoon; he was probably wittering away in his sleep. He certainly avoided any opportunity for temptation: we had pizza delivered, and my mood did lighten a little when Mick produced a bottle of Laphroaig from his overnight bag. I tucked into the single malt and slept well, waking to Mick's enthused chatterings about getting to the hawfinch roost before first light. We made it, and saw both great grey shrikes at Bishop's Dyke, but I was feeling somewhat morose when I got back home.

The girls were already out when I arrived, while Abi was just out of the bath.

'Have a shower and come and join me,' she cooed.

I necked a couple of very large vodkas and jumped in the shower, the alcohol working its tingly magic within minutes. Maybe sex with my wife wasn't going to be too much of a chore after all. Sadly, though, from there on, the evening worsened.

We were soon engaged, so to speak, and all was functioning as it should have done. The vodka was numbing my brain nicely, and I was experiencing a genuine feeling of warm connection with my wife, physically and mentally.

Then I looked down. At the wrong moment.

Abi's fringe had flopped at a funny angle, and in that split second I saw my daughter Lucy beneath me. This was not good for my performance, and my senses were rapidly softening. I closed my eyes, desperate for an image that might perk me up again. Any thoughts of Abi were merging with Lucy, though. Their matching haircuts. They were one.

'Are you okay, honey?'

Oh God – Abi had noticed. Unsurprisingly. Mick sprang to mind. Even worse. But then I thought back to his illicit descriptions of Donna from the Adder Arms. Donna. That was better. Much better. Abi groaned her approval at the change in circumstance. It was great again; I was going to explode, but then at the point of detonation … I couldn't help myself.

'Who the fuck is DONNA?'

I had blurted out her name. Abi was already across the room, screaming.

'No one,' I stammered, in post-orgasmic confusion.

'She must be *someone* – you were fantasising about her!'

'No, I wasn't – I was thinking about Lucy …'

Oops.

'Our daughter …? Oh my God … you sick, sick bastard.' Tears were running down Abi's face as she ran from the room, visibly retching. The shower was running, the toilet flushing.

Oh well, sofa, I thought, *you and I will be getting to know each other pretty well.*

Still on the sofa.

FEBRUARY 28TH 2007

163 SPECIES

How long can a bad mood last?

MARCH

In a month I've added just 21 species. Not good, but at least things with Abi are better, even though she's vetoed sex for the time being. It's been an intense few weeks, though, and the girls have suffered, too. Lucy especially. Poor girl; suddenly Mum goes all stroppy, Dad struggles to be in the same room as her, and she's got absolutely no idea what she's done. She's a sensitive girl, my Lucy-Lou, but has always been tactile around me – lots of hugs and cuddling up on the sofa. I tried to explain that the situation had nothing to do with her, but just couldn't get the words out right. I'm not quite sure what the right words would be, exactly, given the circumstances, but I certainly didn't have them in my vocabulary.

Abi compounded Lucy's sensitivity by going out first thing on the Monday morning after the Saturday before and getting her hair lopped off into a short, dishevelled little number, and then criticising Lucy's style at every opportunity. Abi's cut quite suited her, surprisingly – she looked slightly elfin, and I told her that it reminded me of Halle Berry's look in *Die Another Day*.

She told me to fuck off and die.

That was a long, long week. I managed to forget Valentine's Day on the Wednesday, which further stoked the flames. She didn't speak to me for five days, though she shouted and swore a fair few times. I wrote her little cards, bought her flowers ('Valentine's Day was yesterday, freak!' she spat). I even suggested we went to see a marriage guidance counsellor, but she instead suggested I go and see a shrink. And be castrated.

By the following Monday I was desperate. A weekend of begging had done nothing, and the fact that I had sacrificed the chance of a trip to Suffolk on the Saturday to see a semipalmated plover meant absolutely nothing to her. It would have been a lifer, too. (Mick dipped out on it, which is some consolation.)

Monday lunchtime saw me in Whitcombe's office, pleading for some time off. Of course, he put me through the ringer before he agreed.

'You are a *desk manager*, Edward – a position that comes with responsibility. Your contract clearly states that you give a minimum of four weeks' notice for five or more consecutive days of leave.'

'I appreciate that, Mr Whitcombe, but these are exceptional circumstances.'

He raised an eyebrow.

'Has a golden penguin turned up on the Thames, Edward?'

'No, I'm having some personal issues …' I didn't mean to cry at this point, but the tears certainly helped, '… and my marriage is in trouble …'

Whitcombe stayed silent for some time, before breathing in deeply.

'Edward.' His tone had eased, at least. 'The Department for Work and Pensions has strict guidelines to which I am bound. But perhaps these are exceptional circumstances, and in such a situation I can bend the rules a little.' He prattled on for a couple of minutes showing concern for my lack of ambition, and raised last year's attendance record again. I didn't care too much at that point, though – he had granted me leave, I could patch things up with Abi (though it was going to cost me a fortune to do it) and then I could crack on with twitching in time for the first of the spring arrivals.

I didn't speak when I got home. Instead I laid the plane tickets on the table, under Abi's nose.

'And where exactly is "Male"?' she asked – still curt, but her curiosity had definitely softened her.

'It's pronounced "Marley", and it's in the Maldives.'

Her eyes bulged. Her dream holiday. No expense spared. Of course, she wasn't going to show too much excitement, or let me think for a second that I was off the hook, but a week on an exotic desert island certainly gave me enough time to just about convince her of what was really going through my mind on that fateful evening. I was still going to be in the doghouse for a good while yet, though. I may not have been fantasising about shagging my own daughter, but I had been fantasising about another woman while having sex with my wife, and until she trusted me again, there would be no further hanky-panky between us.

I could live with that fairly happily, to be honest, and the thousands spent on an all-inclusive holiday in the Indian Ocean weren't going to bankrupt us either. I missed a solid week's birding, of course, not to mention the time I had spent grovelling beforehand, but the holiday was a success.

We arrived back at Gatwick to snow and the promise of further cold weather to come, meaning little would be happening on the bird front. We also arrived home to a house that truly had been left in the care of two teenage girls.

Despite our initial assumption, the party had actually been Lucy's idea. She had joined some new website called Facebook and announced the house party to anyone who cared. They think around 150 people turned up, who proceeded to drink my single malt collection, blow the speakers on the stereo and put about thirty cigarette burns into the (now replaced) carpet. The police had turned up at around eleven o'clock, then again at one in the morning, and suffice to say we're probably not getting Christmas cards from the neighbours this year.

The toughest thing, however, was to work out how best to discipline the girls. Lucy had been so unfairly treated by Abi and myself before we went away that it was almost understandable she would behave as she did, and she was mortified at the aftermath. Abi and I talked hard about it, feeling that Lucy must have felt enormous rejection from us both – for a model daughter to suddenly be all but estranged overnight by her parents (when she had done absolutely nothing wrong) must have been devastating.

Holding a party in our house when in a position of trust and responsibility (Christ, I sound like Whitcombe) was indefensible, and yet we knew it would never happen again, and that if ever an action was out of character, it was now.

The disappearance of my whisky was unforgivable, though, and we duly grounded Lucy for six months and Nicola for two.

Two hundred up and in pretty good time, too, all things considered. I got there on the 9th last year, but with far less interruption and a great deal more travelling. Unlike 2006, I've yet to go to Scotland (no need; the biggies will all be there in a couple of months, but the snow won't be), yet to do a big wader hit (though I've bagged almost as many) and yet to tackle the gulls (blurgh).

I enjoy March birding. There's so much going on. It's rapid-fire action, with migrants dropping in daily, rarer species getting blown in from the Americas and Asia, and at the end of the month it's the end of the first quarter, when the leading lists are published for the first time.

New rules instigated two years ago mean that all competitors have to submit a list by April 7th of all sightings up to and including March 31st. From what I gather, this new directive caused a lot of grumblings when it was first imposed. A great many birders liked to keep their cards close to their chest, and kept their lists a secret until the very end of the year – mainly, I think, to protect a few of the more unusual ticks, but also, as Mick used to do, so that they could sit down on New Year's Eve and tick boxes on a complete list, having not necessarily seen the birds in question.

'I *must* have seen a willow tit, and a yellow wagtail, and a little owl,' they would muse, 'can't remember *when* exactly, but I must have seen them.'

Mick now just ticks the boxes for the forthcoming year, though in 2005 a few people got bitten on the arse for doing that. They'd ticked boxes for honey buzzard and nightjar, but with these species being among the latest spring arrivals, when their lists were presented at the end of March, the board had requested further details. The National Board of Birding shares migrant arrival dates with the British Trust for Ornithology and the Royal Society for the Protection of Birds plus some of the regional and county recording bodies, and March arrivals for nightjars in particular raised more than a few eyebrows, meaning rejected claims and even some expulsions from that year's competition.

Mick, with his pre-ticked list, does at least have a bit more savvy about him, and our comparative totals should be fairly even come the end of the month (with the exception of the solitary sandpiper). I know no better, having only seriously competed in the last two years, so I'm quite happy to submit my sightings every quarter. In fact, this year I'm looking forward to seeing exactly what everyone else has got; who I'm up against. My strategy may have to be adjusted according to my competitors' fortunes. I might have to get more involved with their methods and schedules.

The only really missed tick so far this year was the semipalmated plover, but another one's always been on the cards, and I'll find out in a few weeks who, if any, of my main competitors have ticked it. It should also be said that my *own* integrity is such that when I raise that trophy at next year's awards, I'll do so with a clean conscience – there won't be a single disputable tick on my list.

I don't know what's worse: the indignation of a receiving a written warning at work or the humiliation of being well and truly duped by an online prankster.

My pager buzzed just before I got to work on Tuesday morning.

```
-- ALBATROSS SP - MABLETHORPE, LINCS --
```

I was fairly unmoved to begin with. Regular 'albatross' sightings are made all around the coast – normally by amateurs who spend most of their life looking at their feet and are then startled at the sheer size of a great black-backed gull. Or an inexperienced sea-watcher will get overexcited by a passing fulmar and its tubular 'nose', overlook their lack of size perspective and falsely report it as something far grander.

But then the pager buzzed again.

```
-- BLACK-BROWED ALBATROSS - JUVENILE - ANDERBY
CREEK, LINCS --
```

This had a little more substance to it, a point proven by my mobile suddenly bleeping into life.

'What do you reckon?' It was Mick.

'Interesting ...' I was just walking into the office, so tried to sound as blasé as possible.

'I'm due in Nottingham this afternoon – not a million miles away. Might give it a pop.'

'Any idea who called it?'

'None, but I'll keep you posted.'

Mick's initial application for Perry's vacant board seat had been well received, especially with my seconding, and though the final decision wasn't due until April 8th he was already on the brink of entering the inner circle and receiving the kind of solid information that only comes with the privilege of board membership.

I fired up my computer and brought up Google Maps. Anderby Creek was at least four hours away. If the sighting turned out to be true, I had no way of slotting in a trip around working hours. A bleep from the pager again: another sighting, this time aging the bird – a second year juvenile. Mick was soon on the phone again.

'Just spoke to the Guv'nor and he's heading north. Reckons it's a goer. He's seen a photo – says it's poor quality, from a mobile, but definitely an albatross. It'll be a lifer if he gets it.'

Terry 'the Guv'nor' Holden is the vice chairman of the board, and eleven-time overall champion. Nowadays, however, having reached his mid-sixties, he only really chases life ticks; birds he's never seen before. He hasn't officially 'retired' from the annual race and still submits his lists, but he struggles to keep up with the younger guys and didn't even get a classification at the end of last year. If *he* was going, then, this was surely more than just a speculative rumour. It was nearly nine o'clock – Whitcombe's usual arrival time. I had to act fast.

Luke was the only other person on my team already at his desk. I quickly fed him a line that I had a family emergency and had to dash, and made for the door. As I fired up the car engine, the pager buzzed again. A further sighting, this time reporting that the bird was now on the water. What did that mean? Was it dead?

My phone rang. It was Mick, but I wasn't on hands-free – I daren't answer it in Woking. Too many eyes. I would get to the motorway and call him back.

It rang again – my work number. I definitely wasn't answering that. Then Mick again. By the time I reached he M25, I had seven missed calls. I phoned Mick.

'Bird is on the water, but alive,' he reported.

'I'm on my way, Mick – see you there.'

'You're going to get so bollocked, Ted!'

I would, it was inevitable, but I didn't really care. A black-browed albatross. I simply couldn't miss it.

After the usual congestion on the M25, the Focus was eating up the motorway. Ninety miles an hour; nothing was going to overtake me. Thank God it wasn't raining and I had missed the worst of the traffic. I hadn't actually looked at a map, or yet worked out a route, but Mick had mentioned Nottingham and that was on the M1, so that was the way I headed. Still the phone kept ringing. Work calling. Home calling. Mick calling. I would have to stop and sort the hands-free kit out. Watford Gap was the next service station.

Then a text. I glanced down at the phone. It was Mick. One word. **HOAX.**

Shit.

I managed to veer left and across to the inside lane just in time to slip off at the next junction, where I pulled over just off the roundabout, took a deep breath, and reached for the phone. Mick answered immediately.

'Some twat's had a right laugh at our expense.' He was sounding surprisingly calm given the circumstances, but then *his* morning's excursion was going to have far fewer repercussions than my own.

'I just got the full picture from Keith Atkins,' – Mick loved his new board connections – 'he got there about ten o'clock.' I glanced at my watch – it was nearly eleven. 'Reckoned there were cars pulling up all over the place. Utter chaos. Then someone shouted that they'd found it and everyone charged off together. They'd seen it, only "it" turned out to be an inflatable seagull, tied to a buoy offshore. There were two blokes on the water in a RIB, pissing themselves with laughter apparently. Wankers. The photo the Guv'nor saw is probably off a computer screen – hence the crap quality.'

This was very bad news. I wrapped up the conversation and took another deep breath.

'Voicemail has seven new messages,' came the familiar voice.

Four were from Mick, which I deleted without listening to; one was from Whitcombe expressing concern at my abrupt departure from work, while two were from Abi, pretty similar in detail, both asking why my boss had been on the phone asking if there was anything he could do to assist in our family emergency. I was well and truly up shit creek, but the impending shouting wasn't really bothering me. The thing that I was most pissed off about was the fact that I couldn't make the best of the situation.

Missing a made-up albatross was a blow, but at least everyone had missed it: no-one would have that mega-tick edge on me. But the galling thing was that I was sitting in my car, a hundred miles from home, in a place that simply wasn't going to offer me second prize. I was five miles from Northampton. People in those parts got excited about sparrows.

I dug out the road atlas, but that simply depressed me further. Rutland Water was an option but was another hour away, and I didn't even know if any ospreys had turned up there yet this spring, and anyway, they were a bird that I shouldn't have any problem picking up elsewhere. There was little else for it but to turn the car around and head for home – let Abi shout at me this afternoon and Whitcombe have his turn in the morning.

To be fair, Abi was fairly calm about the situation. She had been panicked, basically, by Whitcombe's telephone call, and was worried that something had happened to me or my mother.

Whitcombe, however, took great pleasure in introducing me to the various interpretations of the Disciplinary Procedure over the course of the following few days. It seems I managed to cut him up on the roundabout just outside work at precisely 9.03 on Tuesday morning, causing him great concern for my speed and disregard for other road users. Obviously, something of extreme seriousness must have occurred for me to behave in such a manner.

This put my back up. I hated the whole charade. We both knew exactly why I was speeding away from my workplace within half an hour of arriving; why beat around the bush? So I stirred it up, pointing out that at 9.03, he was arriving late for work, and this was no example to be setting to me and the rest of the office.

I could have been sacked on the spot, apparently – for gross insubordination – but instead I was invited for an official interview the following day to which I could bring representation if required. I didn't bother with representation, and sat for an hour while Whitcombe spouted on about attitude, example and responsibility; attributes I was currently lacking. Meanwhile a woman I didn't recognise sat beside him, scribbling furiously and occasionally interjecting with utterances of correct policy and procedure. It was a mind-numbing hour, only superseded by the following half-hour 'off the record' chat during which Whitcombe sat without his sidekick and played good cop.

'I've always liked you, but ...' He even dragged politics into it, saying it was inevitable that Gordon Brown would take over as prime minister sooner rather than later, that as much as people hated Blair, Brown would be the final nail in the coffin for the Labour government and the Tories would come in and rip the public sector apart. Wide scale redundancies would follow, and members of my team would probably face unemployment.

It was a poorly veiled threat, and I told him so – 'off the record' – and I also suggested that his comments did little to lift my morale and could be counterproductive. I stopped short of telling him to stick his job, and went back in on Friday to receive my written warning, after another 'official meeting' with Miss Scribblealot in attendance. I played the victim at that point, and requested that due to my upset, I have the afternoon off to consider the course of my actions and how best to ensure that such a situation did not reoccur. Whitcombe's face was a picture – he knew I was playing the game, but his little sidekick nodded as he glanced at her for counsel, and he couldn't say no. In truth, I needed the afternoon off; my weekend plans had been blown out of the water.

Mick and I had been due to go to Dungeness on Saturday morning for a couple of days' migrant spotting. There are a few spots along the south coast perfect for incoming migrants, jutting out into the sea as they do, and late March can see a procession of birds arriving from the continent. Portland Bill is probably the most famous of these spots, and popular, but I prefer the mood at Dungeness. It's a bit post-apocalyptic, with the power station and odd little huts and sheds dotted among the pebbles, but it's so easy to spot birds there. The landscape is so flat that you can get a decent scope image from a massive distance. Plus there's a cracking little pub which Mick introduced me to last year.

When I got home from work on Thursday evening, still stinging from my disciplinary meeting, Nicola was conspicuous by her absence. Abi had heard nothing, and her phone was going straight to voicemail, the breaching of her curfew less worrying than the question of her safety. We spent two hours phoning around friends and parents of friends, but no one had seen or heard from Nicki, or, at least no one was admitting to it.

Just before nine, she bowled in – half cut and still in her school uniform. I let rip.

'Chill, Dad,' she kept saying, but I didn't – I'd had a bad enough day. Abi just stayed silent, letting me shout, only speaking when she noticed a wardrobe mishap.

'Nicola, why's your skirt inside out?'

That was enough for me. It was bad enough that she was out while grounded, on a school night, clearly drinking and smoking (weed, perhaps?), but she'd also spent time with yet another A.N. Other in a state of undress.

I poured a very large malt, stormed upstairs, and shut myself in the bedroom with the TV for company. Abi appeared about half an hour later, and of course it was my fault. I always buggered off at the weekend, set no example to my kids – they felt unloved, blah, blah, blah – and, in short, I either stay at home this weekend or I take Nicola with me.

Great.

I called Mick after work on the way home on Friday afternoon in order to let him know the predicament. He was surprisingly relaxed about it. I had worried (knowing Mick as well as I do) that he might see the situation as a bit of a bonus – a chance to lech over a sexually active schoolgirl – but instead, amazingly, he opted out.

'It'll be good for you and Nicola,' he'd said.

Nicola didn't seem at all bothered about the whole thing. She even seemed quite excited about a trip to the seaside. Yesterday's early start didn't faze her either – in fact, after an hour of her non-stop chatter, I relaxed my in-car ban on the station and put Radio 1 on, just to keep her quiet.

I can't say she was overly enamoured with the 'beach' at Dungeness, though, nor the lack of penny arcades and ice cream vans, but credit to her, she made the best of it. The wind was fairly warm off the sea, a steady southerly breeze, and Nicola soon had her nose in a bird book looking up the species as I called them.

Black redstart and firecrest were two early successes, and by mid-afternoon I wondered if my daughter had been bitten by the bug. She'd felt the buzz after a penduline tit put in an unexpected appearance, right in front of one of the hides. There were over a dozen people there at the time, and the tit was a first of the year for everyone – and a lifer for a couple. Smiles all round, with one of the biggest on Nicola's face. She's got sharp eyes, too, something I've never appreciated, and it was she who first spotted the purple heron. Another tick, and I was chuffed to bits, but her interest was quick to wane as the sun began to dip. I suggested we call it a day and head for our room at the pub.

It'd been a cracking day, and my mood was light-years away from that of Friday afternoon, so much so that I surprised even myself when we sat down in the bar that evening to eat.

'To drink, sir?' the waiter asked.

'Red or white, Nicki?' I asked my daughter. She looked pleasantly surprised. 'White, I think.' I wanted red. I turned to the waiter.

'A house bottle of each, thanks.'

'Go Dad!' Nicola smiled with the waiter out of earshot, her eyes on stalks.

'You're not having the whole bottle,' I said firmly. But she did, and saw it off quite easily, too, though she was slurring a fair bit by the time the coffee came out. I was loving her company. We'd spoken more in a day than we had in the last year, and for all her precocious effort, I was finding my baby daughter a damn sight funnier and less bawdy than Mick normally is.

We took nightcaps up to our twin room, where the conversation became more frank and a little more heartfelt. Nicola asked, quite bluntly, what had caused the recent spat between her parents, and I, oiled and free speaking, told her almost exactly why. I left out the bit about Lucy, but admitted to blurting out Donna's name by accident. Nicola found it hilarious and I laughed with her, feeling nicely liberated. Suddenly, though, she gathered herself and paused, an earnest expression spreading across her face.

'It's so great to talk like this to you, Dad,' she giggled a bit, 'and I want to be completely honest with you.' She looked at me in the eye. I was sobering up fast. What could she have possibly done, with her track record, that required this much build up? A wave of paternal responsibility washed through me, and that, coupled with the fear of just what my daughter might want to share, was sufficient for me to steer the conversation swiftly toward more respectable parental counsel.

'You know, Nicola, when I met your mother she was only a year or so older than you …' Nicola frowned.

'Er, yes, Dad – I know …'

'And she was … well, *innocent* …' I felt my face flush red, '… she was a virgin …'

I wasn't sure where I was going with this but I was way out of my depth. Thankfully, Nicola seemed to recognise this fact.

'So am I, Dad …'

She smiled, a slightly embarrassed, crooked smile. I blinked a couple of times and frowned, trying to work out if she actually knew what 'virgin' meant.

'I've fooled around a bit, you know. With guys. I'm not entirely innocent. But I'm only fifteen, Dad – I'm not going to let a sleazy bloke get his way unless he really respects me.'

I was dumbstruck. Nicola could tell, but she was relaxing again – a weight seemingly lifted from her shoulders.

'But …' I needed to get my head around this, 'you've sat there, on more than one occasion, admitting to me and your Mum that you were, well, *engaging* with various boys …?'

'Like I said, Dad, I'm not completely innocent – but I just

embellished the truth a little.'

'Embellished'? Good word. Not sure why she's only been predicted a C in English.

'For whose benefit, though, Nicki? I mean, we've been bollocking you unnecessarily.' Nicola raised her eyebrows – I don't normally swear in front of the girls.

'Mum's …' she said, eyeing me warily.

'You've lost me.' And she had – I couldn't make sense of any of this.

'Okay. Do you remember last year when I was seeing Luke – the one with the Mini Cooper?' I nodded. How could I forget?

'Well – you *hated* me seeing him, and looking back, he was a right prick–' she looked at me for a reaction. I gave none: 'prick' barely constitutes a swearword. 'Well, he was desperate to er, you know, *consummate* our relationship' – another good word – 'and while I did *certain* things, I wanted to wait before doing everything. Which is pretty much why he dumped me. But while I was seeing him, Mum started to talk to me more. Ask questions about the relationship. Where we were at. What we had done. It was like she was enjoying the excitement of it. She even got quite disappointed when we split up, so I made up a story – told her that Luke and me had had a couple more meetings, and ended up, you know, doing it …'

'I don't get it, Nicki – why would your Mum be excited by her daughter having underage sex?'

'I dunno, Dad – but it was nice, you know … Mum paying me so much attention. I've always lived in Lucy's shadow.' I shook my head. 'Get real, Dad, she's Little Miss Perfect – straight-A-but-never-been-boned Lucy-Lou.' She laughed. I did, too – despite the subject matter, I was quite enjoying the candour of our conversation. 'Suddenly Mum'd noticed me,' Nicola continued, 'and it made me feel good. I mean, she did tell me to be careful and respect myself, but she said I should enjoy being young, because you were her first and only …'

It sort of made sense. Abi had only ever slept with me, so maybe it followed that she was getting off on her daughter's tales of the promiscuous youth that she never enjoyed.

'But why keep up the stories, Nicki? You make yourself out to be, a, er …'

'Slapper?' Nicola laughed, and then thrust her head forward, 'Because I can get away with going out and getting pissed!' She pinched me playfully and laughed again. 'D'you know where I was on Thursday, Dad?' I shrugged. 'Only round at Jasmine's. Just us – her parents had gone out for the evening, so we thought we'd sample a bottle from their cellar. I knew I'd be in trouble with you when I got home, so I turned my skirt inside out, knowing Mum would see it and then be more interested in who'd been taking my skirt off, rather than the fact that I was pissed on a school night.'

In hindsight, I should be seriously angry with my daughter, but I actually find her considered deceit rather admirable. She was sheepish in her sobriety this morning, and a little hungover, but we were soon laughing (mainly about my night-time flatulence) even if we glossed over some of the more contentious parts of last night's conversation. I've promised Nicola that I'll keep her virtue a secret, though it'll be difficult to discipline her from now on, knowing that she probably hasn't behaved anything like as badly as she's making out. This weekend's brought us close together, and Abi was right on Thursday – I don't spend enough time with my daughters, a fact which makes it all the more important that I win the bird race this year. That way I can make more family time next year. I'll do it for the girls.

APRIL

I submitted my first quarter's count at 1.07 this morning: 234 species. I'm reasonably happy. Mick said he had 'around' 230 when I spoke to him last evening, which he reckoned would be good enough for the top thirty. Last year I had seen 241 at this point, which placed me seventh, but my strategy since the New Year has been much more economical, and I would certainly expect to make up that deficit with next month's Scottish trip. Of course, any conjecture at this point is wasted – only when the figures are published on April 10th will I know for sure how I'm faring.

I had to make last minute changes to this weekend's plans on Friday evening.

Mick had, without particularly good reason, been undecided all week as to whether or not he could do anything this weekend, and then on Friday morning suddenly decided we should go to Norfolk – bag a crane, maybe a golden oriole; he would drive and sort out the accommodation.

Then Abi dropped the bombshell when I got home on Friday afternoon that the sex ban was over, and we could have our last Saturday of the month hanky-panky as normal. I phoned Mick and he immediately got the arse. Kerrie had agreed that he could go, he'd booked our rooms, and now I'd let him down at the last minute. I had to explain that I had only thought the weekend was free because of my wife's sex veto, and that I was as disappointed as him.

'What the fuck-ever,' he had snapped, before hanging up.

Ten minutes later he was back on the phone, all abuzz and acting like nothing had happened. Andrew 'Cyclops' Johnson (board member, obviously) had tipped him off about a lesser yellowlegs down at Pagham Harbour. It'd been picked up at the dusk wader roost, but wasn't going to be made public until later on tomorrow.

'We can get there at dawn, Ted – bag the yellowlegs, and be back early afternoon.'

And it actually was that straightforward. Mick opted for the A3/A27 route, which is a fair bit further, but with nothing on the roads at six on a Saturday morning we made it in an hour or so. The yellowlegs was bagged. We ticked a few of the empty wader boxes on our lists (Mick is a bit of an expert when it comes to waders – handy, as I struggle, particularly in the winter when they all look the same) and were back home by three o'clock.

The girls had already been packed off to Granny's and Abi and I thoroughly enjoyed one another's company, my wife seeming more at ease than ever before, clearly not affected by memories of our last involvement. In fact, her mood's been positive all week, ever since I arrived home with a smiley second daughter last Sunday. Abi even suggested that we lift the groundings for both girls, suggesting they were already 'technically' out by being with their grandmother for the night. I agreed – I was far happier with Nicola's social life now that I knew the (lack of) intimacies involved in it, although Abi then admitted that Lucy had been allowed out last Saturday night anyway. She has a boyfriend, apparently. Very early days, but they went off to the cinema together. Abi justified her decision to let Lucy go by explaining how much good an evening on her own had been. Certainly, if her mood can be so sparky after just one evening of peace and quiet, I wasn't going to argue the point – though I can't help but feel that my handling of Nicola, and the household karma since, are the real reasons for my wife's contentment.

Twenty-second place (with Mick 27th) at the end of and including March 31st. Mick's missed a couple of warblers, mealy redpoll and the solitary sandpiper, but otherwise we're evenly matched. The results were published at nine this morning, but it's only now, closing in on midnight, that I'm able to properly digest them.

I devised a series of spreadsheets last year into which I can incorporate today's figures and then work out who, realistically, are my main adversaries, and where and when I need to concentrate my strategies for the next quarter. I was at my workstation at around half seven this morning, loading the necessary workbooks from home and renaming them so that, when minimised, they would appear to be innocuous folders and wouldn't draw attention. I got caught last year, Whitcombe sniffing round at an inopportune moment just as I was running my prototype program against the third quarter results. At the time, I was so involved that I didn't notice my boss standing at my shoulder – at least not until he muttered, 'paddyfield warbler?' with a mixture of bemusement and disapproval.

I wasn't going to be sprung today, though. I rattled out an hour's work first thing before anyone else arrived and before the results were published. Thereafter, I had sufficient pages of ongoing statistics and analysis to have active along the bottom of my screen, which I could open the moment anyone came snooping. I needn't have worried too much: Whitcombe hid himself in his office all morning and buggered off at lunchtime, though I was glad to have the escape route in place, as it meant I could focus fully on the job in hand.

After checking through the top twenty or so lists for any spelling mistakes or other anomalies, a click of the mouse would instigate the importation of each list into a master spreadsheet. From this sheet I was then able to eliminate all the species ticks I already shared with the opposition and highlight any of the remaining birds I'd expect to tick (without any major chasing) before the year's end. Then, the remaining figures should show who I really needed to be concerned about.

It was a valuable exercise. Some of the top twenty could be immediately disregarded, like the people who'd already raced around ticking every established species (much as I did last year) but didn't have any significant rarities which might be so important in the final reckoning. With little interruption all morning, I was able to incorporate the next ten lists too, ending up with a complete breakdown of the entire top thirty.

Anyone behind me at this stage isn't going to catch me. The end results hold little in the way of surprises. It's me against eight – disregarding Mick because I should be able to keep my nose in front of him without too much difficulty.

The first seven are all, unsurprisingly, board members, ranked as follows:

1. Rod 'Emu' Smyth. Current champion. 7 species up on me.
2. 'Smoker' Joe Muir. 6 species up.
3. Keith 'Orville' Atkins. 6 species up.
4. Andrew 'Cyclops' Johnson. 5 species up.
5. Mike 'Penguin' Phelps. 5 species up.
6. Cyril 'Terry' Nutkin. 4 species up.
7. Matt 'The Finisher' Carter. 2 species up.

The eighth player is also two species ahead of me, and an unknown quantity – to me at least – so I called Mick on the way home for further info on her. Yes, *her*.

'Emma Kenton? – I shouldn't really discuss her details, Ted.' Mick had today been officially inducted into the board and as such was going to be even more of a twat.

'Don't be a knob, Mick – I just need to know if she's a serious threat.' I could hear Mick drawing his breath.

'Okay, Ted – but this is confidential. I shouldn't discuss anybody's personal details with non-board members …' I stayed quiet. He wasn't going to be able to hold back from telling me. 'She's Claypole's niece. Nineteen years old and on a gap year.' Timothy 'Claypole' Pitt is chairman of the board. Mick continued, 'So in answer to your question – I would say yes, she's a serious contender.'

Damn right she is. Claypole may not compete himself anymore, but he's seven-time champion and knows how to win; plus, he'll be passing all the inside board-member-only info onto this Emma. Being on a gap year, she'll have time on her side, too – no nine-to-five keeping her in check – though on a positive note, she must lack experience, and being a nineteen-year-old girl, she'll be susceptible to distraction. Should she be doing too well come October, I'll anonymously report an early sale at Topshop or an invasion of house spiders, and she'll soon be put off the scent.

Two years ago, when I realised I had a natural aptitude for this
competition, I spent nearly three weeks doing little else but
learning birdcalls and songs. Initially, I just listened to a couple
of free CDs that had come with one of the Sunday papers, but
they only contained around 100 of the more common species
and I soon needed more extensive recordings. Online, I found all
sorts of stuff; from the RSPB website to BBC archive recordings
going back decades, trawling through dozens of websites in
between, all the while tuning my ears and absorbing the variants.

Mick was stunned when I joined him shortly after my
intensive study for a day in the New Forest. I was able to put a
name to every single call and song we heard, without hesitation.
Mick's one of those people who struggles to differentiate a
blackcap and a garden warbler, and has to rely on his eyes more
than his ears, so my sudden ability left him (almost) speechless.

I can't explain why I have such a good ear. I've never been
musical, but can only assume it's a result of hard work and
natural ability. I definitely think that some people, Mick included,
are quite lazy when it comes to birdsong. You really do have
to put the effort in – much like learning a foreign language,
I suppose. During my first competitive year my knowledge
certainly gave me an edge, and the last couple of weeks have
been similar, seeing me racking up species almost daily during
short trips (and there's plenty of daylight for pre- and post-work
outings now) to locations and habitats which should hold freshly
arrived migrants. Short trips after work also mean that Mick
doesn't have to be involved: I can get quite a few species up on
him – species that he'll struggle to find without my ears to help

him – and also, without his constant chatter, I can hear more.

In the competitive birding world, merely hearing a bird and not seeing it is a situation that causes a great deal of controversy. It's something of a grey area, but generally if the species is relatively common (common in terms of unusual birds), the record's accepted, no questions asked; however, should a tick require board ratification, hearing a song or call is considered insufficient. Obviously, with mega-sightings, witness reports and photographic proof are the order of the day anyway, but there are some species that fall in between. Corncrake and quail spring to mind – not common, but highly secretive and almost only detectable by their calls. It was argued some years ago when the corncrake was in danger of extinction that in order to get an authorised tick, the bird might need to be flushed from cover to get a photograph; a practice which was, and still is, illegal. With such a unique and distinctive call, therefore, surely the corncrake could be submitted by sound alone? The board had to agree, but this didn't set a definitive precedent.

With bird populations ever fluctuating, particularly on a small island country with variable climates such as ours, the plausibility of a tick could vary greatly from one year to the next. In some summers, the distant call of a golden oriole was just about all you might hope for, whereas in the last few years, East Anglia's seen a fairly steady population increase. It seems that with so many variables, all the board can do is treat each sighting on its merit, though some competitors are strictly old-school and won't submit anything that they haven't physically seen – an act of martyrdom if you ask me; why deny yourself a firecrest because you've only heard it?

Mind you, if I were on the board I'd put forward the motion of aural testing for the top thirty each year. Nothing too extreme – maybe fifty random species – but it'd certainly sort out a few of the less honest amongst us.

A big, big weekend and the first trip to Scilly of the year, though I'm still stuck on St Mary's as I write.

Mick got the tip-off on Friday afternoon: a black and white warbler had been reported on Bryher, a mega and a half and a potential lifer for both Mick and myself. It'd only been reported to the board as well, not to any of the internet sites, so they decided to withhold the sighting until Saturday morning so that any spare seats on the next available flights could be snapped up. The ferry was always an option, but took about three hours, and when you added on the five-hour drive down to Cornwall that was one heck of a trip at short notice. Mick was taking advantage of the situation, though, and managed to book two seats on the Skybus leaving Bristol Airport at ten to six on Friday evening.

I simply packed up and left work. Whitcombe had done his lunchtime disappearing act again, so I joined him, not really giving my desk any explanation, but acting as if it was perfectly in order. The journey was pretty good. We just managed to beat the worst of the Friday traffic on the M4 and rattled through the airport easily enough, though I really don't enjoy flying on propeller planes – the noise rattles around my head for days later.

Mick had booked us a room in a cheap(ish) hotel in Hugh Town, but we had an hour of daylight spare on Friday evening which we put to good use, taking a stroll down to the grounds of the Star Castle Hotel where a European bee-eater was in residence. Not the most difficult of ticks, but a cracking start to the weekend, nevertheless.

Saturday morning saw us at the quay early: a little ferry runs direct to Bryher on a Saturday, and it was likely to be a popular crossing. Sure enough, a fair-sized group were already assembling on the jetty, many familiar faces amongst them. Of my predetermined rivals, only Keith Atkins and Mike Phelps were absent. I presumed that the young girl getting an awful lot of male attention was Emma Kenton. My first impressions of her relieved me somewhat. She was pleasant enough looking, but too smiley – she certainly seemed to lack the hard edge she would need to become champion. Mick was soon amongst the others, sucking up to his fellow board members and immediately flirting with Emma. I kept a moderate distance. I'm no sycophant, especially when sober, though I took a couple of steps closer when I heard excited chatter about a northern waterthrush. 'Cyclops' Johnson obviously clocked my eavesdropping and saw it as an opportunity to open conversation.

'Good morning, Edward.' He offered a hand, which I shook. 'How's the Rook of the Year faring this year, then?'

This is the sort of question I despise. We all have access to the results just published; we all trawl through everyone else's figures seeing who's ticked what, and yet we all carry this nonchalant air as though it really doesn't matter.

'I'm faring okay, thank you, Andrew.' I half smiled. 'Though not so well as you, as I'm sure you're aware.'

He wasn't wearing his eye patch this morning, and I was struggling to remember which was the bad eye. He was certainly sizing me up – looking for weakness, wondering if my tone was an indication of mild aggression or weak humour. As if reading my thoughts, he shifted uncomfortably and reached into his pocket, scooping out his eye patch.

'Best get this on,' he laughed, forcedly, 'don't want to miss the megas by putting the wrong eye to the telescope.' Of course, the right eye was the bad one – it was obvious now – but no sooner had he covered it up than I wanted to have a good look at it. I wasn't sure if a burnt retina was visible or not, but I was curious to find out.

Mick was there on the day that he did it; a victim of a cruel trick. There were a couple of hundred birders crowded into a patch of scrub on the Gower peninsula, scopes all trained on a small bush where a nighthawk was hiding – some having already bagged it, but all wanting to see it on the wing. At some point, someone, and it was never discovered who, 'knocked' Andrew Johnson's telescope out of position, lining it up instead with the afternoon sun. Everyone was milling around chatting, when the shout rang out, 'It's up!' and Johnson dived for his scope, not noticing in his haste that it was pointing in the wrong direction and promptly staring straight into the solar mass at sixty times magnification.

Mick reckons he must have been immediately blinded, if only temporarily, as it was some seconds before he reacted and in that time the damage had been done. Apparently the back of your eye has no pain receptors, so Johnson managed to completely frazzle his retina without realising. There may have been a chance of saving his sight had he acted sooner, but his main concern was that he'd missed the bird, and he fruitlessly hung around until dusk hoping for another chance. Overnight his rather predictable former nickname, 'Johnno', had been replaced by 'Cyclops', and he became the brunt of many a joke and a warning tale to young birders wielding a telescope for the first time.

I certainly don't know Cyclops well enough to mock his affliction or, for that matter, like him well enough to make too much small talk, but as the saying goes, 'keep your friends close, but your enemies closer', and I do need to keep in with him if I'm going to suss his strategies and beat him. Before I had a chance to pursue a conversation, however, we were joined by Emma, who greeted me cheerily and shook my hand.

'I remember you from the awards night,' she chirped. 'Maybe you can give me some tips and I can be the next Rookie of the Year.'

'*Rook* of the Year,' I corrected her, somewhat sternly, and then, having seen her face drop, added, 'but I'm sure you have every chance.' I smiled, and she giggled a 'thank you', bouncing off back to the main group.

Like I said, no hard edge. She lacked balls.

The ferry trip was short and uneventful, and the fifteen or so of us were soon filing across Bryher, all following Cyril 'Terry'

Nutkin, the man who'd received the tip-off. I tried to mingle a little as we walked; against my natural instinct, it has to be said, but I really needed to infiltrate the clique, separate the individuals from the mass. I kept asking myself why I seconded Mick's application and didn't go for Perry's empty seat on the board myself.

'Smoker' Joe Muir was reasonably affable, between wheezes. The walk was taking its toll on him, but he was frank in his chatter and certainly the most matter-of-fact board member present. I could identify with his single-mindedness, or as he put it, 'bag the humbug,' – he meant the black and white warbler – 'bag the thrush, back on the ferry, maybe home tonight.'

I'm sure part of his desire for minimal fuss – and certainly his curt manner of speech – was down to his ridiculously low lung capacity, and his insistence on carrying half of his life around with him in a bloody great rucksack. Apparently he doesn't do hotels, or B&Bs or pubs with bedrooms. Instead he prefers to save his money (presumably to fund a couple of hundred fags a week) by taking a little one-man tent everywhere he goes. I'd rather kick the habit and have a warm bed for the night.

We'd walked less than half a mile before Joe demanded we have a ten minute 'breather' in which time he puffed through two Dunhills and coughed up half a pint of tar. We did find the black and white warbler fairly easily, though, or at least we found the small band of birders already present who pointed it out to us.

I do like the Scillies. I had five days there last September, but the weather was almost too good; high pressure and blazing sun, meaning little movement on the avian front. This year I'll wait until a little later in the season, when the big Atlantic storms start rolling in. Those storms are the dwindling remains of the hurricane season in the US and, as a result, tend to blow good numbers of American birds across to our shores. The Scillies aren't just one of the first landing points, but are also birder friendly, if you disregard the transport costs. Being constantly windswept, there are few trees, and the landscape's relatively flat. Once discovered, a rarity is normally fairly easy to relocate.

Of course now, in April, with the plant life still thin after winter, the birds are even easier to find. After bagging our humbug, by lunchtime we had sewn up the northern waterthrush and an icterine warbler for good measure. Smoker Joe was going to get his wish – he may get back home tonight, though Mick and I would have to stay, with our flight not booked until the morning.

The bulk of the group headed back to the ferry, but Emma, Cyril and one of the unknowns wanted to stay a bit longer and watch the waterthrush. I could see Mick was torn: he clearly had his eye on Emma, and loitered a few moments longer than the rest of us, trying to grab a quiet moment with her. He caught me up moments later.

'Emma's staying in Hugh Town tonight – some hostel – said we should meet up for a beer later.'

I smiled. Yes, Mick, of course it was Emma's suggestion.

As the little ferry chugged back across to St Mary's, the skipper commented on the unseasonal sea mist which was forming out to the west.

'Don't expect to get off St Mary's if that lot rolls in,' he declared, like some prophet of doom. He was right, though; within an hour the mist had thickened and settled across the island. All flights and all ferry services were suspended, though you could probably have found someone in a little rowing boat with an outboard who'd take you to sea for a fair wad of cash. It meant little to Mick and me: we simply booked into our guesthouse and found the nearest pub. Mick was anxious that those who stayed on Bryher might be stranded there for the night, though his concern was obviously centred around one particular person. Still, there were soon a good few people in the pub. Smoker Joe had appeared, having pitched his tent in a field on the outskirts of town. He was mightily pissed off having to stay the night, but soon loosened up with a few pints of Doom Bar. His relentless bitching about the forthcoming smoking ban was tiresome though. He brought it up every time he lit up, which meant that he spoke of little else.

As darkness fell, it was clear that Emma and Cyril had been stranded on Bryher, a fact with which I was winding Mick up a treat.

'They'll be at it as we speak, Mick – Cyril's wrinkly arse bouncing up and down …' Mick tried his best to laugh it off, but he struggles with jealousy, particularly when pissed, and it seemed he was genuinely irked. Quite why Emma would be jumping into bed with Cyril, one of her Uncle's contemporaries, was surely a situation easily dismissed from a sane mind, but Mick was stewing on it until the food arrived. Then it started getting messy.

Six of us ate, and after the plates had been cleared the waitress appeared with half a dozen Irish coffees.

'Who ordered these?' I asked the table.

'They're on me,' Matt 'the Finisher' Carter was speaking. 'A celebration of today's success – two lifers for me.'

'They're a bedtime drink, though,' Mick argued, before pushing his chair back and making for the bar. I was happy with what I had (a caffeine hit with a whisky background is never badly timed in my book) but soon another drink appeared next to it.

'Tequila!' Mick trilled, in that stupid Mexicano accent that seems to go with the territory of what we were about to imbibe. Joe was straight on it, necking it in one before Mick had fetched the remaining shots. Matt, too, seemed game, and when Mr Straight, Rod 'Emu' Smyth joined the party, I could do little but follow suit.

It was Emu who next headed to the bar. Sambuca this time. By the time I drained the last of my Irish coffee, a further tequila had also passed my lips. It was many years since I'd drunk so much in such a short space of time, and for the next hour and a half or so, I was wondering what I'd been missing out on. The atmosphere changed, seemingly in minutes, from a quiet meal out in a fairly respectable establishment to a full-bore knees-up.

Matt was rattling money into the jukebox; the locals (who were well used to birders, but not normally in this condition) seemed only too happy to join in the fun; someone behind the bar tweaked the volume of the speakers up a notch, and suddenly, Rod Smyth, Champion Twitcher, was dancing on a table to The Proclaimers (featuring Brian Potter and Andy Pipkin). I vaguely recall the landlord locking the doors and closing the curtains at half eleven, and I definitely remember seeing Mick trying his luck with every female in the place, but I have no memory at all of heading back to the guesthouse or what time I got there.

I certainly felt peculiar waking this morning, though. Head thumping, throat dry, I'd been dreaming of drinking pints of milk from the bottle, and now I was semi-conscious I knew why. I stumbled over to the sink and stuck my mouth under the cold tap, gulping down precious, precious water. It was just getting light, a check of the watch confirming it was only a little after six. I'd barely slept, but had obviously sobered up just enough to lift my head above drunken comatose into that horrible cold lonely condition when your mind and body are asking, *Why, Ted? You're in your forties, for fuck's sake.* Mick's bed was empty. Maybe he got lucky. Maybe he was still at the party. Hopefully he would emerge reasonably soon – the flight home was around lunchtime and we really didn't want to be missing it.

As the water hit my stomach, I belched and a rush of acidic foulness reached up my throat. I was going to be sick. I gulped it down – I couldn't vomit here for fear of waking people. I had to get outside. Fortunately, I was still fully clothed: I even had my jacket and trainers on, so it was simply a case of grabbing my binoculars (just in case) and making for the front door.

I'd just made it out of the gateway onto the road when it all came bubbling up. It's an odd thing that when hungover, you do everything possible to prevent yourself from chucking up, and yet, when the inevitable happens, for a short while at least, you feel bloody great. Admittedly it's a feeling relative to your pre-puke state, and the taste in your mouth is none too pleasant, but that moment of calm when your diaphragm has stopped convulsing is really quite soothing. And then a little rush, as your body wakes up again – it set me off walking at pace, and lasted a good five minutes until my head began to cloud again and my throat tightened. I was painfully dehydrated, though someone above was smiling on me. The buzz on the road behind me was that of a milk float. I flagged him down – maybe my dream had been prophetic.

'How much for a pint of milk, mate?' I burbled.

'Sorry, chap. It's Sunday. I've only got a few pints on the back. They're all already paid for. It's papers mainly on a Sunday.' I didn't need his life history; just a fucking drink. I fumbled in my pocket and pulled out a crumpled fiver and some shrapnel, poking it around while my brain attempted to tot it all up.

'I'll give you seven quid for a pint,' I offered my hand, hopefully, 'and 8p.' The milkman took the money, jumped out of the cab and handed me a bottle of silver-top.

It was the best milk I had ever drunk.

As he hummed on down the road, I wandered over to a gateway in order to prop myself over the bars while I enjoyed a drink. It was still foggy, but I could make out a dishevelled shape in the field before me, a little way off and curious in its form. Through the bins I could make out a half-collapsed tent, and someone poking out the front of it. It was Smoker Joe, and I climbed over the gate to go and see him.

I can only imagine that Joe had tripped over a couple of guy ropes trying to find the zip and taken half the tent down with him, because he was now hanging out of his sleeping bag, which was poked into the flattened doorway of the tent, looking pale and snoring loudly. He, too, was fully clothed and comatose; a couple of nudges with my foot proved that fact. Inches from his dribbling mouth was the remnants of a cigarette, burnt down to a perfect line of grey ash in the grass.

'Silly sod,' I muttered. He could have burnt himself alive. And then my thoughts darkened. It was half past six on a Sunday morning on a foggy Scilly Isle. If Smoker Joe were to burn himself alive with no witnesses, or at the least burn himself sufficiently for long-term hospitalisation, I would have one less competitor to worry about.

I crouched and closed my eyes for a moment, before slowly shaking my head. I couldn't do it. Not that. Joe was an oddball as well as a rival, but being burnt alive with a hangover wasn't a nice way to go. As I surveyed the scene, though, I still felt compelled to take advantage of the situation in some way.

Joe may have been hanging out of the tent, but his bag wasn't

– his bag containing his notebook; field records; days and dates of rarities and megas. Joe's always been a pen and paper man. I imagine he's got a computer at home, but I doubt he could do much beyond turning the thing on. If his tent were to catch fire, his year-to-date records would go up in smoke. There was no way he would have made copies, and his challenge for the title would dissolve into the fog around him.

A box of matches lay on the grass next to his open cigarette packet. I picked it up carefully and, though it was damp, could feel enough roughened strike to spark a flame. Mick had once shown me a trick he used when the wind was blowing hard, taking three matches together and striking them downward, giving a swift and large flame that crackled as the phosphorus ignited. I readied myself and struck the matches. Nothing, but a second strike caused a sizzle and then a flame. A mass of thoughts shot through my mind. Was Joe still sleeping? Would I get away before he saw me?

Ouch! Shit! My fingers were on fire! They had blackened as the matches blazed, but still I plunged them into my mouth to soothe the burning. I glanced at Joe – he was unmoved and still dribbling. The rush of adrenaline that'd come with the pain had temporarily cleared my head and seen off my hangover, but it was quick to recede. I took my fingers from my mouth – they were sore, if not blistered. It was strange, though; the burning sensation seemed to have spread to my left knee. My nostrils suddenly tickled with the smell of burning material, and as I glanced down I saw a coil of smoke trailing up my leg. Fuck.

Time suddenly slowed down.

A periwinkle-blue flame was licking up from beneath Joe's sleeping bag, and in the split second before I ran, I pieced together what had happened. I'd dropped the matches right next to the neck of the open bottle Joe had been lying on. Whatever was in the bottle (and judging by the image of flaming Christmas pudding that had shot into my head, I presume it was brandy) had ignited. I had to get out of there.

I glanced back when I reached the gate. I'd heard nothing, but could just make out a fuzzy orange glow through the fog. As I leapt over the gate and into the road, I heard the first shriek. Joe had finally woken up.

I ran, sprinting back towards the guesthouse as the shouts far off behind me grew stronger and turned to screams. A million thoughts were rattling through my head; the second surge of adrenaline had brought remarkable clarity to my mind.

Your footprints are everywhere, I thought, slowing down to a halt, *and your DNA must be somewhere.* I had left my milk bottle behind. *Shit!* I thought, and breathed deeply. I had to go back and help him. That would explain my footprints.

I glanced at my trainers. How common were they? Not common enough. And besides, there was the milkman – he wasn't going to forget the face of a man who paid seven quid for a pint of milk.

I began to jog back. The screams were now blood-curdling. Proper pained, gargled, helpless wails. As I reached the gateway I could see a mass of orange and red, zigzagging towards me. It stopped moving as Joe fell, and the screams became whimpers before they became silence. Through the fog I could see the still, amber glow, but it was rapidly reducing in size, and as I climbed the gate and moved towards it I realised another person was there, beating down the flames.

It was Mick.

MAY

A slow start to May, but Mick and I are off to Scotland on Friday, so we should boost our totals by at least seven species, hopefully more. I've bagged the honey buzzard and nightjar, though – both yesterday and both down in the New Forest. A pre-dawn start was good enough for the nightjar, though I didn't see it. It chirred away unmistakably, however, and I was able to head up to Acres Down with a hope that a honey buzzard may drift over, which, by lunchtime, it did.

I had to be home by mid-afternoon in time for Lucy's party. Eighteen! It doesn't seem quite possible. The family came round for an afternoon barbecue – my mother, Abi's parents, plus her brother Tom with his wife Sam and their two kids. A couple of Lucy's friends came round too; I can't recall their names, but there was no sign of the mysterious boyfriend, though Lucy saw him last evening. Nicola made up for the lack of teenage males by introducing us to Simeon, her latest interest. I caught Abi giving him the once over, giving Nicki a suggestive glance and a little nod of approval. I thought he was a bit of a prick, all hunch shouldered and angst ridden with his jeans halfway down his arse. He did charm Abi, though, suggesting her and Lucy were sisters (Abi took Lucy out this morning for matching haircuts again – the Rihanna look is back).

Mick was invited but declined, blaming a dicky tummy, but really he's kept his head down ever since the Scilly Isles. He was detained for questioning for two days all told: first in the local nick, and then back in Penzance. I hung around for him on the Monday – managing to bag a yellow-browed warbler and a hoopoe for my troubles – but didn't wait around when he was taken over to Cornwall.

My prolonged weekend also delayed the inevitable bollocking from Whitcombe, though he resisted further disciplinary action due to the 'desperate tragedy' that I'd witnessed. I couldn't have cared, to be honest. I can scrape by without that job. There's nothing owing on the house, and when my dear mother passes the remainder of Dad's estate will be winging its way to me and I'll never have to work again.

Mick also got quite a bollocking from work, similarly for having gone AWOL on the Friday afternoon, not to mention missing Monday and Tuesday to 'help the police with their enquiries'.

My own questioning had comprised little more than a straightforward request for a statement. I duly recalled that I had woken up poorly, gone for a walk to get some fresh air, and heard Joe's screams – by the time I had got to him, he was already unconscious or dead, and Mick was trying to beat out the flames.

Mick, though, had to explain why he was in the tent, and he couldn't actually remember. He said that he could recall leaving the pub, but wasn't certain whether he had gone back to Joe's tent to carry on the party (an empty bottle of brandy was found at the scene, I was told, the police believing that some of the contents of which had soaked into Joe's clothing, hence the fireball) or had got lost and ended up with Joe because he had nowhere else to go. Either way, the first he knew of the fire was waking to Joe's screams and getting out of the tent just before it, too, burst into flames.

The police suggested that he had gone back with Joe for some gay sex, their inquiries in The Chapel Arms having pointed to the fact that Mick had all but begged every female in the place for some old-fashioned heterosexual action but, having failed, had gone back with Joe as a last resort. Of course, this stung Mick's pride a treat, though his greater concern wasn't the false allegation of his bisexuality, but that Kerrie might find out about his very real flirtation-bordering-on-sexual-harassment in the pub.

The inquest was opened and adjourned, probably for some months yet, and the pathologist has yet to release the body, so there's no funeral date set. Joe's a Londoner though, so the service will probably be somewhere in town, meaning little value in me taking a day off to attend.

Obviously, I've applied for his vacant seat on the board, and with Mick seconding me, it should be a formality.

Absolutely knackered. It's close to midnight and I've only just got home, having been on the road since ten o'clock this morning. Next year, I am definitely driving us *there*.

We tossed a coin on Friday: Mick won, and at the time I wasn't too concerned. After a week at work the last thing I fancied was a five hundred mile drive, but as it was, I couldn't get my head down in the car anyway. As we passed Lancaster, I suggested that we take it in turns; if we were to be travelling through the night, I might as well be driving if I couldn't be sleeping. Mick would have none of it, however – he was taking us all the way to Oban, and I could get fucked.

He was charged up on Red Bull. He'd necked four cans before we'd even hit the M6; it was probably the fumes keeping me awake. I did nod off eventually, but can't have been asleep for more than an hour and a half because I woke up when the motorway ran out around Glasgow. Windy roads and roundabouts are no good for maintaining sleep, so I gave up, dug the thermos flask out from underneath the seat and poured a tepid coffee.

'Save me some!' Mick snapped, making me jump.

'Alright, Caffeine Boy – calm down …'

We shared the coffee and began to chat, Mick finally opening up a bit about the events of last month. It was clear that he was still mightily disturbed, and he'd been receiving counselling in order to address his trauma and insomnia.

'It's all well and good though, Ted – I mean, they can get inside my head, maybe stop me from seeing flames every time I shut my eyes. But they'll *never* get that smell out of my nostrils.

Never. I came home from work the other night and Kerrie was cooking pork chops. It all came flooding back. I threw up and promptly fainted, there and then. I can't even stomach bacon any more.'

I said little as Mick talked. To be honest, my mind was elsewhere, running through the schedule for the next two and a half days. If we could nail all of the Scottish specials and maybe a couple of bonus ticks at the same time, I would be well on course for this month. Joe's demise meant there were only seven others I had to seriously worry about, and, in all honesty, I really couldn't see Emma Kenton being involved in the final shake-up, so realistically it was me against six. The odds were improving.

Mick spoke in circles of self-pity for the remainder of the journey to Oban. Fortunately we made really good time, and by half three were only a couple of miles away with a four-hour cushion before the ferry set sail. Time enough for some sleep, for me at least, because as soon as we parked up Mick wandered off, hands bepocketed and a sense of moroseness shadowing him. He told me as we boarded the ferry that he had walked right round the harbour and out to the ruined castle, where he watched the sun rise over the town and wept for Joe, who would never see another dawn.

Thankfully he lightened up as we took our seats in the café on deck, partly due to the cooked breakfast he was tucking into (no bacon, sausage or square sausage, but four hash browns and three eggs) but also because he had accepted my offer of a pint of McEwans with which to wash it down. I never normally drink in the morning, but I was willing to give anything a go to lift Mick's mood, and three pints later we were ambling along the pier at Craignure and heading towards Bryn Davies, our guide for the day.

Last year, and it was my decision, we dispensed with Bryn's services and came up to Mull in February. It was naïve on my part, but I was a little excitable in the early part of last year. I had figured that, having paid Bryn to show us the birds in 2005, it would be a simple case of retracing our steps the following year and saving ourselves the cost of a hired hand. What I hadn't considered, however, was the cost of the ferry; the cost of fuel on the island; the fact that Bryn was (in 2005) taking us to nest sites which wouldn't necessarily be active or in the same place the following winter, and that Bryn, despite his name, had lived on Mull for thirty-odd years and knew it rather well. We might also have been more fortunate last year had we – or rather I – considered the fact that there were so few hours of daylight in February, and the weather was liable to be, quite frankly, shite.

We ended up on the island for three days and, having failed to spot a single eagle in that time, called Bryn in order to join one of his tours anyway. He showed us half a dozen golden eagles and at least as many white-tailed eagles, and though we were relieved, the lesson of that year meant that we booked him exclusively this time round.

What we did *not* want to be doing was sitting by the side of a sea loch oohing and aahing at a bloody otter curled up on a bit of kelp for two fucking hours. Honestly, our fellow tour members last year were gone in the head. It's an otter. It's asleep. Can we get a shift on, please? But no – they wanted photographs, and then they wanted to watch it swim, and catch fish, and look all furry and cute. It was just as bad when we clocked the first golden eagle, too. Bryn had pulled into a little car park up some glen, which overlooked a couple of lochs and some seriously high mountains. Within a couple of seconds he had spotted a goldie hanging over one of the ridges, got the scope on it, and we all had a peek. Mick and I had jumped back into the minibus at that point, tick achieved and ready to move on to the next spot. But everyone else seemed content to sit and watch this distant bird for three quarters of an hour.

'Oh it's gone …' they would cry. 'No, there it is! And another!'

It was far, far too cold to be standing on a mountainside, in February, watching the same bird soaring round and round and round.

This year, we had it sussed. There would be no hanging around to admire the view. Mick had pushed the hard sell on Bryn with his newfound status. As a member of the board, Mick suggested, it would be great business sense for Bryn to take us out on our own for the day at no additional cost. It would be good publicity for him, Mick and I being top birders, and if he could produce the goods in the morning, he'd get the afternoon off. We'd risked a little by booking accommodation for Saturday night way up near Aviemore – a three hour drive north-west – but that way we'd have more time the next day with Finn Paterson to take us around the Highlands, and it was likely that Finn's guided trip would prove a lot more unpredictable than Bryn's.

Bryn greeted us with great news. A white-billed diver had appeared in one of the sea-lochs at the north of the island, and was showing well: the bonus tick we'd hoped for. It was the diver we headed for first, Mick and I chatty after our early morning lubrication but Bryn relatively quiet. I don't think he really gets it, though I suppose he's used to carting round the otter lovers day in, day out; the kind of people who get excited if a deer takes a dump on a distant mountainside. We're certainly more serious and dedicated customers than he's accustomed to.

As we dropped down a narrow track towards the diver site, Bryn pulled over and pointed out a golden eagle above the cliffs on our right.

'Magic!' Mick was rubbing his hands and wearing a big grin. 'Onto the diver, driver, and then a sea eagle, and we'll be back in Oban before lunchtime.'

As it turned out, we arrived back in Oban at half one, having picked up the white-billed diver and white-tailed sea eagle with ridiculous ease. Bryn had to drive like a nutter to get us back to Craignure in time to make the 12.45 ferry, but he did it with minutes to spare, and Mick was soon tucking into another pint of McEwans. I refrained this time round and took the driving responsibility instead – day one had run perfectly, and I could wait until we reached Aviemore before I had another drink.

The drive was fairly uneventful, broken only by Mick's steady snoring and a telephone call from Abi. I had plugged my mobile into Mick's Bluetooth, and he woke with a start upon hearing Abi hallooing cheerily on the loudspeaker. Normally Mick had plenty of time for my wife and enjoyed the kind of flirtatious banter that would offend if I didn't know him as I do, but his grumpy mood had returned on waking and he barely acknowledged her.

Abi didn't seem concerned and was chatting away about her plans for the evening. She was going to go out with Lucy and some of Lucy's girlfriends, apparently. Down to the White Hart with all of the other student drinkers – she'd be twice the age of all of them, but would no doubt be happy to let people believe she was Lucy's elder sister.

Lucy's younger sister would be staying in on her own. Poor Nicki. Since Lucy's eighteenth, she's no longer flavour of the month in her mother's eyes. Simeon's long since left the scene, and she has a new boyfriend, Jake, who's not only quiet, well-kept and polite, but also her own age. It would seem Abi's less keen to hear about her younger daughter's (made-up) sexual exploits with a fellow minor than she was when Nicki would have been (theoretically, at least) the subject of sexual abuse by men a few years her senior.

Mick's mood remained gloomy until another couple of pints had perked him up, and by the time we sat down to eat he was as sparky as he had been all weekend. We propped up the bar after our steaks, and Mick did the round-up of board texts and phone calls as we tucked into a couple of large Speyside malts. The white-billed diver was a principal topic of conversation; its increase in appearances in recent years not detracting too much from what was a significant tick. The validity of the sighting was not in question, of course, and Mike Phelps for one was now considering a trip up to Mull himself.

Graver news came of my board application, however. Cornish Tom had emerged as the most likely replacement for Joe Muir's seat, having narrowly missed out to Mick last month. His credentials should have been questionable, as technically he didn't have sufficient grounds for eligibility. True, he'd finished in the top twenty on eleven separate occasions, but never for five consecutive years, and only once since the turn of the century. Obviously, he was well thought of; not least by Rod Smyth, who (according to Mick) has an interest in Tom that runs a little deeper than Tom realises. This was bad news, though. I would remain at a disadvantage for as long as I wasn't in the board loop, though the only saving grace was the fact that Cornish Tom wouldn't present any sort of threat to the leader board, even with the privilege of board membership – he only left Cornwall a couple of times a year.

Sunday morning's headache was particularly unpleasant, though Speyside whisky tends to have that effect. We'd barely finished breakfast when Finn rolled up outside the hotel. Mick'd used Finn's guiding services for some years, and he knew exactly of our requirements.

'Ptarmigan first, lads,' he announced, as we hopped up into the Land Rover. He normally ran a minibus, like Bryn, but with Mick having booked him exclusively for the day he was able to use his Land Rover, which was tatty and well used, but had a double cab as well as four-wheel drive.

We had four 'must-sees' on the day's agenda: capercaillie, ptarmigan, Scottish crossbill and crested tit. The off-road capability of the Land Rover proved invaluable, particularly for the capercaillie, which was proving elusive deep within the forests. The rain didn't help matters and didn't aid our spirits either, and by mid-afternoon we had only clocked the ptarmigan, the easiest of the quartet to spot. Finn proved his worth, though, and led us to a small flock of crossbills, before almost flattening a capercaillie as he took a short cut through a mass of Douglas firs. The crested tit was a gimme, Finn merely taking us round to his mother's for a cup of tea (Mick and I both had something stronger) where we sat and watched the garden bird table for half an hour. Finn's mother had been feeding the local Highland birds a mountain of peanuts through the winter and had a mass of species as a result: we saw three crested tits together, though one was all that was needed.

It was the sort of day that I really struggle with. We'd walked for miles, been bumped around in a cab in between stomps, and were soaking wet. People actually pay Finn to do this for *fun* – there are some strange folk in the world …

I've been 'invited' for a disciplinary meeting on Monday – a second written warning looks inevitable. Whoopee shit. It's a small price to pay for a buff-bellied pipit.

The pager buzzed on Wednesday afternoon with a pipit sighting, and Mick was on the phone about half an hour later, for once his inside info coming after the general populace were let in on the spot. It'd been seen around the top of South Stack, near Holyhead, a six-hour drive from home. Though it hadn't yet been confirmed by photograph, South Stack is such a well-watched area that I felt it worth a punt. Mick was going to try and get there at some point on Thursday, but was due in Birmingham at midday for a meeting. I didn't wait for him, and instead drove up overnight and was on site before dawn.

Abi hadn't been best pleased. Nicola had been in a strop all week, and Abi felt she was suffering from the lack of a father's influence. I really didn't have time for an argument there and then, but did agree to take Nicki away with me this weekend (still not sure where, as yet – I'm going to wait and see what's about tomorrow morning).

There were a fair group of people already assembling at South Stack when I arrived; at least thirty, and by dawn at least another dozen had arrived. There were no board members present from what I could see, though Emma Kenton appeared, greeting me like an old friend. I exchanged pleasantries with her, but I was really tired, and more concerned about getting the tick and hoping someone might get sufficient photo evidence with the lack of board presence.

I needn't have worried. The pipit showed as soon as the sun

came up, or so I was informed. It looked like any other pipit to me: small and brown, with a spotty breast. My research into potential species and the identification thereof hadn't included this little fella, so for once I was glad of the numbers there who knew what they were looking at. Emma was ever so excited, but I was finding the situation difficult. There were far too many seagulls around for my liking, and though I'd intended to get a couple of hours sleep before I headed home, there was no way I would relax enough with all those gulls about. Instead, I pointed the car south-east and headed for home, missing the pipit's demise as I did so. It took to the air, got caught by a gust of wind that threw it out over the sea, and was promptly thwacked at a hundred miles per hour by one of the resident peregrine falcons. I heard the story from Mick, who'd made it almost to the Menai Bridge when he got the news. Not a single board member had ticked it, Emma being my only challenger also to bag it. Result.

I ended up taking Nicola to Suffolk. The buzz came on Friday night (over the pager) that a sandhill crane had been spotted at the RSPB reserve at Minsmere; potentially the biggest bird of the year so far. I called Mick, who was in a peculiar mood.

'Yes, I've heard about the sandhill,' he said, more than a bit dismissively, 'there are no photos yet, but one of the wardens witnessed it, so it sounds solid.'

'I've got to bring Nicki along, Mick – do you mind? I'll happily drive ...' Mick went quiet.

'I can't go tomorrow, Ted. Problems at home. I might go on Sunday instead. Do it in a day.'

I can't pretend to have been too disappointed by this news. Mick was such hard work in Scotland that it was something of a relief not to have him maudlin in the car for hours on end. I jumped online, found a twin room in Aldeburgh – 'there's been a sudden rush, dunno what's going on,' the women had said – let Nicki (and Abi) know the weekend plan and then headed for bed. It would be an early start – pre-dawn, maybe earlier – since there would be an awful lot of people descending on the reserve on Saturday morning, and I couldn't afford to miss out.

I was up at half one in the morning, too wired to sleep any more. I found Nicki downstairs, still awake and watching some trashy film on DVD.

'You're having a laugh, Dad ...' She was open-mouthed.

'I said we'd be leaving early. Grab your bits, you can sleep in the car.'

She was asleep before we reached the M25, and the journey was smooth. I kept my toe down, but eased up as I overtook people on the motorway, peering in to see if I recognised any faces. I couldn't believe that any of my rivals weren't going to be en route, if not already on site. Some may have already bagged it. I hadn't pressed Mick for further details, for fear of him diverting the conversation around to himself. I really couldn't be arsed with any more of his self-pity. Joe was dead – he should get over it.

It was still pitch black when I rolled into the reserve car park, but there were only a couple of spaces left. Nicki stirred as I switched off the engine.

'Are we there? I need a pee …'

'You'll have to squat by the car, the reserve isn't open.' I wasn't overly sympathetic to my daughter's needs, but I was far too concerned with the other occupants of the car park. A small group of people were huddled around a little gas stove in the corner – it looked like Keith Atkins, something of a self-styled bushman, and his cronies.

Nicki sat bolt upright, suddenly wide awake.

'I will *not* piss by the car, Dad! There are people *everywhere!*'

'Slight exaggeration, Nicola, and please do not use that sort of language.'

"Piss" is not swearing. "Fuck" is swearing.' She folded her arms. I smiled. She's a prickly thing in the morning.

'Okay, Nicki – let's go and check the visitor centre.'

We did, and though it was all closed up as expected, someone at the RSPB'd had the foresight to hire in a couple of Portaloos, which were already well used. Nicki's face as she came out from her visit was a picture.

'That is fucking disgusting!' she snapped, screwing her nose up.

'Just because I let one "fuck" go, Nicola, doesn't mean you can get away with another.' I tried to sound authoritative, but the words sounded daft as I said them and I couldn't help but laugh. Nicki looped her arm into my own.

'Come on, Dad – let's get your telescope and go and find this *fucking* bird …'

Matt Carter was loitering around the car when we got back.

He looked up, saw me, and smiled.

'Hey, Chip!' he said, shaking my hand a little too eagerly, 'I thought this was your car. How are things?'

I hadn't seen or spoken to Matt since the Scilly Isles, and despite what'd happened on that occasion, I could tell by the tone of his question that what he was really asking was, 'what have you ticked?'.

I skirted the obvious.

'Not bad, Matt, all things considered. Mick's struggled to come to terms with what happened.'

Matt nodded.

'Poor old Joe, eh? I always told him smoking was bad for his health.' He turned and winked at Nicola. 'Do you smoke, darling?'

Matt's something of a Jack the Lad. I'm not sure of his age, but he could be in his twenties or his forties for all I know. He's full of smarm, well-kept, gave himself his nickname ('The Finisher' – sounds like a bloody darts player) and clearly liked the look of my underage daughter.

'I don't smoke, no … do you?' Nicola cooed, clearly taken in by Matt's charm.

I interjected.

'Nicola's too young to smoke.' She pinched me hard. 'At least she is for another month.' My disclosure of Nicki's age didn't seem to deter Matt – he was still on the charm offensive.

'So you're nearly sixteen,' he said, smiling. 'You look older.' Nicki smiled too, enjoying the attention.

'People do say I look older than Lucy, and she's eighteen.'

'So there's two of you, eh?' Matt gushed, 'a lovely pair of Bangers.' He laughed hard at his own joke.

'It's pronounced Bayn-ger,' I said, firmly.

'I know, I know, Chip – sorry, just a joke.' He cleared his throat and changed the subject. 'It's getting light – we need to get moving. I'll go and wake Emma up.' He gave me a little wink as if to confirm that, yes, he was referring to Emma Kenton, and, yes, there may well be something going on between them. I felt a pang of jealousy. Only very slight, but undeniable nevertheless, though my thoughts then ran immediately to the positive aspect of such a situation. If Matt and Emma were romantically involved, they were *both* likely to take their eye off the prize. It could work out very nicely in my favour.

Emma bounded over and greeted me with a big hug – slightly over the top – and then introduced herself to Nicki and squeezed her as well. Nicki warmed to the company of someone of her own sex and generation, the two girls giggling and chatting as the mass made its way along one of the boardwalks and into the swathes of reeds. I just went with the flow. In this sort of situation, and with most if not all of my main rivals in attendance, it was more important that I didn't miss anything. I could go off and do my own thing, potentially bagging a bird or two for myself, but I would be likely to miss the big prize.

With a few hundred eyes searching every inch of the reserve, it wasn't long before shouts were going up. The sandhill crane wasn't immediately on anyone's radar, but plenty of other odds and sods were. Bearded tits, marsh harriers, bitterns – all birds I already had, of course, but at around nine o'clock came an almighty result.

'Semipalmated!'

There was a mad clatter of tripods and excited chatter as the hoard descended upon the source of the shout; I shoved my way through them and clocked it straight away. A semipalmated plover – having missed it in March, this was a corking result, and a massive two fingers up to the people who had smugly bagged the first bird. I texted Mick with the news, but heard nothing back – he must have been so sore.

That sighting kept the crowd buzzing for the rest of the morning, and our numbers were swelling by the minute. It had to be the biggest single-day twitch of the year. I was painfully aware of how tricky it would be to get out of this place if or when the crane appeared, so warned Nicki to be ready to dash immediately. She didn't seem to care, and was still giggling away with Emma, the two of them rather enjoying the inevitable male attention from such a masculine-dominated crowd.

It was lunchtime when the shout went up and the sandhill

crane sauntered out of a reed bed into a blitz of camera shutters and telescope lenses, but having had my glimpse and got my tick, I was true to my warning and simply grabbed Nicki's arm, ushering her back to the car park.

'What if something else appears?' she argued, seemingly affected by the buzz of the morning, but more likely upset that I had rushed her away from her new best friend without time for a proper goodbye.

'Nothing else is likely to appear,' I said, 'at least, nothing that I haven't already got, and, if it does, we'll get the call and come back.'

We made it to the car park well ahead of the main rush, and minutes later were trundling towards Aldeburgh. We grabbed saveloys and chips for lunch, before checking into to the hotel and falling into our room. Through habit, I flicked the television on. The Cup Final was underway – Chelsea against United at the new Wembley. I'd completely forgotten it was on. I was exhausted, but the thought of a dozy couple of hours watching the Blues was rather pleasant. Nicki, though, was full of questions.

'Why do they call you "Chip", Dad?'

'It's short for "Chipolata",' I answered, without considering my dislike of my nickname, 'Mick came up with it years ago. From our surname. Banger – sausage – chipolata …'

'Do they call you "Chipolata Dick"?' Nicki sniggered. I snorted, slightly shocked at my daughter's crudity, but also finding the conversation and its direction mildly amusing.

'They do, yes – but you shouldn't laugh, you've got the same fecking surname!'

'Not for ever, Dad – I'll get married and the Bangers'll be finished.'

'Lucy has to get married, too, don't forget. Perhaps this new mystery boyfriend will pop the question one day.'

Nicola's expression changed.

'I doubt that,' she said, raising an eyebrow and fiddling awkwardly with her sleeve. She knew something.

'Have you met him?' I was eager to know. 'Do you know who

he is?' Nicola looked straight into my eyes. She looked confused and wary.

'I think I do ...' she muttered. I nodded and opened my eyes wide, prompting her to continue. 'Don't be mad, Dad ...'

'Just tell me, Nic!' Nothing and no one could be *that* bad.

'Well, I was in town the other day and saw Lucy down the street. She was a long way off, but I'm sure it was her ... anyway, she was with this guy and he had his arm round her, and then they had a little kiss and she went one way, while he came up the street towards me.'

'And ...' I was getting a little impatient.

'Well, he didn't see me, but I saw him clear enough. He came right past me ... it was your mate, Mick.' Nicola looked at me with a pained look.

I needed a drink.

Cornish fucking Tom's been confirmed on the board. What a joke.

JUNE

Three hundred: up in good time; nearly a fortnight ahead of last year – but this is a big month. I don't expect to be setting the world on fire – no one does through the summer – but I must hit *everything* that shows if I'm to keep up with the pace.

Mick called last night, after yet another weekend spent at home, and bigged up the challenge of Keith Atkins. He's this year's dark horse, apparently. I'm not sure how a guy who was champion less than four years ago can quite be considered a dark horse – surely he's a frontrunner? Nevertheless, I'll have to keep tabs on him when I'm able. The next results will be unveiled at the beginning of July, and they'll be the more accurate indicator.

Mick seemed more normal on the phone, more himself. Perhaps Kerrie had laid back and thought of England for a few minutes on Saturday night. Perhaps someone else had suffered the indignity – though surely not my Lucy.

No matter how much I trust Nicola, I simply refuse to believe that Lucy would see anything in Mick. I don't doubt that it was Mick that Nicki saw that day, but she admitted herself that the girl she saw was a good distance away, and I think she got herself confused. And while Lucy may be straight-laced and almost a little prissy, she enjoys hanging out with friends her own age and has no need for a 'father figure' – she has me. No, I'm confident that Nicki has called this one wrong. In fact I'm certain she has. I've kept close eye on Lucy throughout the last fortnight, and her behaviour hasn't been unusual. I pressed her a couple of times on the identity of her mystery boyfriend and she was quick to blush, though she reddened in embarrassment, not shame.

By last Friday, Lucy was definitely avoiding my probing, and

I realised that I wasn't going to get the definitive truth for the time being at least. More importantly, I was allowing myself to be distracted from the matter in hand. Thank God this diversion happened now and not in the autumn when the twitches will be coming thick and fast and my schedule might be severely compromised.

Fortunately, I didn't miss the only twitchable bird of this weekend. A red-footed falcon, in Essex of all places. Not the most unusual of ticks – in fact, one I would have expected to have already made this year – but it was showing well near the golf course at Burnham-on-Crouch, and with a large weekend crowd assembled and doing the hard work of finding the thing, I was there and back within six hours.

I've had better days.

I decided to chat to Abi about the Lucy and Mick situation and she exploded. I didn't mention Nicki as my source, but instead suggested that a work colleague had seen them together and recognised both (barely feasible, I know) and that I felt it best to discuss it openly with my wife … just as we were going to bed.

'Are you out of your mind?' Abi had asked, calm voiced, but with a frightening glint in her eye.

'I know – it seems ridiculous, but –'

'Damn right it's fucking ridiculous!' she screamed, toning her voice down as she remembered both girls were home. 'Is this one of your sick little fantasies? Done enough fantasising about screwing her yourself, so you're picturing your mate doing it instead? Your daughter, in the thick of her A levels, studying like mad, and you think she's sleeping with *Mick*? Have some respect for her, Edward!'

I don't like it when she calls me Edward. It normally signals a lengthy spell in the doghouse. Worse still, she was right. I shouldn't doubt my daughter. I'd wanted desperately to believe it wasn't true, but because I know Mick so well and know that he probably would, given half the chance (with either of my daughters), I'd let the possibility form a little seed in the back of my mind.

Abi was still shouting. Low-pitched, whispered shouting.

'Perhaps if you actually spent some time *at home with your family*,' she hissed, 'you might have a better idea of what we're up to.' She calmed a bit, and continued. 'Lucy's seeing a nice lad called Josh. They're in the same history class. He's eighteen, and they're taking their relationship gently until they've finished their exams. I've met him. He certainly isn't your mate, Mick.'

'Right,' I said, aware from her stance that although her tone had eased, I was still very much in the mire.

'Should I, er, sleep on the sofa tonight?'

'I don't care where you sleep, Edward – but it will not be in this bed.'

Maybe Nicola made the whole thing up. Maybe she's been lying to me about everything? No. She was being honest with me. I know her well enough to tell when she's lying. She made a mistake, and I shouldn't blame her. I definitely felt better for having mentioned it to Abi though, despite her reaction and the uncomfortable night I had on the sofa. My mind had been far too clouded by the very idea of Mick and Lucy together, to the point where I was losing my focus. With a clear head, I can get back to more important concerns.

Abi soon had other things to worry about anyway, albeit of my creation.

She totally blanked me this morning. Even when I went into the bedroom to grab a clean shirt, she simply buried her head under the duvet and ignored my apology. She didn't ignore me an hour later when I came back through the door.

'What the hell are you doing home?'

I was totally honest with her.

'I've been suspended from work. For two weeks.'

'Suspended?' Abi flumped onto the kitchen table with more than a slight touch of melodrama. 'What about money?'

'I'm suspended on full pay.' I was a little dismissive at this point, irked that her first consideration had been the financial impact. 'Until they conduct an inquiry and decide whether or not to sack me.' I wandered out of the kitchen, loosening my tie and chucking it onto the back of the sofa – that was something I wouldn't miss wearing for a fortnight. Abi was following me as I walked.

'Sack you?' Her voice had risen a couple of octaves. 'What the fuck for?' I was fiddling with the loose broadband wire by now, firing up the computer so I could get online and get busy, my indifference probably fuelling Abi's ire.

'My attendance record,' I muttered, 'mainly.' I could sense Abi required further information. 'I've missed a few days this year that I shouldn't have – but they were big twitches …' the bogus journey to Lincolnshire chasing that phony albatross suddenly sprang into my mind, '… well, most of them were.' I glanced up at Abi, who was silent but operating the kind of body language which requires no verbal communication: hands on hips, head slightly cocked.

I like the way her nostrils flare when she's angry. It reminds me of the younger Abi – the one who'd struggle to get angry with any conviction; who'd stamp her feet and grit her teeth like a child. For a moment I was struck with how pretty my wife was, though more pressing thoughts soon returned.

'Sorry Abi – I can't talk now. I need to email Whitcombe, get him to confirm the exact length of my suspension.

'What?'

'It's Tuesday, if you haven't noticed, and I've been suspended for two weeks. Does that mean I have to go back in on Monday 18th or Tuesday 19th? I forgot to ask at the time. And I need to know before I plan the next fortnight. Whitcombe's chosen two of the crappiest weeks in the birding calendar to give me a holiday, but I intend to make the most of it.' I turned back to the computer, opening a couple of the Bird Alert websites from my favourites. Abi was still standing beside me – stock still. 'And don't worry about money,' I said, deliberately patronising, 'I have plenty saved, plenty to come to me, and if needs be I can always get a mortgage.'

The last thought sounded particularly tempting as I said it. If I were to lose my job, I could take out a small mortgage on the house and go full time twitching for the remainder of the year. Very tempting. For now though, I needed some birds to see.

Three days of nothing. Mick says I should see it as a good sign. Apparently there are a fair few people charging around this week chasing birds I've already ticked. My lack of activity would suggest that my list is comprehensive and competitive. Maybe, but it also tells me that other people are rapidly gaining on the lead I may have had while I sit here twiddling my thumbs.

I could have hiked it up to south-west Scotland for a Ross's gull, but a couple of factors stopped me. Firstly, it was initially unconfirmed with no photographs yet to surface, and secondly, it was a seagull – albeit a very small seagull, but nevertheless, I didn't want to risk the trip on my own.

I've considered avoiding the rarer gulls until as late in the year as possible. There's a chance that I may not need them, and I'm also likely to pick them up on other twitches. At worst I would miss out on three or four ticks, and if I tick the majority of the remaining megas, I should be safe.

It's so frustrating to have so much time and so little to go at. I do need an eagle owl, and I know where a pair is rumoured to be nesting, but the area in question is the Forest of Bowland, which is vast and inhospitable. If nothing much surfaces by early next week I may give it a shot, but I'd rather wait until Mick's free for a jaunt, or we happen to be passing. The board will no doubt know the exact nest site, but Mick won't tell me unless I'm with him as he'll be just as apprehensive about making the trip on his own.

There was a pair in Sussex that Mick and I ticked for the last two years, but one too many people found out and the birds were shot. Selfish bastards. There's some loophole (I think because they're non-native) that allows eagle owls to be hunted as vermin. Now, thanks to some trigger-happy yokel, I'll have to troop to the other end of the country rather than my neighbouring county.

At last, another tick. It's probably been my longest drought since January, and I have a lot more time on my hands now.

A squacco heron turned up in Somerset yesterday – or at least, that was when it was reported. Rumours are rife that it was found over a week ago, before the weather settled, and that the guy who found it decided to keep it for himself. This chap (and Mick suggested this evening that he knows who it is) obviously got a bit of an ego trip by keeping the details hushed up, but Mick got the tip-off last night from Mike Phelps, and he picked me up this morning and drove us down the M4.

It was a bit of a roundabout route, the actual location of the bird being fairly near Glastonbury on the river Brue, but Mick reckoned the A-roads would be clogged up with traffic involved in setting up Glastonbury Festival.

'You ever been to Pilton Festival, Ted?' Mick had asked en route. He knows I haven't and yet he still asks every time we're anywhere near the place. He also has to refer to it as Pilton, not Glastonbury, because that's what the locals call it.

'No, Mick, I still haven't.'

'And you'd best keep it that way, Ted. Biggest load of over-hyped shit I have ever experienced.'

I can't pretend to be particularly into 'contemporary' music, but Mick makes me look like a culture nut. He skipped Radio 1 when we were kids, jumping straight into Radio 2 and maintaining the middle-of-the-road safety net into which his parents had borne him.

Mick was openly a fan of Cliff Richard until secondary school, when he was mercilessly bullied for the fact. The seventies, to Mick, never got wilder than The Carpenters or Barry Manilow, and he's been stuck there pretty much ever since. Then, in 1985 I think, he was captivated by a girl who was barely out of school but seemed ever so worldly wise: Mick pursued her for a couple of months, getting no further than a snog and the briefest of fondles. She was in her first year of sixth form and Mick was twenty-one and very used to girls dropping their knickers as soon as he flashed a smile, but she (and I can't remember her name, but it was something hippyish; Sky or Cloud or Dandelion or something) was headstrong and self-respecting, and a little aloof with it.

She was into modern music and the CND and had spent the previous summer camped with her Mum at Greenham Common, so it was natural that she would fancy a trip to Glastonbury Festival. Mick spied it as his chance to finally deflower her, and bought the tickets, a tent and a large box of condoms.

They went on the Thursday, and by Friday night Mick was back home. He kept a low profile for a week or so, and then appeared down at the pub with his usual swagger. He told us that he'd had his wicked way on the Thursday night, but she'd been about as responsive as a lump of coal and he had no intention of repeating the experience over the remainder of the weekend.

However, our friend Eddie reckoned he saw the girl a couple of months later and she had asked after Mick with some concern. According to her, Mick had struggled to put the tent up in the rain, getting soaked to the skin in the process, and had sat huddled and crying in his sleeping bag for 'hours and hours'. With a half pitched tent and a sad, sodden boyfriend, she had sought shelter in a friend's tent for the night, and then returned in the morning to find no sign of Mick, and not a word from him since.

I like to believe the second story, and think it rather more likely to be true – so, though Mick always raises the 'Pilton Festival is shit' argument every time we go near the place, I do always have a little smile to myself.

Mick didn't pursue the subject too far this time. I mentioned the fact that Nicola had expressed an interest in going to

Glastonbury for her school-leaving treat, and the mention of her name swung Mick's attention.

'She's legal soon, isn't she, Ted?'

I paused, briefly.

'Your goddaughter will be sixteen in a couple of weeks, yes – and you still haven't responded to her party invite.'

'I'll be there, Ted, don't you worry. All those ripe little sixteen-year-olds running around. Can't wait.'

'So you won't be bringing Kerrie and Scott?'

'They'll be coming, but it won't stop me *appreciating* young, unspoilt female forms. In fact, it'll give me something to think about when I get Kerrie home.'

'You're a shameless man, Mick.' I was smiling as I spoke, but then he overstepped the mark.

'They won't all be unspoilt, of course. Your Nicki must have had a couple of dozen pairs of hands over her – as Roger Mellie would say, she must have a fanny like a wizard's sleeve …' Mick still found the inane musings of *Viz* magazine a constant source of humour, but referring to my daughter – his godchild – in such a manner was a little too much. I was just about to let rip when the twitch came into view.

We'd been cruising along a long straight road getting ever closer to Glastonbury town, all the while keeping an eye on the river to our left, which was currently home to the squacco heron, and hopefully a small gathering of birders who could point it out to us. We weren't expecting quite such a *big* crowd.

'Bleedin' heck,' Mick muttered, 'they better not have spooked it.' There were at least a hundred people gathered, all jostling for space on a little farm service bridge that led off the road. Cars were littered everywhere, on both sides of the road. At some points there was barely room for Mick to squeeze through, and he merely added to the mess by pulling his car onto the verge just below the bridge, blocking in a couple dozen other vehicles as he did so. 'We won't be here long,' he offered as way of explanation, 'at least, we better not be.'

We got the scopes out and pushed our way through the masses, soon finding ourselves on the bridge and behind Mike

Phelps. Mick leaned over and spoke into his ear.

'You let the cat out of the bag then, Penguin?'

Mike spun round, knocking his scope off-balance as he did so. Fortunately for him, the sheer squash of people meant that his prized toy merely rested against someone's belly and didn't smash into the floor.

'Mick! Chip! – great to see you both.' Phelps was as ebullient as always, shaking our hands vigorously. 'Someone else must have gripped it last night. My source told me and only me, but when I arrived this morning there were already a couple of dozen people here.'

'So where is the thing?' Mick asked, disregarding Phelps's chatter.

'Tucked up in the reeds at the moment. It caught a fish about an hour and a half ago – either a roach or a rudd – but then it saw us lot, got edgy, and retreated out of sight. It hasn't flown, but it might need to get super-hungry before it says hello again.'

As ever, Phelps was using dozens of words when just a couple would suffice. This was mixed news, though. Positive in the fact that the bird was still here, but something of a worry that it was nervy and hiding up as a result. I set my scope up and reached into my pocket for a mint. Bollocks – I had left them in the car. I needed something to suck on while we waited around, especially with Mick blowing fag smoke in my face.

I tapped Mick up for his keys and pushed my way back towards the car, but I hadn't gone more than about ten paces when I was grabbed from the side.

'Chiiippie!' It was Emma and Matt. 'You been here long, Chip?' Emma was giving me an overfriendly squeeze as she asked the question.

'Minutes,' I answered. 'You both?'

'Half-hour, tops – we haven't seen it yet. Matt's already seen one this year, of course, but he phoned me this morning with the news and insisted he drove me down here.' Emma was prattling. Matt wore his usual smarmy expression over her shoulder. 'How's your daughter Nicki? Is she here?' Emma's eyes darted around the crowd.

'No, no, she behaved herself this week …' I said, adding, and God only knows why, 'it's her sixteenth birthday in a couple of weeks and we're having a party – you'd both be welcome to come.'

It felt as though someone else was speaking the words. I certainly didn't want this pair round at my house, though, in fairness, I couldn't imagine either of them would be over-enthused about coming to the birthday party of a girl they barely knew. Emma's face certainly confirmed the latter. She smiled weakly and opened her mouth to speak.

'Don't worry if you can't.' I had regained my senses and was making Emma's refusal less awkward for her. 'It's a long way to come and you hardly know her.' Emma's smile widened with apparent relief, only for Matt to lean forward and shove his size ten into the equation.

'We'd love to come, Chip – it'd be great to meet the whole family. What date is it and what time do you want us?'

Emma and I were both momentarily speechless. I was about to murmur something when we were interrupted by a single tone horn coming from the road: someone was pissed off and they weren't going to display the fact quietly.

The local farmer was trying to force his way through the mass of cars and people in the biggest tractor I'd ever seen. He'd obviously already lost patience with the lack of cooperation around him, and was inching forward with his hand constantly on the horn. He was nudging towards the bridge, surely making enough of a racket to spook the squacco. I pushed my way back to where Mick and Phelps were standing; they had both folded up their tripods, but seemed intent on staying where they were, quite understandably, too. They had the prime location for seeing both banks of the river downstream. Leave the bridge and it might be impossible to get such a good vantage spot again.

There was reasonable room for the tractor to get through, but as it kept coming people pushed and shoved to gain and regain their previous positions. The jostling was getting more vociferous and, as the tractor drew alongside me, it was all I could do to stay on my feet.

Opportunity knocked in that instant.

I feigned a shove from behind and clattered into Phelps, sending him sprawling forward. Unfortunately, my impact was insufficient to knock him off his feet, but in keeping his balance, he had to plant one foot directly under the rear wheel of the tractor: I got second prize.

In hindsight, the noise was rather surprising. Less crunch and more pop. Phelps's subsequent scream was a bit girlier than I would have expected. I went to ground, too, with a bit of a footballer's dive – I needed to ensure my role in the event would also be that of the victim. There were shouts; screams; the tractor driver stopped and clambered out of his cab, holding his mouth in fear of what he had done. Mike's foot looked as though it belonged in a cartoon. It was almost flat, though his brown leather shoe was already staining red.

I saw a flash of movement above me. Someone (I later found out it was Mick) had laid one on the tractor driver, who promptly spun round and clobbered the wrong person back. There was a rush of bodies as tempers flared and voices were raised, and as I struggled to my feet, I rather feared that the tractor driver might get lynched. But then a different shout, from behind the melee.

'Squacco! Squacco!' There was a scramble for telescopes and binoculars, as, sure enough, the squacco heron looped its way downstream and away from the madness of the bridge. Result.

We had to move off the bridge to let the paramedics on, and the police took a statement from me and as many other people that had hung around and were willing. Mick and I slunk off as soon as we could, grabbing a quick pub lunch in Glastonbury itself before heading for home.

Mick texted tonight with an update on Phelps. They haven't amputated his foot, which was apparently a strong possibility, but he will be in hospital for a little while as they'll have to use an awful lot of metal in the rebuilding job. I can't imagine Phelps's challenge will be up to much after this weekend. Even when he's released from hospital, he'll be in plaster for a long, long time, and won't be fit to drive for at least a few months.

I might just pour myself a glass of single malt.

After a dismal Monday, full of thunder and lightning and needless texts from Mick, the last few days have been epic.

I really didn't care too much to have hourly updates on Mike Phelps's condition on Monday, but, as with Smoker Joe, Mick seemed to have borne himself an obsession out of another's misfortune. True, Phelps's foot was properly mangled, but it was only a foot, and modern science would rebuild it as good as new. Mick set up a relay system with Mrs Phelps from the hospital, and phoned around the rest of the board – and me – with the most menial of changes in condition.

'He's going into surgery in an hour …'

'He's entered surgery.'

'He's still in surgery.'

'He's out of surgery.'

'He's contracted MRSA.'

Actually that final update didn't come through until Tuesday, by which time I'd all but stopped looking at the phone when I saw Mick's name, but, as I said in my texted response, hospital was the best place for Phelps to have picked up MRSA. I think Mick misunderstood me a little; he called me a heartless bastard, telling me not to make jokes at such a sensitive time. But I wasn't making a joke, and nor was Phelps seriously ill. True, he had to be put in an isolation ward, but the only real effect of the MRSA would be the delay in the foot rebuilding operations and, frankly, that was music to my ears, especially with some of the goodies he missed this week.

Monday's storm obviously stirred up a movement of birds across Europe because my pager sprang into life early on

Tuesday morning and it's been buzzing ever since. The coast of Norfolk was where the initial action was, with a pallid swift being the first twitch: I arrived on site at lunchtime on Tuesday, by which time a good few dozen other birders were there. Despite staying until dusk, the swift remained elusive, though I did have the bonus of a red-rumped swallow, which rather conveniently disappeared about five minutes before Matt Carter arrived. He was without Emma, and didn't seem too fussed to have missed the swallow.

'There'll be more by autumn,' he said dismissively.

The pallid swift is a little less usual than the red-rumped swallow, but there have been years when neither have appeared, so Matt's complacency shocked me. As it turned out, the swift put in a dawn appearance on Wednesday, meaning both Matt and I got our tick. Matt raced off back to London for work (he'd slept in his car – alone – and he didn't mention Emma at all, apart from the fact that 'they' were very much looking forward to Nicola's party next weekend. I'm glad someone is).

I was soon heading south into Suffolk where a glossy ibis had just been reported. Matt must have been sick when he got paged with that sighting, and there were no board members present when I arrived at site. There must have been fifty people there, though, and the ibis was showing well. I soon had another tick and was trundling back towards Surrey. The whisper among the ibis crowd was that the bird had shown up on Monday, and had been suppressed until Wednesday morning. I gave Mick a call on the journey home and he was a little coy about the whole thing.

'Haven't really heard too much about the glossy ibis to be honest, Ted …' he had murmured, with more than a hint of aloofness, before quickly changing the subject to Nicola's party. Scott, his son, wouldn't now be coming, but Kerrie would, and they were happy to provide the Pimms if we had the lemonade and 'salady shit'.

Nicola's party is getting out of hand. It's her sixteenth birthday, and it's got bigger than Lucy's eighteenth. Fortunately we haven't put an invite out to the wider family, though I've lost count of the people coming. Nicola's promised to limit her invites for friends to ten – plus Jake, the boyfriend – but that still means over twenty people descending, plus Emma and Matt. I just hope to God that the day's dry; I can't plan much beyond a barbecue in the garden, not with that many guests. I've told Abi to stock up on burgers, bangers and cheap rosé, not that she seems to be in the best of moods with me still.

She had the arse when I got home this evening.

'Nice of you to drop in,' she snarled, by way of a greeting. I can't work her out sometimes; one day she's full of support and actively encouraging me to get out to a twitch, while the next I'm in the doghouse for not spending enough time at home. I just ignored her tonight. Poured myself a drink and grabbed my journal.

I've done an awful lot of miles over the last two days, even managing another hop over to Scilly, for a whiskered tern of all things. A Bonaparte's gull also put in an appearance, which was worth double in some ways as it's one of the dreaded gulls that I don't have to go looking for later in the year.

Ironically, I'd found myself on Scilly on the same day as Smoker Joe's funeral in London. His final, flaming moments seemed an awfully long way away now, though it was reassuring to think that most of my competitors would be tied up at his wake and not gripping the whiskered tern.

I'm seriously hungry now, though. Abi didn't bother cooking me any dinner tonight, though, in fairness, I hadn't let her know I'd be back (almost) in time. I'd better go and soften her up a bit – see if she'll knock me up some bacon sarnies.

I've dated this the 24th, but we're a good hour or so into Monday 25th. Sleep's been a real struggle tonight, mainly due to tomorrow's meeting at work. My 'suspension' was increased by another four days, due to the fact that the Human Resources department hadn't been correctly informed of the suspension and hadn't organised a back to work meeting as per the Disciplinary Procedure. It all sounds like a load of balls to be honest, but I wasn't too bothered, particularly as it meant that I got to pick up an aquatic warbler and a Radde's warbler (among others) during the back end of last week.

What had pissed me off was the fact that no one from work told me of the situation until I rolled in last Tuesday morning. I found some speccy little teenager sitting at my desk and received a less than enthusiastic reception from my team, going into Whitcombe's office only to find his number two, Wendy Parsons, sitting at his desk and obviously enjoying her moment of power.

'Ah, Edward ... do sit down. Mr Whitcombe is on leave.' She spoke the words as she peered at me over the top of her glasses, and as I sat down she leant back, pursed her lips and brought her fingertips together like some kind of spiritual guide. I listened to her drone on in a monotone about 'ongoing HR issues' and the need for further investigation and discussion between herself and Whitcombe regarding the steps they were going to take, and then suggested I take the remainder of the week off – fully paid – and reconvene for a meeting on Monday morning.

I forgot to ask who the kid on my chair was or whether they were ensuring his acne didn't erupt over my desk, but, to be honest, I was more aware that if anything had shown that morning, I might have missed it unnecessarily.

As it turned out, Tuesday was fairly quiet on the bird front, though Wednesday and Thursday brought me a couple of ticks each. The weather stayed settled after Wednesday, though, which meant few new arrivals worth gripping. At least that meant we could go ahead with the barbecue plan for Nicki's birthday, although someone still managed to puke all over the lounge carpet and one of the sofas.

I blame Mick. He turned up with four litres of Pimms yesterday. To a sixteenth birthday party. It was no surprise that Nicola's giggling friends wasted no time in getting stuck into it. By four o'clock two of them were already upstairs, sleeping off the effects; I had to light the barbecue early just so as to get some food into their stomachs.

Nicola herself seemed to be oblivious to her friends' antics, and instead seemed intent on playing tonsil hockey with Jake. I barely saw her during the afternoon until she appeared by my side as I was flipping burgers, putting her arm around me and playing the cute little daughter.

'Daddy,' she half whispered, 'can I talk to you?'

'What do you want?'

'Well … Mum said it was okay if you said it was okay …'

I left the burgers and turned to Nicola.

'Spit it out, Nicki.' My words could have been better chosen. After her numerous afternoon disappearing acts with Jake, I dreaded to think what she might spit out.

'Can Jake stay the night?' She was still hushed, but fired the words out in a quick breath. I looked at her slightly blankly. She glanced around, and then, seemingly happy that no one else was within earshot, leaned forward and continued. 'I want tonight to be the first night, Dad … if you know what I'm saying.' She glanced around again. 'Mum thinks that Jake and I did it weeks ago, but until today I haven't felt ready … and now I do.'

I was a little stunned. A mixture of embarrassment, awkwardness and a tinge of repulsion had rendered me speechless. I turned to the barbecue and to the burgers; a few had caught and I began flipping them furiously.

'Dad …?' Nicola was still there. I needed to think. Part of me was touched, really proud and pleased that my daughter felt able to be so honest with me, but the thought of her fumbling around and losing what remained of her innocence with just a single wall between us was difficult to stomach. I pictured myself lying awake trying not to hear things that I desperately didn't want to.

In a moment a thought sprang to mind, and I pulled my wallet out of my pocket, turned to Nicola, and counted five twenty-pound notes into her hand.

'Go and grab the phone and get the number for the Premier Inn place over at Horsell. I'll book you a room for tonight, if they have one. You can get a taxi over there later.' Nicola's eyes widened, and she smiled broadly.

'Wow! I mean … thank you.'

She hugged me, and I suddenly realised how easy fatherhood can be. You just need to keep some cash in your wallet. Our moment of bonding was interrupted by a hand on my shoulder and a shout in my ear.

'Chip! Good to see you!' It was Matt and Emma. They'd brought presents for Nicola and more Pimms. It was going to be a long night.

The barbecue was a welcome distraction for the next hour or so. I kept the meat moving, and in doing so, avoided tedious small talk with my 'guests'. Matt and Mick had soon found one another and started talking shop. Not just about birds, but clearly board business, too. Every now and again they would lean close to one another and whisper behind their hands, darting their eyes around shiftily. Slightly over the top – I doubt any of Nicki's friends would really care to hear any of their secrets.

Emma had allied herself first with Nicola, then Abi and Kerrie in the kitchen (who were in the process of creating the most slowly prepared salad in history), before bumping into Lucy and Josh in the conservatory and realising that her opportunity for decent conversation lay with people closest to her own age. I just maintained a low profile, enjoying a light Pimms-fuelled haze and keeping an eye on my pager. This was one time that I didn't want it to buzz. I was over the limit, and frankly couldn't be arsed to charge off anywhere, but fortunately, it only buzzed with birds I'd already twitched.

The food did, temporarily at least, sober and straighten up proceedings, but as afternoon became evening, the drunken giggling of teenage girls was getting ever more tedious and louder by the minute. I shifted the party focus into the conservatory and shut the door, worried of a neighbourhood complaint and another visit from Plod. Inside, though, the atmosphere just became more raucous. Bottles of spirits were appearing, and Matt was soon leading the calls for shots to be downed – everyone concurred. Except Emma. She sidled off at around half eight, sharing a taxi with Nicki and Jake, who dropped her at the station en route to their evening's love nest. Nicki said the next day that Emma had always intended to leave early as she was off to another party up in town, but Matt had barely acknowledged her departure, so I can only presume they'd had a tiff of some sort.

The drink continued to flow, and my own head began to fuzz. Abi was in a very tactile mood and grabbed my hand around midnight, leading me upstairs to 'reward me' for the generosity I showed Nicki in funding a hotel room for the night. I was properly pissed by that point, and maybe it was the afternoon sunshine, but I was feeling pretty damn amorous myself.

Abi rewarded me a couple of times with a vigour I hadn't seen before, and by one in the morning I was an exhausted but sated wreck of sweat. I needed a pee, though, and a sit down – a feast of meat and a bucket of booze tends to have that effect. As I sat in the en suite, my head just starting to throb as the drunkenness subsided into hangover, I could make out the sound of sex elsewhere in the house. I had to strain my ears to hear it, but there were definitely male and female moans in harmony. It was an intriguing distraction from my headache, though I was baffled as to the location of the noise's source. Mick and Kerrie were in the spare room (a sofa bed in the study) and a possible source, but having been an unwilling witness to plenty of Mick's past sexual efforts, I was far from convinced it was them.

I couldn't remember Josh having left. It could have been him and Lucy, though I was beginning to wonder if it might in fact be Matt and one of Nicki's friends. Last I'd seen of of him (before Abi dragged me upstairs) he was trying to coerce the girls into a game of spin the bottle. They were certainly drunk enough to have agreed, and one thing could very easily have led to another.

The tempo of the moans began to change; rising, presumably, as they approached a crescendo. I strained my ears hard to listen – it wasn't that I was getting a kick out of it myself, but I simply wanted to know who it was. I was listening too intently to hear Abi padding across the bedroom floor, however, and jumped out of my skin as she burst through the door and vomited all over my lap.

Three hundred and twenty-one species submitted at halfway. Surely, *surely* that will put me top with plenty of room to spare.

July

Fifth? I'm fucking *fifth*? And not only that, I'm *joint* fifth – with Cyclops Johnson. A guy with *one eye* has kept up with me.

This is outrageous. Rod Smyth, Keith Akins, Cyril Nutkin and Matt 'Paedo' Carter are all ahead of me. And I'm only a few species up on Mike Phelps, who's been incapacitated for a month.

I need to crunch the figures into my spreadsheets and work out exactly where I stand …

They've covered everything I've ticked. *Everything.*

The glossy ibis in Suffolk – which Matt Carter 'missed' – well, he's got it. They've all got it. The day before I did. And Matt didn't even tell me about it at the pallid swift twitch.

And Mick? Utter bastard. He's been a right sneaky fucker. So much for friendship. I called him a couple of hours ago to have words.

'Ted? It's one in the morning …'

'I'm surprised you're not out with your bum-chums twitching ostriches and pterodactyls.'

'What …? I'm asleep, Ted …'

'You're sleeping easy enough then, Mick? Clear conscience? Don't feel you need to tell me something?'

'Er …' Mick sounded dozy and confused.

'A scarlet tanager, Mick? A *cagebird.* Surely an escapee, but no – you've ticked it, along with the rest of the board.'

'Oh, you're pissed off about the *birds.*'

What else would I be talking about?

'Damn right I am, Mick. We're supposed to be mates. Best mates. And you've been swanning around behind my back, twitching megas left right and centre, and not had the decency to let me in on it.' I was fuming, not least because Mick seemed so indifferent to my upset.

'Ted, I couldn't tell you. Not about all of them. The tanager was there for a day, maybe two, on private property, and the board decided it was best to keep the location hushed – wait and see if it stuck around before releasing some details. It didn't. It flew. Of course I went to see it. What fool wouldn't? A lifer, just outside Bristol …'

'And you didn't think that I might fancy twitching a lifer? Thanks a bunch, Mick.'

'I couldn't, Ted – just couldn't. Not that time, at least. And I wanted to tell you. I hated myself for not – I feel like I've been carrying around a dirty little secret. But the board made the decision, and if you'd suddenly turned up my discretion would have been called into question and I would've risked expulsion.'

I fumed, silently. I could understand Mick's predicament, but friends come first. Mick paused. I let out an audible snort, and he carried on, knowing I was far from placated.

'Cornish Tom was kept out of the loop, and he'd been accepted onto the board by then, just not sworn in. That's how strict the rules are.'

'Bristol's a little bit out of Cornish Tom's range, though, isn't it, Mick? He gets terrified crossing the Tamar, let alone putting a couple of counties between himself and home. It didn't matter if you told him or not.'

'Exactly, Ted – and we didn't tell him. So how could I possibly have justified telling you?'

The mention of Cornish Tom had now diverted my anger.

'Cornish Tom shouldn't even be on the board in the first place. He certainly seems to be doing rather well considering he never leaves Cornwall.' In truth, I hadn't noticed Cornish Tom on the list, my only real interest being those above me.

'You know Cornish got in through the back door, Ted. Literally. But you're at the top of the contender list. You'll be the next one in, no question.' Mick laughed. 'You just need some other poor sod to die!'

Mick's words have played heavy on my mind. He is, of course, completely correct: I can't win this competition without being on the board; I think that's fairly plain.

Only one tick so far this month, but July's notoriously quiet, so I doubt any of my rivals will have squeezed any further ahead. Of course, being out of the loop could be costing me dearly, but I'm hatching plans to get my foot well and truly inside the door.

I did have a cryptic text from Mick this morning. **Aquatic: TF 38993 12020. Not from me.**

He's clearly feeling guilty – as he should. His loyalty's been severely misplaced, particularly as it was my seconding that bought him his seat on the board to start with. Even now though, his efforts are pretty thoughtless. **Warbler?** I texted back.

Yes – not from me came the response.

Aquatic warbler. Thanks Mick. I think we were actually together when we ticked that one earlier this year. It just goes to show how little interest he has in my efforts, and how little attention he actually pays to this competition. For the last couple of years, I've held his efforts in high regard. He's appeared committed, focused and sharp eyed. This year, though, I've realised that most of his success is either pure fortune or the result of someone else's hard work; he's still in the running for a top twenty finish at the very least, but he has no hope of winning the thing, and I can't understand why he doesn't seem interested in pushing himself that little bit further.

I've stepped up to the plate this year. Gone to the next level. And I've left Mick wallowing in my wake. It's obviously apparent that I have the greater application, the greater strategy and the greater commitment to the cause. Like a lion rising through the ranks of a pride, I've done my apprenticeship, sniffed around the edge of the carcass, bided my time and cast the dominant male aside. The very fact that Mick forgot that I'd already ticked aquatic warbler – that *he* had ticked it – is proof enough of his failing.

He's inadvertently done himself a favour today, though. I'd been considering cutting him out completely and maybe telling the board about his false ticks – I'd yet to think about it properly – but as it is, I think Mick's more use to me at the moment as a friend, especially when he's this apologetic. He'll definitely second my application when a board seat becomes vacant, and though I'm confident that my profile and popularity among the rest of the board are sufficient to guarantee my acceptance, I can't risk another Cornish Tom sticking his wrinkly mitt into proceedings.

So, I need to create a vacant seat – but it won't be Mick's. What I might do, however, is use him for a trial run of something I've been considering. I can't rely on an opportunity to present itself as it has in the past: I need to create my own, get thinking. And on that score I have, this week, got my arse into gear and sorted out the time conundrum, at least for a couple of months.

On Sunday night I drafted up my resignation and went to sleep convinced that I would be shoving it under Whitcombe's nose first thing on Monday morning, but during the night I thought of a better plan. I would play the game.

I got up at seven, called in sick and then made an emergency doctor's appointment. I hadn't seen my doctor in years, but I felt confident I could convince him of my 'anxious' state. I turned on the waterworks in the surgery – just a little though, I tried to focus more on appearing jittery and aloof – and played the victim well, talking of my plight at work, being singled out for attention due to my being one of the old guard. I blamed my suspension on Whitcombe's personal vendetta against me. I spoke of the upset of finding my desk filled by another, and then, when finally allowed to return to work, finding myself demoted; forced to sit in isolation, where my work was monitored by Whitcombe himself. I felt scrutinised and marginalised. Alone. A helpless victim of a ruthless Civil Service, which was lining up people like myself for inevitable cutbacks.

The doctor began talking about employment law at this point, and suggested that I approach ACAS in order to further my claim of discrimination. I didn't want that hassle, so I wound in the conspiracy theory and played instead on my own state of mind. He soon bought it, and presented me with a sick note for two months.

Job done. Sick note in the post, recorded delivery, and I've bought myself two months before I need to worry about work again.

The week's continued to be quiet on the twitching front, but that at least has meant I've been able to put a hasty and rather sly plan of action together. I'm testing it out on Mick tomorrow morning and have sown the seed tonight. I'm confident it'll work.

The location has been key. I spent all of Tuesday and Wednesday sussing out where and when. I've yet to tell Abi of my sick leave – I just haven't got time for the endless questions – so instead I've been going off in the morning with a shirt and tie on and scouring the local area for the perfect spot for an accident.

I found it last evening. There's a lot of heathland around Woking; some of it common land, some of it MoD land, but all in all a sufficient amount to be able to find a small area that's seldom walked or played. Not far from Bisley is a little lane that eases into the heath, fizzles into track and then … nothing. People must use it to park and walk from, but in the two days I spent sussing it out, I didn't see a soul. As luck would have it, at some point in the last few months someone's taken a car up the lane and set fire to it; I can only presume it was joyriders, but I owe whoever it was a drink, because it makes an ideal landmark. About ten paces beyond the burnt-out car, a little deer track winds up the slope and into a copse. It carries on climbing through the trees and bramble before opening out onto a plateau. About three-quarters of the way through the copse, the path takes a left turn and climbs sharply through a tight little mass of trunks: it creates a distinct zigzag up the slope, and if someone were to slip, they could potentially fall around ten feet or so into a mass of brambles and probably do themselves a bit of damage.

I don't want to hurt Mick badly; I just want to see if my plan might work, and I don't mind if he gets a bit knocked up in the process, so I took a garden fork and a rope up today, tied myself to one of the tree trunks and then worked my way beneath them, letting the rope take my weight. The earth was dry, but sandy – easy to work loose, and within ten minutes or so I had exposed the bulk of the roots of the tree I was tied to. It didn't work quite as I planned, but when I pulled myself back up to the path to admire my work I could see I had done even better than I hoped. In the middle of the lower section of the path now lay a deep hole and a tangle of solid roots that could surely tweak an ankle.

I searched around the nearby area grabbing twigs and dried grass, and laid them all as gently as I could over the hole. It took a good half-hour to achieve, but eventually I was satisfied. Unless you looked hard, there was no obvious change of ground beneath your feet. True, I had put a lot of debris into the hole in order to disguise it, but a size ten boot would smash through the lot.

The next step was to apply the bait. A quick check online got me a grid reference for the plateau on the heath; then, and I waited until ten o'clock this evening before I did so (couldn't risk anyone popping up tonight and spoiling the trap) I texted an anonymous sighting to one of the bird report services. **Masked shrike – Bisley, Surrey.**

It could have been a risk using my own phone to text from – I certainly won't do so again – but I've been thinking on my feet somewhat.

Next, I needed a little bit more subtlety. I knew that the grapevine would very quickly begin to tick, but that the general response would be dismissive. I'd chosen the species in question carefully. A masked shrike is a serious mega – but one was on Scilly last year, which gives a hint of plausibility, and the bird itself is pretty distinctive. If someone was claiming it, a misidentification would be unlikely.

Next, I needed to sow a further seed. I gave Jon 'King' Arthur a call and fed him a line. Jon's one of the Cornish birders – a mate of Tom, and a similar age. His days of trooping up to Surrey to see anything are long gone, but that was what I was banking on. Instead, I acted as though I was looking to him for information.

'You've heard nothing then, Jon?' I asked.

'Not a thing. But why would I?'

'It was just that I heard a rumour that it was spotted by a couple of the Cornish lads, and they got a picture, but waited until they got home before getting a positive ID.'

'Hmm ... odd one this, Ted ...'

'Someone gave me a grid reference and reckoned there's a burnt out car down near it. They followed the path next to it, through the trees ... I thought if it was any of the Cornish lads, then you would be bound to know. Not to worry though, Jon - I'll give Tom a shout, instead.'

'Just a minute, Ted – I was due to give Tom a call anyway ... what's this grid reference of yours?'

Bingo.

I made the call to Jon at half ten this evening and before eleven, the grapevine had done the job. I wasn't worried about the paper trail coming back to me. It simply wouldn't. People like to keep their sources quiet, no matter how vague they are.

Mick called me at 10.57.

'Got a big one, Ted – and don't tell me again that I leave you out of the loop. It's local, too, really local – someone's reported it online, but there's positive info coming up from Cornwall. They have photos, too. A masked shrike, Ted. Here. In bloody Bisley!'

'Never! Are you sure, Mick?' I worried for a second that he could sense the breadth of my grin.

'Good sources, Ted. It's hush, though, for the moment. So let me get to site first. I'll go up about four o'clock – just as it gets light. I'll phone you as soon as I arrive and give you directions. That way, if anyone else from the board's there, I can't be accused of letting you know already.'

'Thanks, Mick.'

I was beaming, and I still am. It's nearly one and I can't sleep for the anticipation. Will it work? Mick couldn't have taken the bait any better. He'll be up in a couple of hours and phoning me soon after. I need to try and get my head own.

I woke with a start this morning. The sun was already up and casting a shaft of light up the wall through a small crack in the curtains. I reached for my phone. Nothing. No word from Mick, and it was nearly six.

Maybe he'd overslept? No, surely not. He stood to gain far too many plaudits from the board if he was first on site this morning calling a masked shrike. It must have worked. He must have snuck straight up the path before giving me a call and gone straight into the trap. He would be stuck there now, in pain. Maybe with a broken ankle twisted under a root or a broken wrist as he put out an arm to break his fall.

I smiled. The idea of Mick in pain was slightly amusing. He would be crying, of course. Blubbing like a child, feeling desperately sorry for himself. I felt a pang of guilt. Actually, no – guilt's too strong a word. A touch of remorse. Remorse? No, still too strong. I felt a tinge of *concern*. Yes, that's better.

I pondered, on the short drive to the heath, the best way to explain to Mick how I had come to find him. He'd mentioned the Cornish link, so it would be easy to convince him that I'd tapped up Cornish Tom for the exact location. It probably wouldn't matter though. Mick would just be too relieved at my arrival to concern himself about how I came to be there. And as it turned out, none of my ponderings mattered anyway.

The police were already there. Two cars and a bike, plus an ambulance – though there was no sign of the paramedics. Mick's car was just beyond the burnt-out wreck, and another car was tucked in beyond that. It was quite a gathering. One of the policemen strode over, grim faced, and my window was already down.

'Sorry, sir – I must ask you to leave. There has been an incident.'

'I think it's a friend of mine involved, though,' – the policeman didn't seem to be listening – 'that's his car. The Mondeo. Mick Starr?' I said his name with a slightly sharper tone, which caught the policeman's attention. He put a hand on the bonnet and leaned in, looking severely pissed off.

'Sir. I must ask you to leave.' His voice was sterner now. 'If you leave your details, we can contact you later and inform you of proceedings.'

I sat for a second and then wound up the window and slipped the car into reverse, attempting a three-point turn on the narrow track. I was two-thirds of the way through the manoeuvre when there was a bang on the roof. I jumped, looked round, and there was Mick – at the passenger window, white as a sheet, with one of those space blankets around him.

I wound down the window again.

'You alright, Mick?'

'Cold. Shock.' He was visibly shaking.

I turned the engine off and got out of the car, glancing towards the policeman as I did so. He seemed to have lost interest in me now that Mick had come over. Mick was murmuring.

'Matt ...' he said. 'Matt Carter. The Finisher. He's dead in the woods.'

This was a turn up. I looked over Mick's shoulder towards the burnt-out car. Yep, that certainly was Matt's car beyond it.

'What happened, Mick?' I crouched down and signalled for Mick to do the same. He really did look quite pathetic. Here he was on a lovely warm summer morning, shivering and wrapped up in tin foil, looking not unlike one of those post-rave pill-poppers who'd appeared on the news in the nineties.

'I got here at four this morning ... and found Matt's car here already. I didn't even know he'd be here ...' Mick looked at me anxiously. I think he was worried I'd be upset that he'd tapped up Matt and not let me join the party. I wouldn't be surprised if he'd arranged to meet Matt here; two board members, bag the mega together, and then let the common riffraff like myself in on the act. But I half smiled, encouragingly, and he continued. 'I went up into the woods and found him. Face down, but twisted. He'd fallen. The path's quite steep through the trees …'

Mick started to cry. I let him have a few moments and then touched his shoulder.

'Go on Mick, it'll do you good to talk about it.'

He wiped his face with the back of his hand.

'I tried to turn him over, but I couldn't move him. And then I noticed this lump pushing up his t-shirt. I thought it was his elbow at first, but no, it was a lump of wood. A branch. It'd gone straight through him …'

I struggled hard to remind myself of the scene I'd left last evening. Though I was delighted with my handiwork, I couldn't recall a dangerous looking branch that could have done that kind of damage to Matt. I tried to visualise the scene as I'd left it. I must have been so focused disguising the pit that I hadn't properly surveyed the area. Still, I shouldn't beat myself up. It had gone way better than I could have possibly expected.

Mick was sobbing again, but his expression changed slightly and he looked at me with a puzzled frown.

'Why are you wearing a tie, Ted? I thought you were off sick?' I automatically loosened my tie and undid my top button.

'I haven't told Abi yet. She thinks I've been going off to work every day.' Mick nodded and smiled. He'd be alright. I was suddenly anxious, though. I was in my work clothes, but I still had my change of clothes in the car. The clothes I'd worn yesterday. Oops. Poor planning, Ted. I'd left them in the boot. What if the police wanted to check my car – 'Just a routine check,' they would say. They would find the muddied clothes.

And – the sodding fork! The garden fork was still in the car. God God, what a twat I was. I had to keep calm, though. Not draw suspicion.

'Gotta go, Mick. I'll speak to you later …' Not the coolest of partings, but Mick was still in shock and oblivious to my sudden haste. I thought it best to acknowledge the police before I went, and tried to catch the attention of the guy I'd been talking to earlier. He didn't seem aware of me, though, so I slipped into the driver's seat and eased off down the track.

Seat belt! I put it on quickly. That would have been a stupid way to have been rumbled. I rolled slowly down the track, eyes practically glued to the rear view mirror. No one came running after me, though. No sirens were wailing. I'd got away with it.

It was still early, but the roads were already filling with commuters and I needed to get shot of the fork. I would hang on to the clothes – bung them in the wash when I got home. Time to tell Abi I had been signed off sick; that was one charade not worth maintaining.

The Basingstoke Canal was an obvious dumping point. I knew a quiet spot near Mychett where there was a little car park next to the towpath. It was only fifteen minutes away, and though there were a couple of cars parked up, there were no signs of the occupants. Dog walkers, probably. I checked up and down the canal and heaved the fork into the middle. The splash was excessive and could have drawn attention, but as I headed back towards Woking, I felt a rush of relief – a kick of adrenaline. I pulled into the first garage I passed and bought myself a lottery ticket for tomorrow night. I don't normally waste my money, but with my luck, I might just win.

Won a tenner. That's nine quid profit. I'm on a roll.

It's been hard work this week, and I've done a lot of travelling for just four ticks. It's been good to keep out of Abi's way, though. She exploded when I told her I'd been signed off sick.

'What'll we do? We can't afford you not to work!'

'Erm, actually we probably can, Abi – and at worst I'll get Statutory Sick Pay, which is something …'

'SS bloody P? That's no way to support a family!'

That comment put my back up.

'Abigail.' (She hates being called Abigail.) 'I have supported you from the moment we met. Look around you. Four walls – a half-million pound house – and what have you paid towards it?'

I hurt Abi with these words. Really hurt her. And at that moment, I really didn't care. She's always carried guilt for not paying her own way; or rather, other people have made her feel guilty. Friends, her brother, even my mother at times. Mostly it'll be light-hearted little jibes, poking fun at the fact that Abi's never done a day's work in her life. And to be fair, it isn't really her fault. She was only sixteen when we met, and she was fresh out of school. I was already in my twenties, working at the Employment Service, and a homeowner – even if that was largely down to the fat cheque I received after my father had died.

I saw her in town one Saturday afternoon. She was with some friends, but she stood out from the group. Her hair was shoulder-length at the time, and she had a sprinkle of freckles across her nose. I smiled at her, and she smiled back, before blushing. I walked on and into the pub where I was meeting Mick and the other boys. Mick was either still living in Bristol at the time, or had only just moved back, but either way I spent an hour listening to his endless sex exploits and realised I wasn't really listening to a word. I was thinking about the dark haired girl with the freckles. I guessed she was about seventeen, but in my head made her eighteen – it seemed less pervy. While Mick was waffling, I was placing a life around that cute smile. I decided she was at college and did have a boyfriend, though he was a bit of a dick. She wasn't a virgin (I was wrong on that assumption in the end) but she'd only ever slept with one person, her current boyfriend, who had a tiny cock and not much else to back it up. She would now be thinking about me. An older guy. Experienced. She was ready to move on to the next step in her life. To develop her sexuality.

I was at an age when I would think about every girl I met in a sexual manner within minutes of meeting them, and still had that unquenchable stamina that you take for granted in your youth. True to form, I was standing at the bar creating images of that girl in my head, when – boing – I had a hard-on. I shuffled awkwardly and tried to subtly manoeuvre my hand into my pocket in order to disguise the bulge. Touching it simply increased the problem, though, and I found myself arching my back in order to stop my cock from bursting out of the top of my jeans.

'You alright, there, Ted?' I think it was Mick who asked.

'Yeah, okay – just got a dicky tummy. Got some cramps. I need the toilet.' I headed across the bar.

'Needs a tommy-tank more like!' Whoever cracked that one was received with hoots of laughter, but I was thinking they might be right. Self-relief was the only answer.

The path to the toilet led me past the open door of the pub. I glanced out. It was fated. There she was: the same girl. And she smiled again. Before I knew what was happening, I was speaking to her.

'Can I buy you a drink?'

She stopped walking and blushed, her friends walking on and giggling together like teenage girls do.

'Erm, now?' She sounded painfully shy, and young. Then her

expression changed to concern. 'Are you okay?'

I was still bent awkwardly, with my hand stuffed into my pocket. Except now the source of my problem, the girl who'd inadvertently given me a stiffy, was looking directly at it. Though it would have seemed impossible, the problem got even worse.

'Don't go anywhere,' I said hurriedly, 'please. Give me two minutes.'

I stumbled through the toilet door and thanked fortune that a cubicle was empty. Such was the advanced state of my condition, it took only around half a minute to resolve it. The relief was immeasurable. I breathed deeply, tucked myself in, rinsed my hands and went back out into the bar. She was still there, just outside the door, scratching the pavement with her foot and looking desperately self-conscious. She tried to compose herself.

'I'm just with my mates at the minute – but you can buy me a drink another time.' Her line had clearly been rehearsed, or maybe advised by a friend – the gaggle of gigglers were still only twenty yards or so up the street.

'I'd like to,' I said, feeling rather cocky. 'What's your number, and your name?'

'I'm Abi.' She smiled, and then took a pen out of her pocket. 'Give me your hand.' I obliged, and she wrote a number carefully on my palm. It was the same hand I had just used to relieve myself, and as her fingers brushed against it, I momentarily pictured her hand doing the relieving. By the time she had rejoined her friends, I was back in the toilet cubicle.

I took her to the cinema a few nights later; we saw *Ferris Bueller's Day Off*. Some of my friends had raved about it, but I found it a bit dull to be honest – and far-fetched. Nevertheless, Abi and I were soon kissing in the back row, and continued kissing as I walked her home. She wanted me to come in and meet her parents, but I declined. Finding out as I had on the walk home that she was only sixteen was one thing. Looking her parents in the eye there and then was another.

As it turned out, Abi's parents were delighted with her new boyfriend. To them I was clean-cut, successful and offered the promise of a safe, secure life for their only daughter, and they weren't wrong. Within months they all but pushed Abi out of the door and into my house. It was weird when we first lived together: she would get home from college, make dinner, and then spend the evening writing essays. I had it made, popping down the pub most nights, a few beers with my mates, and then back home to my cute little girlfriend, who, at the time at least, was insatiable.

By the time Abi turned twenty, she was two years married and had Lucy. She hadn't needed a job at any point up to then – and I did always enjoy spoiling her – and ever since she's been a full-time mother. Though the sarcastic comments she's received over the years haven't been too barbed, they have affected her, and in recent years she's got upset more than once about the fact that she missed out on her 'chance of a career'.

Seeing her on Friday, tears welling up after I'd caused them, gave me the chance to make a suggestion and deflect the attention away from myself.

'Maybe *you* could get a job,' I said with a calmer tone, smiling as she looked up at me.

'What?'

'A job. Nothing major – we don't need the money. But something for you. Something you want to do.' I put my arms around her. She stopped crying. Situation appeased.

I've always struggled with the definition of irony, and try not to refer to things as being ironic too often. I used to sing along with that Alanis Morissette song when it first came out, quite unaware of people sniggering behind her back. I've steered away from the term ever since. Until now. This may be coincidence, but if so, there is an undeniable ironic edge to it.

Mick called yesterday morning, sounding sombre.

'Just to let you know that Matt's funeral is next Tuesday, Ted. Eleven o'clock at Kensal Green.'

Another London funeral venue. I'll be giving that a miss.

'Any news on my application, Mick?'

This was a far more pressing issue. I'd waited a couple of days until after Matt died before putting my name forward as his successor, but the response had been painfully slow. Mick himself took over a week of nagging before he seconded it.

'We're meeting after the service. It'll be discussed then.'

Ten minutes later, Mick was back on the phone.

'I haven't told you this, but I've got a tip-off from Cornish Tom. They've clocked another masked shrike – probably the same bird, but this time on Scilly.'

Is that not a coincidence with a nice ironic coating? The sad thing is, I've had no one with whom to share the peculiar parallel, which is maddening. It's just such a funny thing.

At least, though, I've been able to tick a masked shrike for myself – I missed last year's bird, so it's a lifer to boot. Yet another trip to Scilly. I'm still there now, back in Hugh Town, supping a pint of Doombar.

I've seen surprisingly few birders down here this time. The

shrike was easy enough to find – I just stumbled around until I found a sea of tripod legs and set mine up alongside – but there were only a couple of dozen other people there, and no board members in sight, though I'd imagine they would have all been down yesterday or the day before. For whatever reason, the shrike has only been reported nationally this evening. There are far too many games going on.

AUGUST

AUGUST 1ST 2007

331 SPECIES

It was gone nine o'clock when Mick finally answered his phone last night.

'About time, Mick. Your phone's been off most of the day.'

'I've been at a funeral, Ted – and then the board meeting. I've had my phone switched off.'

'I thought you might have died!'

Mick didn't seem to be in the best of moods.

'What's the word from the meeting, Mick?'

'You're in, Ted, but it's not official until the meeting next Tuesday when you can be sworn in. Obviously you need to be there, Ted – and it was somewhat frowned upon that you didn't make it to Matt's funeral.'

'Crisis at home, Mick – you know how it goes.'

Yessss! Finally. I'm on the board.

I managed to hold off on the celebrations last night, though I did sink a couple of single malts. I suggested to Abi that we open a bottle of fizz, but she didn't much appreciate the idea.

'For God's sake, Ted, I'm working tomorrow.'

Today was her first ever day of employment – she's taken a job at one of the charity shops in town, I forget which one. Two days a week to start with, half eight 'til five, with an hour's lunch break. She came home for lunch today, though I doubt that'll be a regular thing. She'd gone into town by bus this morning, leaving the Ka at home in order to avoid the ridiculous parking costs. By the time she made it back here at lunchtime, though, she had less than half an hour of her lunch break left. She was too anxious to eat, and I ended up having to drive her back in. Then she asked if I could pick her up as well, at the height of bloody rush hour. I did, this time, but made it quite clear that it can't be a regular thing. For one, I'm off sick, and if anyone from work spots me, questions might be asked. Far more important, though, is the fact that I can't commit myself to be in Woking town centre at half five when I might need to be anywhere in the country on a twitch. She can be pretty damn thoughtless sometimes.

Mind you, Abi's certainly found out how tough a day's work can be. She was in bed by eight, absolutely wiped out, and Lucy had to make us all dinner. A bit of an anticlimax all round really. I'd already cracked open the fizz, thinking it was something of a double celebration, and Abi only managed a couple of sips. Lucy turned her nose up (she has work tomorrow as well, office temp work for the summer) so it was left to me and Nicki to drink it. I know Nicki's always happy to have a drink, and I ended up opening a second bottle after Lucy went to bed, the two of us sat outside on the patio looking up at the stars with bubbles tickling our noses.

'So what's this board thing you're so chuffed about, Dad?'

I was amazed that Nicola needed reminding, but at least she was showing an interest.

'It's *the* board, Nic. The adjudication panel who sit and rule over everyone in the bird race each year. It's an unbelievable honour to be invited to sit. No one ever resigns or retires – the only way in is in a dead man's shoes.'

'And Matt's the dead man?'

'Yep.' I held my glass up, 'Cheers, Matt!' I turned to Nicki, but she wasn't joining in with my toast – instead she wore an awkward expression.

'You don't seem to bothered that Matt has died, Dad – did you not like him?' Whoa! Heavy stuff.

'I didn't really know him to be honest, Nic – and, well, if I'm honest, he did get on my nerves a little …'

'But he made such an effort to come to my party. Him and Emma … and he made such an effort to get on with my friends, too …' *He certainly did that,* I thought, and snorted, trying to stifle a laugh. Nicki shot me a look, so I quickly turned the snort into a feigned cough. '… he really did, though, Dad – especially after me and Jake left. He looked after Bryony really well; held her hair for her when she was sick, and cleaned up after her too.'

Hmm … so it was most likely Bryony and Matt I heard copulating in the middle of the night. She's a pretty thing, I suppose.

'He didn't clean up *that* well, Nic – we had to get the carpets cleaned because they were so matted up with puke.' Nicola managed a weak smile, and took another gulp of Prosecco.

'It is sad, though, Dad. He was too young to die.'

I could tell that until I shared some of my daughter's upset, she wasn't going to leave the subject alone. I suppose you've not had too many experiences of death at sixteen. None of her close family have gone during her lifetime, though my Mum can't be too many years away.

'You're right, Nic. It is sad. And it must be very sad for Emma, too. She must be struggling a great deal at the moment.'

I'm not sure just how sincere my sentiments came across, but they seemed to satisfy Nicola, at least enough for her to open up a bit.

'Emma *will* be sad, but she'll be a tiny bit relieved as well ...'

'What do you mean, Nic?' I was curious. It was a distinctly cryptic comment for my daughter to make.

'Sorry, Dad. I shouldn't say anything.'

I topped up her glass.

'You've got to tell me now ...'

It's odd, I suppose, but I felt (and feel) absolutely no responsibility or guilt for Matt's death. This was the first occasion since he died that he or his actions had even held any real interest for me.

Nicki drained her glass, and offered it to me for another top up. I obliged. She can seriously drink, my younger daughter.

'Well, he was a bit too *serious* for her. A bit full-on. She was happy just taking it easy, having a bit of fun – she's going to uni in the autumn, and wouldn't have wanted Matt cramping her style ...'

'And she told you all this?'

'Well, yeah ...' Nicki shrugged, as though it was common practice for people who barely knew each other to share their innermost secrets, and continued, '... and he – Matt – wanted to get serious. Get engaged, probably, but definitely live together and cruise the land looking for birds together, the Posh and Becks of birdwatching ...' Nicki laughed, but I was mildly affronted.

'It's a serious thing, Nicola. The bird race. There's hell of a lot of prestige involved.' There was a hard edge to my tone, which I instantly regretted. Nicki didn't know any better – she's only a teenager, for God's sake. How can she possibly understand fully the true values and worth in life? I was going to apologise – try and lighten the mood again – but Nicola did it for me.

'Oh, get you! Get over yourself, Dad! Have another drink ...' She tipped the bottle this time but filled my glass too much, the excess spilling over and dripping down through the gaps in the table.

'Are you drunk, my girl?' I feigned an angry tone this time, and Nicki beamed. She really is a smart girl. She could easily have reacted to my earlier comment; taken umbrage and flounced off in a strop. Abi certainly would have – and Lucy too. But Nicola's less volatile. More thoughtful. Certainly more laid back and grounded. In fact, she's a lot like me.

August 8th 2007

333 species

It's the day after my official induction and I must say, I was a little underwhelmed by last evening's festivities. I put a suit and tie on for the first time in weeks and even popped into town during the afternoon to get my hair tidied up – at least I bothered.

Mick picked me up at half six – he was still in his work clobber and still in work mode, talking business over the Bluetooth headset from the moment I got into the car until we were almost at High Wycombe. The meetings are usually held in a pub, a hotel or even occasionally a village hall, but that night we were to assemble in the lounge of the chairman's country house.

Timothy 'Claypole' Pitt, chairman for many years but of zero threat to me, lives in a small village in the Chilterns in a seriously large and imposing old rectory.

'Christ on a bike …' I gasped, as Mick steered us up the gravel drive.

'Nice pad, eh Ted?'

Mick had said few words since the end of his business calls. I thought he might have been feeling envious, seeing as tonight was all about me, but his tone now seemed okay.

'It must be worth an absolute fortune, Mick … bloody hell, no wonder Matt was so keen to get a ring on Emma's finger – some serious wedge in this family.'

'Looks can be deceiving, Ted.' Mick had stopped the car and was loosening his tie. 'From what I've heard, Claypole's got himself plenty of debt. Any money from this place would get swallowed up.' He'd now undone his tie and chucked it behind him onto the back seat. He clearly wasn't too concerned

about his appearance. Nor should he have been, it turned out –
Claypole answered the door in his slippers and what could easily
have been his pyjama top, though it lay largely hidden beneath a
tatty multicoloured cardigan.

'Evening lads, come on in … sherry?' His greeting was warm
enough, and he showed us through the hall and into a side room
where a selection of chairs formed a vague semi-circle around
a fireplace in which, despite it being August, a fire was burning.
'Getting chilly, lads, isn't it?'

'Er, a little,' I murmured. No it wasn't. We'd had the air
conditioning on in Mick's car, which was just as well because the
temperature was nudging the mid-twenties. This room, however,
with the windows shut and a fire chucking out heat, felt like a
bloody greenhouse. I'd met Claypole a few times in the past and
he'd always appeared well-dressed, very well informed and an
altogether ideal chairman. Today, though, he seemed doddery
and old, and, well, *disappointing*.

He had poured us both a sherry, and was handing them to us
when the doorknocker rapped again. As Claypole left the room, I
sidled up beside Mick.

'Is this normal, Mick?'

'What do you mean?' Mick knew full well what I meant, he
was just enjoying the power he still held over me.

'The lack of formality …'

'Well, it's a lot less formal than normal, Ted. But it is a *meeting*
of formality …' Mick was smiling to himself. He was obviously
pleased with his turn of phrase, but it just left me pissed off.
Before I could comment, though, the door opened and in strode
the vice chairman, Terry Holden. 'The Guv'nor'.

'Evening, Mick, evening, Ted – great to see you both.' He
shook our hands firmly and I was relieved to see him in a shirt
and tie; perhaps the mood would be more official now. Terry
helped himself to a drink – a malt judging by the colour (wish
I'd had that option) – and stepped over to the bay window,
loosening a couple of latches and heaving two of the windows
open, turning to Claypole as he did so.

'Good God, Tim, it's like a furnace in here!' He was almost

overfamiliar and certainly seemed to be making himself at home, but I was grateful for the movement of air, even if the temperature didn't drop. My shirt was clinging to my armpits.

Rod Smyth was next to arrive, unexpectedly followed – for me at least – by Emma Kenton, who was dressed sharply with her hair tied back into a bun. I hadn't recognised her initially. She smiled weakly at Mick and myself and sat down in the corner of the room.

'Emma,' Claypole announced as he ushered us to sit down, 'will be minuting for us tonight.' He turned to Emma. 'We shouldn't be late, dear, and you needn't note all of the induction detail.' Emma nodded and lifted a notepad from her bag.

I couldn't believe she was there in such a confidential circle. It had taken me so long to break into this clique, and all she needed to do was put on a smart blouse and bring a pen and paper with her. We would, no doubt, be discussing matters of a delicate nature; strictly need-to-know, and she, one of my main competitors (albeit one of the less fierce) was privy to every word.

What upset me even more was the fact that the meeting then commenced, with less than half of the existing board present.

'First, this evening, apologies.' Terry Holden was speaking. 'Obviously poor old Mike Phelps is still all but incapacitated, while Cyril, Keith and Andrew have all got prior engagements this evening and are unable to attend …'

Prior engagements? This was my fucking induction. Where the hell were they? Unless, of course, they were all together twitching some mega. I glanced around the room. Rod, surely, would be in on a conspiracy, but it was probably a bird he already had …

'… Tom Spargo,' Terry continued, 'having made it all the way up to London last week for poor old Matt's funeral,' (did he flash me a snide look then?), 'is unable to make the same sort of journey again this week, and I'm sure we all understand that.'

'Hear, hear,' Rod affirmed, tapping his hand on the arm of the chair as he spoke.

So, my point about Cornish was well proven. If he couldn't be arsed to do the mileage, he was unfit to be a board member. I sank the remainder of my sherry, wincing slightly as I did. It was sweet to the point of being sickly.

'Erm, another drink, Ted?' Claypole was standing now, offering his palm in the direction of the drinks cabinet.

'Thank you. Don't mind if I do.' I went for the whisky this time. It was a blend, unfortunately, and looked a bit odd sitting in a sherry glass. As I sat, Claypole began to speak.

'Gentlemen. Sadly, we have yet another extraordinary meeting amidst a desperately extraordinary year.' Claypole's tone had shifted dramatically – suddenly he was commanding and oozing authority. I sat up straight. 'The tragic loss of Matthew Carter has left a gaping hole in our society and our hearts …' he looked across at Emma. I followed his gaze, but she had her head down and was scribbling. '… though it was wonderful to see so many faces at his funeral service last Tuesday – I'm sure he would have been humbled and proud.' That was definitely a little dig in my direction. 'As I mentioned at the unofficial meeting last week, we have been fortunate to accept such a deserving individual to fill Matthew's seat as we have here in Ted …' I glanced at Mick, hoping for a 'hear, hear', but he said nothing, '… but due to the tragic circumstances surrounding this appointment, it seems inappropriate to celebrate tonight as we may do normally. Ted, I trust you are in agreement with us?'

'Er, yes. Of course.'

Was I bollocks. Mick joined the board in identical circumstances, and though he was being a secretive sod at the time, he told me enough of his induction for me to know I was seriously missing out. His night was more of an initiation: drinking games, silly hats, rites of passage; all I got was a glass of cheap sherry and a blended whisky that I had to pour myself.

Then came the book. Mick had mentioned this bit, too, but it was a minor detail at his party. Terry opened a small wooden chest and lifted out a parcel of cloth, bringing it over in front of Claypole, who was working his hands into a pair of leather gloves. I was ushered to join them, whereupon I too was given a glove, just one, for my right hand. I put it on. Claypole then unfolded the cloth to reveal the dusty tome beneath.

'*The Natural History of- Selborne,*' he said, with an air of
grandeur. 'First edition ...' I looked down at the book before me,
squinting slightly to read the author's name. There was no sign
of one – just scribbles in Latin. Luckily, Claypole was still talking.
'... by Gilbert White.' Gilbert White? I'd never heard of him.
Or her – was Gilbert a boy's name? I'd heard of Gilbert Grape.
That was a crappy film with Johnny Depp in it, by which logic I
could deduce that Gilbert White was most likely a man. 'Just rest
your fingers lightly on it ...' Claypole had turned from college
professor back into gibbering lunatic. He seemed so in awe of
this dusty book that I wouldn't be surprised if he took it to bed
with him, and not to read. I rested my gloved fingers on the
cover. Claypole cleared his throat. 'Now then, Ted. Repeat after
me. I, Edward Banger ...'

He mispronounced it.

'I, Edward *Bayn-ger,*' I corrected him.

'Oh, sorry, Ed. I mean Ted.' Claypole chuckled to himself.
''Ed Banger – Head Banger! That is rather unfortunate!' I forced
a smile, but I'd heard that particular joke about a thousand times
before I started school, which was when the real piss-taking
started.

Claypole composed himself again.

'Do here vow ...'

'Do here vow.'

'To see and share ...'

'To see and share.'

And so it went on – I can't remember it all, but it was a darn
sight longer than my wedding vows, and to be honest, after that
first line, 'to see and share', I zoned out and parroted the rest
back. It was utter hypocrisy. The board see plenty, but only share
amongst themselves, dribbling out the info when they (I should
say *we*) have had their fill.

Claypole finally rounded off the vows and passed the book
back to Terry.

'Well, Ted, that's it – you're officially one of us! Sorry about
the muddle with the name.'

'No problem.' I felt as though I was expected to say something.

'Do say some words, Ted,' Claypole said, sitting down. So I did have to speak.

'Erm, thank you all. Er, it has long been an ambition to sit on the board ...'

I really don't like public speaking. In fact, I don't much like the public, and I had no idea what to say.

'... It is, er, a very sad circumstance by which I have come to sit, however, and I, erm, would like to raise a glass to Matt ...' There were murmurs of approval and a rush of movement as everyone reached for or recharged their glasses. Mine was refilled for me, with the blended, and I held it up. 'To Matt,' I offered – not much of a toast, but it would do. Expectant faces looked at me for more, however, so I muddled a few more words out.

'I'm very sorry to have missed Matt's funeral ...' I looked in Emma's direction, but her head was still down, focusing on her scribbles – I couldn't believe my 'speech' was being minuted – '... but I, er, had something of a family emergency last week ...' I was treading water by this point, '... one of my daughters – my youngest, in fact, had a, erm, pregnancy scare.' I'm not sure why I said that, but it prompted Emma to glance up, a look of concern on her face.

'No surprises it was your Nicola!' As usual, Mick shoved his tuppence-worth where it wasn't welcome. I thought it best to tie up my speech, so I rose my glass again, took a sip and sat down. Claypole stood up almost at once.

'Bravo, Ted, bravo. Now! On to business!' He retook his seat and Terry took the proverbial floor.

'Not too much to discuss this time round, gentlemen. And with only a few of us here, it shouldn't take too long. First up, the great bustard ... but enough of our new board member!' I managed a token smile at this awful joke, though Rod and Claypole laughed heartily.

And so the meeting drew on. The great bustard was discussed – principally the reintroduced bird's validity in this year's competition – and the final decision was to adjourn the final decision until September. There were a couple of mega reports that required ratification, both of which were rejected (a short-toed eagle and a nutcracker). I say rejected – officially, 'further information is requested', which is as good as a rejection; if you haven't already got sufficient photographic proof, you're unlikely to suddenly come upon it.

The final mega-sighting up for discussion was the masked shrike, the one on Scilly. With four board members having made it down to see it (five, including myself), it was quickly approved, though the next few comments forced me to bite my tongue.

'Obviously, the accepted masked shrike in Scilly gives validity to the sighting in Surrey earlier in the month – it being more than likely the very same bird.' Terry was still the man talking, and talking now about my phantom shrike. 'We will never know whether or not poor Matthew had managed to tick it before his dreadful accident, but as was suggested at last week's meeting, we shall be awarding Matthew a posthumous tick.'

Unbelievable! Matt was already ahead of me, and now he'd managed a tick from beyond the grave for a bird that never existed. It got worse, though.

'Similarly, in the private ballot held after last week's meeting, it has been unanimously agreed to also award the tick to Mick Starr. Congratulations, Mick.'

I was absolutely dumbfounded. Talk about a frigging boys' club. Mick had barely pulled out of the drive before I could help myself from commenting.

'So you saw that masked shrike the day Matt speared himself, did you, Mick?'

'As I said to the board last week, I saw *something*, Ted. And even though I couldn't be a hundred per cent sure, the general jizz was that of a medium-sized shrike …'

I let out a snort, but could say nothing. The cheating bastard. Of course, I was a hundred per cent certain that Mick had seen bugger all – there was no shrike to see. But I couldn't say anything; I had to let him get away it. I'd spent hundreds of pounds and two days going to and from Scilly to bag *my* masked shrike, but Mick just told an almighty porky. Shocking.

A big day in the Banger household. Lucy picked up her A-level results this morning: three As and a B. She's quite rightly over the moon, especially seeing as she only needed four Bs or better to get into York, her university of choice. I took the family out for dinner tonight to celebrate. We went to the Chinese restaurant in town, which the girls have loved since they were little. It's far from cheap, and only normally a venue for birthdays, but we did have a double celebration today: not just Lucy's results, but also the arrival of my 'official' board member dossier and communication kit.

It came this morning via courier, finally putting me on an even footing with the remaining board members. Mick had always been a little cagey about what he'd received – an elusiveness that had suggested slightly more than the boxful that arrived this morning – but I was still pleased to finally feel like part of the inner sanctum.

The mobile phone I received was surprisingly basic, though a note with it suggested that what it lacked in features it made up for in coverage, according to the bumf – 'selected for the purpose of vital communication anywhere within the British Isles, this piece of kit is used for national communication by MI5'. Really? I couldn't quite see a special agent wielding this brick. I supposed it might make for a useful red herring, though. It certainly wasn't flashy enough to risk being stolen.

I had a little play with the phone. It didn't have any manufacturer's name on it, let alone a model name or number, with the SIM card apparently inaccessible without the use of a large hammer. I couldn't add or delete any contacts, and the existing contacts, of which there were nine, didn't display any actual telephone numbers – just the individual's nickname. I scrolled down to 'Superstar' and hit the call button. The ensuing ring tone sounded as if I was calling someone abroad, though Mick was quick to answer.

'I take it you have your toys then, Chipolata.'

I fucking hate my nickname.

'This phone seems a bit basic, Mick … and what's this crap about MI5?'

'True, apparently, Ted. Sourced by our president – he's got some pretty tasty contacts by all accounts.'

'What president, Mick?'

'Ah, so you haven't read the letter yet.' Of course not. Play with the toys, read the boring stuff later. 'Don't bother asking, Ted – I don't know who it is. Only Claypole does, and possibly the Guv'nor. Matt reckoned it's someone famous, but that was only speculation. Packham, Soper, Oddie … who knows.'

I dug the letter out of the box. The envelope was embossed and sealed with wax – all a little OTT to be honest. Inside, Claypole's signature sat at the bottom of two pages of waffle. I scanned through the bulk of it: a recap, really, of the vows I had taken and the responsibilities and trust I now commanded. Midway down the second page was a smaller, separate paragraph:

*The presidency is an unelected position relinquished only on the death of the current president or in extraordinary circumstances, whereupon the nominated successor is appointed in his or her stead. The identity of the president's successor will, until this time, remain anonymous to all but the existing president, who will have indicated their favour in their last will and testament or other such legally binding document.**

The asterisk corresponded with a mark at the bottom of the page. Here, handwritten, was the following scribble:

*Our current president has chosen to maintain anonymity throughout his or her tenure. This identity will remain withheld, even after their passing or succession.

– Timothy Pitt.

'His or her' tenure, Claypole had written. Was that a red herring, or merely Claypole trying to sound legally authoritative? The paragraph in the main letter only referred to 'his', not 'his or her', but the format of the letter looked like a well-used template. The fact that he'd bothered to add the last part seemed to suggest that the current president could, in fact, be female.

I was fascinated. Not only had I been utterly unaware of the very existence of a president until this point in time, the very fact that it was so confidential had me wondering why. This wasn't some secret Masonic society, and yet whoever was at the very top – whoever had sourced these MI5 superphones – wanted absolutely no connection with any of it.

The unmistakable trill of a nightingale sprang from my new phone. Nice touch; I had received my first text. It was Mick. **Bet ur wondering who!!!**

I certainly was.

I emptied out the remainder of the box in search of any further clues, but found no more reference to our president. Instead, there was another pager to add to my collection, a couple of chargers – one of which was for the phone and again, carried no manufacturer details – and a folder containing a heap of paperwork which looked decidedly uninteresting. I had a token flick through the folder, spotting contact details, codes of conduct and a great stack of past records, but nothing of any great relevance and certainly nothing so important that it required any reading now on my part.

Just as we were about to head out this evening, the new pager sprang into life.

-- BUFF-BELLIED PIPIT - ROMNEY MARSH --

Not particularly exciting, and besides, a tick I'd already made earlier in the year. What *did* impress me, though, was the text that accompanied another nightingale trill around five minutes later. It was from Emu Smyth. **Buff-bellied ID confirmed by personal source. Text for further details. Will suppress info until morning unless otherwise advised.**

This was more like it. I might have already seen the thing, but here was proof that board membership was going to keep me up with the game.

Since we got home from dinner, I've checked every national and regional website for any details of a buff-bellied pipit and found absolutely nothing. A week ago – in fact, a *day* ago – I would have been completely in the dark, but today, should I have wished, I could have picked up my tick before the rest of the country had any idea.

Another week, another family meal out. This time it was Nicola's turn to be the centre of attention, and though she didn't live up to the achievements of her elder sister, she managed to bag nine GCSEs – the bulk of them at C grade – and that was achievement enough to warrant another outing to the Chinese.

Nicola insisted on bringing Jake along with her, and the two of them were nuzzling up to one another all evening. Lucy and Abi have seriously chummed up over the last few weeks, coordinating their lunch breaks and consequently blowing their wages as soon as they land in the bank. With five at the table this week instead of four, I played not only the gooseberry, but also the sucker who had to put his hand in his pocket having only spoken about three words all night. I'd tried to muscle in on Abi and Lucy's conversation, but struggled to understand a word. Lucy did seem to be inferring that she might take a gap year, presumably because her relationship with Josh is picking up pace. I imagine they're sleeping together. Lucy is far more private than Nicola, but her and Josh have spent a few nights away at music festivals this summer – in a tent, admittedly, but I can't believe that at eighteen they can be keeping their hands off one another.

Most of Lucy and Abi's chat, however, focused around clothes and music. Abi has become a right little singles chart obsessive recently – tuning in every Sunday like I used to when I was about ten. She has a special affinity for McFly, a boy band seemingly aimed at girls considerably younger than Nicola, but instead snaring the attention of her near middle-aged mother. Embarrassing, really, but she's unashamed. Whenever I make the slightest derogatory comment, I get shot down for being out of touch. A boring old sod. Well, frankly, I'd rather be seen as a boring old sod than a woman past her prime trying desperately to act cool. Abi doesn't seem to remember that she's a mother to Lucy (and Nicola), not a contemporary. Her role is that of a guide. With principles. Not some wannabe teenager trying to reclaim her youth. A 'milf', as Mick puts it – a phrase he's become fond of this year. I'm not sure what it stands for, but he uses it when referring to women of an age – with kids, basically – that he would still shag … hang on, M.I.L.F. – ah. I think I've got it now. Anyway, I don't much like the idea of my wife being seen as such. And her current behaviour is liable to encourage exactly that.

I suppose the one positive aspect is that she's become so focused on her youthful regeneration that she barely notices what I do, which means that while I may feel a bit unwanted on family meals out (apart from when the bill arrives), I can at least jump in the car at half six in the morning and drive myself a hundred and sixty-odd miles to Blakeney, north Norfolk, without the slightest murmur of disapproval from my wife. In fact, I texted her a few hours ago to say I may as well find a B&B up here and head home tomorrow morning rather than fight through the Friday night traffic, and she came back with, **Of course – makes sense – might pop out with Lu and the girls tonite. love A xx**

Her newfound independence is a bloody godsend. She no longer berates me for blowing 'our money' on my 'obsession'. She earns her own money now, and spends it all as she pleases. New clothes, kitchen tools, a rug for the hall – and yet she puts nothing into the joint account. The one that funds the food bills, the utility bills, the car bills. The one to which I'm the sole contributor.

Abi knows she's onto a good thing, and I'm quite happy to let things slide along exactly as they are. An entirely unplanned and unspoken mutual understanding has developed. I'll leave her alone and she'll leave me alone: quite how long it continues is really down to me. I have every right to ask for a little help bankrolling our family – especially having funded Abi's entire adult life until this point – but I'll certainly not be pulling her up on anything until the New Year, when (if?) I've got the title in the bag. And today's dark-sided flycatcher will certainly help toward that goal.

It turned up yesterday, one of the Norfolk Nutters (a self-titled group of twitchers – I'm not being derogatory) tipping off Keith Atkins last evening. My board phone buzzed at half five this morning, and off I headed.

It was lovely to turn up at a mega-twitch with so few people jostling for position. A fair few Nutters were there, a dozen maybe, while the only other souls were board members; Cyril Nutkin, Keith Atkins and Andrew Johnson. I expected Mick to be there – he'd texted that morning to say he hoped to wangle his work so as to end up in East Anglia – while Mike Phelps was absent, still hindered by foot problems, and Rod Smyth turned up almost at dusk, when the bird hadn't shown since mid-afternoon. Word was getting out by that point, and a biggish crowd was assembling – mostly locals – but there's every likelihood that the bird will either scarper or lie low, meaning a possible dip-out for Emu. That really would be something – me bagging a tick that the champion has missed.

Mick called tonight to say he was in King's Lynn, having sat in a jam on the M11 for nearly four hours. Apparently someone jumped off a bridge; a bit selfish on a Friday afternoon, but more than a bit amusing that Mick had suffered for it. He's had to fork out for a hotel room, while I'm enjoying free accommodation courtesy of one of the Norfolk Nutters. My newfound board member status certainly does open doors. A chap calling himself Leighton Buzzard all but begged me to share his whisky and use his spare room. His wife fed us supper, too, and promised me a fry-up in the morning.

Magic.

SEPTEMBER

September and October will be pivotal months. The migrants are all on the move and some dramatic weather systems can throw them miles off course, particularly the youngsters, who don't really have a clue where they're going, instead just reacting to an instinct and flying. Just about anything can turn up anywhere, and I absolutely *have* to keep my eye on the prize. Stay focused. Keep my wits about me. I can't afford to miss a thing.

I called a family meeting last night in order to express the importance of the next couple of months (Nicola spied the chance to demand a takeaway, so I obliged and picked up a Chinese, along with a few bottles of wine – all the better for aiding my pitch).

Abi was quick to raise a negative point before I'd even filled my plate.

'What about work, Ted?'

I was expecting that question.

'As you all know, I'm currently signed off work due to stress and anxiety,' I said quietly, but firmly, 'I'm due back to the doctor this Wednesday, and I'm sure he'll sign me off for another couple of months.'

I glanced around the table. Abi was flicking her eyes back and forth between the girls, as if she wanted one of them to interject. Money was her concern, but she would rather have someone else ask the question, for fear of having to start putting her hand in her own pocket. Lucy and Nicola seemed indifferent, but I wanted to push the conversation along and so answered the fear that Abi dared not mention.

'I'm still getting full pay while I'm off sick, and I'll continue to for at least another four months. The Civil Service doesn't offer many perks, but it does look after the sick.'

'So, Dad, are you just pulling a monster sickie so you can go birdwatching?' Nicola was as blunt as ever. I finished my mouthful of chop suey before I responded.

'First of all, Nic, I'm not "pulling a sickie". My job has become increasingly demanding, and as a result I've been medically assessed and deemed, by my doctor, to be unfit to work –'

'– but well enough to go twitching?' Nicola wore a smug grin.

'That's enough lip, Nicola – your father has worked very hard for this family.' Abi was my welcome, if unlikely, defender. I glanced at her in order to smile my thanks, but she had returned her attentions to her food.

'Sorry, Dad …'

'No problem, Nic.' I sipped at my wine and continued, 'the next couple of months will be crucial to my hopes of winning this year's title. At the moment, I'm among the front-runners. It's unlikely that I'll be in such a strong position again …' I paused for a mouthful of food and in case anyone wished to comment. They didn't. 'Normally around this time we'd be looking to book a family holiday abroad in the autumn, but, unfortunately, I don't feel I can commit my time this year …' I paused again. Still silence from the table. '… so I won't be going on a family holiday this side of Christmas.'

Should I have been so absolute? 'This side of Christmas' suggested that I'd be up for a holiday in the New Year, but should I fail to win the title, I'd want to work doubly hard in January in order to kick-start next year's challenge. No, I should stay positive. I was going to win.

I glanced around my family. No one seemed to be too concerned by what I was saying – in fact, no one seemed to be listening. Nicola was already helping herself to seconds.

'Er, does anyone have any thoughts …?'

Lucy finally spoke.

'Well, Dad, if I were going to uni, I probably wouldn't have time for a holiday, but as it is I'm going to take a year out, which means I'll be working and *definitely* won't have time for a holiday.'

'And I don't want to let the girls at work down,' Abi piped up. 'It'll be busy in the run-up to Christmas. Maybe we should look at a holiday in the New Year …'

I glanced in Nicola's direction, awaiting her input. Abi and Lucy followed my gaze. Nicola felt all eyes upon her, put her fork down and shrugged her shoulders.

'I couldn't give a shi- monkeys, to be honest. Me and Jake might go away together if we can save up enough …'

'And if we let you,' Abi added, firmly.

Great: all my anticipation of family upset over a missed holiday was for nothing. No one bloody wanted to go anyway. I helped myself to more takeaway and topped up my glass, feeling rejected.

'Well, that's all fine and good, then …' My tone was a little flat, and prompted Lucy to speak.

'To be honest, Dad, the next couple of months won't be much different to the last couple, or the last few years. Or ever.' She let out a nervous giggle. 'You're away most evenings and weekends chasing birds, and before this it was your model boats, and model planes, and the stamp collecting and whatever else you got into …' Lucy lost her momentum and with it her confidence, smiling at me weakly, but I struggled to return a positive expression. 'What I mean, Dad, is that it's fine. You get out there. Find those birds. *I* definitely don't mind …' She looked at Abi and Nicola for support. Nicola was still shovelling Chinese food, but Abi nodded enthusiastically.

'Of course,' Abi said hurriedly, 'Lucy's right, you have all of our support.'

'Okay …' I was confused.

I ran through the last few strands of conversation in my mind. It was so out of character for Lucy to be outspoken about anything, and I mentally noted her dig about the time I spend on my personal interests. But she had, after that, offered her support, as had Abi. Nicola's silence was down to her love of monosodium glutamate, not a reflection of her opinion. I smiled.

'Thank you. All.' Nicola finally looked up from her plate.

'No sweat, Dad.' She gave a quick thumbs up. 'You get out there and win the title. Go. For. It.'

She returned to her meal, and I returned to mine. Within a minute, Lucy and Abi were chatting away about Louis Vuitton – a man, I presume, who apparently has a handbag fetish – Nicola had finished gorging herself, helped herself to another glass of wine, and had taken it and herself away to the lounge; leaving me alone with my thoughts, which was no bad thing.

The doctor was a breeze. I barely needed to play up at all before he was scribbling out another sick note. He did, however, recommend a course of anti-depressants – only a mild dosage, he assured me – which I felt it wise to accept. I took the prescription, but screwed it up and chucked it in the bin outside the surgery. I might let my doctor think I'm going to pop pills to improve my health, but I'm buggered if I'm actually going to take them. Prozac's for whackos. Still, I had the important thing – the sick note – and another two months of work-free twitching. Mick seems keen to make the most of the autumn, too. He drove us to last night's board meeting, my first proper one, and was full of plans on the journey home.

The meeting itself wasn't particularly inspiring, though there was a better turnout this time round. Only Cornish Tom (surprise, surprise) was unable to make it, using illness as his excuse. It still makes me fume: he has no commitment whatsoever, and should never, ever have been given a seat before me.

Mike Phelps made it, and he still can't drive. His wife gave him a lift and sat in the pub car park for two hours while we discussed business. I wouldn't have objected to her coming in, to be honest; Emma Kenton was there taking the minutes again, so another pair of unworthy ears wouldn't have affected matters too much.

Last month's dark-sided flycatcher caused a bit of a stir and some dissent among board members. Rod Smyth raised his concerns: he, along with Mick and everyone else present, had failed to pick it up on the Saturday (get in!) but he *had* seen an unusually dark-plumaged spotted flycatcher. Perhaps, he argued, there had been a misidentification.

Keith Atkins spat his dummy straight out.

'How dare you question me or the Norfolk Nutters!' he snarled. 'You're bitter because you dipped the thing. Have you *seen* all the photos?'

Emu was quite taken aback.

'My apologies, Keith. I didn't mean anyone any disrespect. I was merely raising a concern aired by people on the Saturday twitch.' Keith visibly calmed. Emu continued. 'And I was totally unaware of there being any photographs. I'd love to see them – not to question them, of course – just to admire the bird.'

Emu may have smoothed things over, but I'd seen a side of him that I hadn't expected. For the current champion, and seemingly such a humble and genial chap, he's clearly a seriously sore loser. He misses one bird and then gets the arse about it.

For my part, I kept quiet throughout the meeting. I had little, if anything, to add to proceedings and so, instead, was able to sit and glow inwardly at the fact that I'd missed nothing all month. Throughout August I'd bagged all I could have, and I'd even managed to get a tick up on Emu.

The only matter that did stir me up, however, was the final topic on the agenda: the decision to withhold the third quarter results and not publish any further updates until the decisive list in the New Year. This was a matter that had been discussed at length all year (thanks for the info, Mick) and the decision was down to the sheer workload involved in publishing so much data. It was proposed, therefore, that as of 2008, just the six-monthly results would be revealed, and that publication of this current quarter's results would be scrapped. I couldn't believe it, and did raise my concern.

'This seems a little unfair on all of us – sorry, *those people* – competing at the top end, though; aren't we moving the goalposts mid-match?'

Terry Holden raised his hand.

'A fair point, Chip, but this is no sudden decision. As you're no doubt aware, we've been mentioning this likelihood in the monthly newsletter since April, and we've had next to no negative response.' Terry clocked my confused expression. 'You do *read* your monthly newsletter, don't you, Chip?' He laughed, and a snigger rippled through the rest of the room. I forced a fake laugh, too.

'Of course I do! I was just worried that some people might have missed it.' Terry winked with a slightly patronising sneer, and turned to Emma.

'Emma, please disregard this exchange from the minutes.'

Bollocks did I read my newsletter. I never had. Well, not since the first one dropped into my inbox: a few hundred words of nothing studded with births, deaths, marriages and birthdays, and nothing of any consequence. I didn't even bother to open it now, and doubted that anyone else did either. Now there would be no way of knowing where I stood when the end of the month arrived. I would enter October, the absolutely critical month, blind. I might even have to get out there and track down a couple more gulls to be on the safe side. Good God, please, no. Not the bloody gulls.

I missed the rest of the agenda as I gently stewed about the news and the threat of seagulls, and was more than ready to head for home as soon as Claypole brought an end to proceedings. Mick, however, wanted to stick around and have a pint with Keith Atkins, who was staying in the pub for the night rather than trooping straight back to Norfolk. I was feeling far from sociable, but had little choice in the matter. Emma came over before she left and gave my hand a squeeze.

'How are Lucy and Nic?' she asked. 'Is Lu still taking a gap year?'

It seemed as though I was always the last to know what my family was up to.

'She is, yes – she's carrying on temping so she can get some cash together …'

'And spend some more time with Josh,' Emma smiled, 'there'll be wedding bells at the rate they're going.'

I frowned in shock. What an odd thought.

'Only joking, Ted!' Emma laughed. 'Though I am a bit gutted

that she won't be at York this year. We could have had a right laugh together.'

Lucy? A 'right laugh'? Really?

'So when are you off to uni?' I had forgotten Emma was going.

'Moving up on the fifteenth, ready for Fresher's Week, and then lectures start the week after.'

'And what about the bird race?' I was amazed that Emma was prepared to give up such a strong position.

'Oh, I'll get out when I can.' She sounded almost dismissive. 'I've saved a fair bit this last year; I can afford to blow some of it chasing the twitch. After all, I've got a genuine chance of making Rook of the Year – I might just be your successor!'

I felt a little disrespected by that comment. I'd worked hard to get Rook of the Year, and here she was, almost flippant about the title. She was in a good position to win, yes, but she also got the chance to sit in and eavesdrop on board meetings every month, getting all the inside info. I did it the hard way. Before I could get too pissed off, Mick was thrusting a pint into my hand.

'Get your chops around that, Ted!' He turned to Emma.

'Hey Em! How are you, darling?' Emma's lips tightened.

'Fine. Thank you. Anyway, I'm off. Bye Ted, say hi to the girls.' She barely glanced in Mick's direction and was gone.

'Bloody hell, Mick – what have you done to upset her?' My first sip of beer had seen half a pint disappear.

'Dunno, Ted – she must want my cock. She might get lucky one day.'

I took a seat. There were just Mick, myself and Keith Atkins remaining, and talk soon reverted to birds.

Until last night, I hadn't paid much attention to Keith – nor anyone else for that matter – but he's alright. A pretty decent bloke, and potentially a very handy resource. I'd always seen him as a bit of a tree-hugger; an ex-hippy who viewed life through rose-tinted glasses and a haze of pot smoke, but despite the wispy beard, he has a little more to him than that. I'm not too interested in a complete personality breakdown, but his little outburst at Emu suggests that he's got balls, as well as being in touch with nature. He does get a little too wishy-washy for my liking, though – a bit too romantic. A bird is a bird, not some piece of priceless art that needs to be admired for hours on end. Still, his chat about weather patterns and the effect they have on Norfolk, his patch, was surprisingly interesting.

Keith reckoned that many people were wasting too much time in autumn waiting at the regular spots (Scilly, Shetland) for the big drops, whereas if they watched the weather and the wind patterns, they would see that the big, cold easterly blasts were dumping all sorts of goodies down the east coast, especially in Norfolk – and it looked like this month promised to be better than ever.

The long range forecast promised a succession of weather patterns forming over Russia and Eastern Europe, which would roll the winds straight across the whole of Northern Europe and across the North Sea. The week of the seventeenth, he reckoned, could be a biggie, and if Mick and myself fancied joining him, he could guide us round the best of Norfolk.

I was immediately sceptical. Keith was one of the main players, I argued on the way home, so why would he want to help one of his main rivals (and Mick)?

'Who gives a fuck?' Mick said. 'Keith's too nice for his own good – he's happy to share. Plus he already won the title back in 2003. He probably won't be as driven as he used to be.'

Another point well made by Mick was that there might be ongoing tensions between Keith and Emu. If Keith couldn't win the title himself, he'd want to make sure someone other than Emu did.

Regardless of all of this conjecture, though, it looks likely that I'll be spending a few days in Norfolk this month. And Mick certainly will – he texted today to say he's booked that week off.

Things are beginning to hot up.

Thursday saw me charging up to Northumberland where I dipped out on a Siberian rubythroat (as did about a hundred others – and according to Emu, the photos taken on Wednesday are a bit dodgy) but did pick up a Ross's goose for my troubles. A shore lark (a bird I've dipped up 'til now) led me over to Deal on Friday, while Saturday saw me in North Wales, successfully bagging a Wilson's snipe.

The big problem now isn't just the amount of twitchable birds turning up, but the amount of misidentifications. So many of the migrants are LBJs (Little Brown Jobs; small birds that to the untrained eye may appear to be exactly the same). While I'm no expert, it gets my goat that so many people go out there, particularly at this time of year, see something unusual and, rather than consider the obvious, they start off considering the obscure.

'Oh look, is that an eastern black redstart?'

Er, no. It's a bog-standard black redstart – regular enough. But because you aren't used to seeing either, you plump for the mega, report it as such, and then keep a low profile when the proper guys arrive on site and make the correct identification.

To be fair, I suppose, the bulk of the birders out there are reasonably clued up, certainly respecting both the value of accurate identification and their place in the birding hierarchy. As a basic rule of thumb, at the bottom of the chain you have the fair-weather birders and the part-timers; those people who decide on a Saturday that it's a nice day to go birdwatching, so off they go, to somewhere local and pretty, and then they stroll around with a bird book in one pocket, a thermos flask in the other, getting excited about a kestrel or a blackcap – birds that may look nice, but are ten a penny. Then they'll watch those same birds for as long as they're in view, normally through a pair of cheap binoculars that they clutch tightly as they walk. They don't own telescopes, let alone decent cameras, and, as a result see little of real interest; should they report anything especially unusual, it'll be acknowledged with a large dose of incredulity.

Next step up are the patch birders. The big fish in little ponds. Some of them may be reserve wardens or recorders; others just locals to a site of marked borders where they can get to know every individual blade of grass. These people are more scientific. At least, I think that's what drives them. They get terribly excited about the first willow warbler of the spring, or the first swallow, and hope all year that a bittern may take winter residence in their local reed bed, whereafter they'll make a daily pilgrimage to see it and take yet another photo of it skulking among the reed stems. These birders will often be on site daily, counting everything. 'Gosh, there were three different magpies today, two garden warblers singing, and a flock of two dozen woodpigeons. Then two robins appeared at exactly the same time. Amazing! I got a slight erection …' The thing is, they spend so much time fussing over the same birds in the same bloody location that they wind up having to look at other things to stave off boredom, like butterflies, or flowers, or even trees – 'Good Lord, the dog rose has flowered two days earlier this year than last!'

To give them their due, though, they are pretty sharp if something good turns up in their manor. They get so excited about showing off a mega on their patch that they'll be there from dawn 'til dusk, for as long as the bird hangs around. All you need do is turn up and straight away they'll point the thing out, and at this point, they'll be rubbing shoulders with the county counters; those folk with a bit more of an adventurous streak. In fact, county counters will drop anything and go anywhere, any time, just as long as it falls in their county border. Now, I can understand – to a point – why some people get off on this. If you live in Cornwall, cut off from anywhere, or East Anglia, or the Isle of Wight, where it's not affordable to go chasing birds nationwide – in those places, I can see why a county list might be worth ticking. But in *Surrey*? Please. But still, they do exist. 'Oh yes, I've already seen dozens of hen harriers this year, but now one's turned up near Blackbushe and if it crosses the border, it'll be a county year tick!' And off they go, to waste days hoping that a bird flies from Hampshire into Surrey. Bizarre.

Again, though, and I really should give them their due, the county boys know their birds, and generally know if something out of the ordinary is amongst them. They tend to be as obsessive with their life lists as their year lists, so should something big show, they'll be out in force. They're also fairly happy to share their knowledge, meaning we can all get in on the act, though some cliques do exist. The Somerset Suppressors were one such group, though before my time. By all accounts they were a small band, formed as a splinter group from the Somerset Seers, tired of their parent group's open-mindedness and willingness to welcome all and sundry across their borders. The Suppressors took it as their life mission to find rare birds in the county and then keep it a secret, only letting snippets of information slip when the bird had gone. Then they would get off on the buzz of rumour that would subsequently surface. They might let a poor quality photo 'accidentally' appear on one of the websites, and as the rest of the county – and country – were gossiping about what may have been, they would sit smug, stroking their cocks and their egos. They started to give Somerset birding a bad reputation, though, and the Seers decided to take action. They released false details of a serious mega (an albatross, I think) and gathered en masse the following morning on site. Naturally, the Suppressors, showing complete hypocrisy by chasing someone else's sighting, all turned up, scopes at the ready. The Seers managed to ID them all, promptly outing them on the internet and making them instant pariahs. Mick reckons they gave them a right pasting too, but either way, they sank back into their sad little worlds and Somerset became a happy place to twitch again.

There are still plenty of political games going on nationwide, but the bulk of people respect the likes of me. I'm Premier

League. Top division. While the majority of birders are content with local rarities or counting the sparrows in their local park, we're the big boys at the top of the tree. The truly committed, taking it to another level.

Mick said that on his first couple of big twitches alongside Emu, he lost count of the autographs that he had to sign. He thinks it might have been as many as a dozen. That's a serious amount of respect and admiration. That's basically celebrity. And with myself potentially being in the same situation in a few months' time, I've already practised my autograph technique. I've pictured the scene: a young impressionable kid, out with his Dad, giving me a double take. He'd tug his old man's sleeve, and whisper something to him. I'd give him a smile, and maybe a wink, let him know (humbly) that I was he. The champion. Over he'd trot, clasping a pen and his favourite bird book, and I'd oblige, scribbling, 'Happy Bird-day, E. J. Banger'.

At this point I realised that I would have just presented the lad with my exact signature, so I spent a couple of hours working on an autograph that would suit. Something readable – he needed to be able to show his mates and them clock it without prompting – but also something far detached from the squiggle on my credit cards. I settled for a simple 'Edward Banger', twirling the lines of the first 'E' in an exaggerated series of loops. I toyed with adding 'Chip', but couldn't bring myself to include it. I dislike the name, and, besides, it's quite an ugly word to write. My own name will be quite enough.

Day one in Norfolk – well, day two, technically, though Mick and I didn't arrive at Keith's until around seven last evening. Anyway, I already have a distinct feeling that this is a big mistake.

The Atkins family home is pleasant enough; in fact Cherry, Keith's wife, is more than pleasant. I'd put Keith in his mid- to late-fifties, and he's certainly no looker. Short, grey in hair and complexion with a peculiar little wispy beard, he dresses quite smartly – always in a collar, and never in jeans – but even so, I wouldn't expect him to be married to someone of Cherry's stature.

She can be barely thirty. Tall, full-figured, lovely smile, though her accent is off-putting. I'm not sure if it's local, but it's certainly yokel. She sounds like one of the Wurzels – lots of 'oo-arr'-ing, and 'moi luvver'. Mick's obviously smitten. He thinks her accent is endearing, though I think his ears have been fooled by his eyes, and most of all the shape of her chest. Cherry doesn't appear to wear a bra, and yet they sit high and firm without.

'They could be fake!' Mick was full of it again tonight (we were on fold-up beds in Keith's study) and spoke of little else before he started snoring. 'Have you ever felt a fake tit, Ted?' I shook my head slowly, but Mick was already speaking on. 'I quite like the feel. Solid. They remind me of the first few tits I ever squeezed back at school, nice pert little cannonballs …' and so he droned on.

Keith and Cherry have certainly made us feel welcome. There was a chilli waiting for us when we arrived, and a cracking stew tonight. I don't know what the meat was, but it was just the job after a fruitless day in an east coast hurricane. As we washed down our food with homemade wine, Keith kept enthusing about the weather. That wind was going to bring goodies galore.

I probably won't sleep too much tonight. The wind's blowing hard outside and my mind is racing. Where's Emu? And Cyclops? And Cyril Nutkin? Maybe they've paid Keith off – got him to bring me here for a week, take me away from the real action. Keith's motive certainly is confusing. He's feeding us, guiding us, giving us free accommodation – and for what? Nothing? Out of the goodness of his heart? He said last night that he would get us five ticks this week. How does he know what either of us need? It's two and a half months since the last results were published; we could already have ticked every bird he thinks he'll find us. Something isn't right.

And another thing. This room smells. A mixture of cinnamon and, well, skunk. And a heavy must – though that's probably the shelves of old books.

I feel physically sick. Cherry dished up casserole tonight. *Game* casserole, she called it. I've never been a big fan of game – it tastes too … well, gamey – but I persevered and managed about half of it before Mick pushed the point of what we were eating.

'Can I taste pheasant, Cherry?' He was smarming.

'Er, yes, I think so, luvvy …'

Keith interrupted.

'I think it was partridge in this pack – partridge, pigeon and squirrel.'

I beg your fucking pardon? I didn't say this out loud, but the look on my face clearly spoke volumes.

'You alright, Ted? Not allergic to anything in the stew, are you?'

'No, Keith, no, no – and it's very nice. I've just never had squirrel before.' Or partridge. Or pigeon. Though they at least are semi-respectable foodstuffs.

'It's all fresh, Ted … well, freshly frozen; picked up, butchered and frozen all in the same day.'

'Picked up …?' I ventured, tentatively. I wasn't sure I wanted to know more.

'… from the road, yes. It's all free food!'

Christ, I was eating roadkill. I folded my knife and fork and pushed the plate away.

'It's very … filling,' was all I could muster. I glanced in Mick's direction. He was still chomping away, flashing almost indiscernible looks in Cherry's direction. He clearly fancied a bit of Cherry pudding.

Then Cherry took her top off. After dinner, sipping sloe gin by the fire. It was warm in the room, and Cherry obviously felt it cosy enough to take her jumper off. Mick and I were both briefly rewarded as Cherry's vest top rode up with her jumper and flashed, albeit briefly, a fine, shapely breast. Such momentary gratification was shattered by the next revelation, though. I wasn't sure at first, thinking I was seeing things, but then Cherry lifted her arms to run her fingers through her hair and there they were. Two hedgehogs, one under each armpit. I immediately glanced down at her legs, which were still (happily) betrousered, but I had seen enough to shatter my own lecherous thoughts, and judging by the glazed, shell-shocked expression he wore, Mick felt exactly the same.

Despite the tragedy of Cherry's bush, though, it's been couple of very fruitful days. The Nutters are a keen bunch, and on Tuesday morning it seemed as though most of Norfolk was out on the hunt. I don't much like searching, so was chuffed when the first call came through at around half eight. An eastern yellow wagtail had shown up with a small flock of yellow wagtails. The positive aspect for the Nutters was that with three board members among their number, any decent sighting was going to be ratified without a problem, and this meant we – or rather Keith – would be the first port of call for everyone.

For the last day and a half we've barely stopped, and though we've charged around after a good many birds I'd already bagged, I've picked up six that I hadn't, including two more lifers – Siberian chiffchaff and barred warbler. We have missed a few, but they were quite likely incorrect IDs – though a call's come through tonight which is pretty exciting. Leighton Buzzard has reported (only to Keith at present) hearing the call of a Tengmalm's owl in some woodland near Cromer. My first thought, since bird calls are something I do know a fair bit about, is that he may have misheard a snipe, but Keith is completely confident in Leighton's knowledge and is planning a sortie tomorrow evening.

I'm game – though I'm not overly excited by the rigmarole that will go with it. Keith has been bustling about all over the place for the last hour or so, sorting out a camping stove and a tent along with other bits and pieces. It seems his other love is foraging, and tomorrow evening he'll enjoy the best of both worlds.

Lovely. I arrived home to a germ-riddled shithole. Abi and Lucy
have both been off work with a stomach bug which seems either
to have affected their ability to clean up after themselves or cloud
their brains into believing that Nicola will do all the housework
on her own.

Either way, the kitchen was a disgrace when I arrived back this
morning, dirty crockery piled up everywhere. Abi and Lucy were
both still in bed, still claiming illness, though their sick buckets
were both empty. Nicola was nowhere to be seen, but appeared
after I'd already got one load into the dishwasher, clutching bread
and milk and sporting an alarming air of indifference.

'Alright, Dad. It's a puke-pit here. You had a good week?' I
murmured something in reply, but was too involved with the
cleaning to enter into involved conversation.

It's taken most of the day to get the house straight, and I'm
the only member of the household with an actual certified
ailment: not happy. And nor is my stomach. After a week of
eating vermin and God knows what else, I wolfed down fish and
chips tonight and it's not sitting very favourably.

In truth, I've eaten next to nothing over the last few days. Last
night's meal was Cherry's finest effort of the week, a vegetable
lasagne, but there was little of it, and I ate less than a mouthful
when, as it transpired, I should have stuffed my face.

The morning had been quiet, with just repeat sightings or
pre-ticked birds on the move. Keith got us over to Cromer
mid-afternoon, where we met up with Leighton Buzzard. Emu,
Cyclops and Cornish Tom were all apparently in the county and
seeking out some of our past grips, but we'd agreed to keep the

Tengmalm's owl quiet until the morning, convincing Keith that we didn't want to waste anyone's time should it not reappear.

Keith was happy enough once we reached site, and had soon rustled up a makeshift camp in the field adjacent to the woods. I sincerely hoped that we wouldn't need the tent – that we would bag the owl and be back at Chez Atkins by midnight. I imagined Mick shared my view; he hadn't slept under canvas since Joe smoked his last.

I followed Keith as he padded off between the trees in search of dinner, partly from ennui-driven curiosity, and partly to make sure that no hedgehogs or stoats ended up in the pot (God, I can't think of hedgehogs without picturing Cherry's mass of underarm hair and retching). As it turned out we were hunting mushrooms, and it was quite good fun. I had no idea just what was out there: Deceivers, which look dodgy but are edible, while Brown Rollrims look alright but can do you some damage. Keith was picking away, half-filling his basket within an hour, and though I forget the names of most, there was one species that did excite me. Deadly Webcap.

The name says it all.

Keith was gushing with excitement when he found them – three small and innocuous looking little toadstools. Apparently I was looking at a rare specimen; indeed, the first that Keith had encountered in Norfolk. He warned me not to touch, and spun a yarn of a near-deadly triple poisoning in Scotland a few years ago. As he moved away from the spot, I gently hoiked one out of the ground and snuck it in my pocket. It seemed daft not to.

In hindsight, I could have made far better use of that little mushroom. I should have offered to dish up and then popped it on one specific plate, because as it was, I simply chucked it in the pot just as Keith was gathering us together to eat, and then realised that I was leaving far too much to chance. I took a small bowlful myself – had a cautious nibble, poked the rest around to check the webcap hadn't found its way to me, and then, satisfied it hadn't, sat back to watch events unfold.

Mick, Keith and Leighton all seemed to be enjoying what may well have been their final meal, and as they shovelled forkfuls in the gloom, I pondered whose bowl I most wanted the interloping mushroom to end up in. Certainly not Mick; he was giving me a lift home for starters, and, besides, he was a useful friend. Leighton Buzzard I barely knew, and was no threat in the competition. It had to be Keith – in fact, I knew deep down as soon as I picked the thing that it was Keith I intended to fall foul of it. He'd given me some top ticks this week and was a generous host, but I still didn't trust his motives and, more to the point, he was a major, major rival.

Two hours passed before I began to suspect that the Webcap had avoided everyone. I had a little play with the cooking pot, feigning disinterest when I was really searching for a rusty-coloured alien amid the leftovers. I couldn't see it. Maybe Keith had misidentified it in the first place? A shame, really. It would have rounded the week off nicely – another man out of the running.

I did get one wish, though. The Tengmalm's owl began calling around eleven. Unmistakable: a strange, almost mechanical plopping call, and, though Mick was keen to try and flush it in order to get a good sighting, Leighton had brought a Dictaphone along and got a lovely crisp recording. We agreed that that was certainly evidence enough of its existence – and with three board members present, who else was going to argue?

OCTOBER

The weather's pulling in this week: finally the Atlantic's throwing a couple of storms our way, promising fruitful pickings, though the biggest dilemma on most people's lips is the same. Shetland or Scilly? Which will throw up the most? Every autumn when the wind starts throwing birds off their American migration routes, the two opposite ends of the British Isles are inevitably the busiest.

There was little in it last year, and Mick and I spent a week in Shetland, bagging plenty and having a laugh as well. Mick was set on pulling a local girl, any local girl – he fancied a bit of Viking, apparently. They were bound to like it rough. His efforts got nowhere, though, the few local girls we encountered showing not a shred of interest in Mick's Anglo-Saxon charms.

This year the general consensus seems to be very much one or the other. A lot of forum pages on the internet have filled with arguments for each venue and, in truth, there's little objective opinion – it seems to come down purely to a personal preference for either dark, damp Scottish days, or warm, dry Cornish ones. Me? I've got the distinct advantage of time and, to a degree, money. In other words, I'm going to do both.

This really is make or break time. If I batter the credit cards so be it, but my bag's packed, my telescope stowed, and on Thursday morning I'll head west: first to Scilly, figuring that the first birds to drop will be doing so there, it being the first point of call on a transatlantic crossing. I'll leave the following week or so up to chance – just follow the pager. I don't care if I end up on a non-stop hop to and from Lerwick and Bristol airports, just as long as I keep bagging.

One person definitely out of the autumn equation – and all but out of the title race as a result – is Keith Atkins. Poor old Keith is on a life-support machine and it's touch and go as to whether he makes it – complete kidney failure, apparently.

I'm sipping my third Doombar as I write – back in Hugh Town, and back in the Abbey Arms. I've spent so much time here this year that the barman recognised me as I wandered in, and I have to say it was comforting to see a cheery face.

Abi kicked off big time last night, apropos of *nothing*. I was just looking through my bag, checking I hadn't forgotten anything, when she wandered into the bedroom and exploded.

'I can't believe you're fucking off AGAIN!' she screamed.

I was speechless. She knew where I was going and she knew when I was going. I'd been a bit vague about my intended return, but suggested it would be a week or so, and, besides, she'd offered me her support at our family meeting last month. My argument calmed her a little insomuch as she left the room, trying to take the door off its hinges as she did so. I couldn't be arsed to follow her, and instead sat and stewed for the best part of an hour, getting myself seriously worked up. When the door creaked open again, I was ready for war.

Except Abi had brought a peace offering. Not the steaming mug of Horlicks that she placed on the dressing table, but the glass of cold malt that she fetched straight after. I caught a whiff as she offered it to me: Laphroaig – a fine choice, though she'd left it neat and I usually prefer a drop of water.

'Malt for us both …' She smiled weakly as she spoke. 'Sorry, love – I'm just tired at the moment.'

Then came the tears. I gulped a mouthful of whisky, put my glass down and offered my arms, and Abi fell into me.

'I know that I said I supported you.' The words were tricky to decipher through the sobbing. '… and I d-d-do support you.

And I know you support me. *My ex-horse died …*'

I may have misheard that last comment, but I got the general gist. As she calmed she talked more rationally: she was exhausted, work was so busy (she should try a full-time job in the Civil Service), the house was a mess and the girls didn't help. To be fair, she made not one further disparaging comment about me, which I was pleased about, and having worked Abi out of my embrace and onto the bed and laid the top blanket over her, I told her I would go and talk to Lucy and Nicola in order to ensure they pulled their weight while I was away. She gave me a watery smile.

I nipped into the bathroom before going downstairs in order to water down the whisky. The next gulp slipped down a lot more smoothly. The girls listened, flashed little sideways looks to one another, but promised to do their bit while I was gone, so, fatherhood duties complete, I found the bottle of Laphroaig and poured another glass. I should have left it there, but had a third, fourth and fifth glass, and a nagging headache this morning.

Flying's no fun at all when you're even slightly hungover. The air conditioning dries you out like a prune and you end up gasping for air. I keep some rehydration crystals in the bathroom cabinet, the ones designed for the squits, and on waking, had a rummage around to find them. I had one sachet left, thank God, which I quickly tipped into a glass and topped up with water. As I chucked the empty packet at the bin, I thought of Abi's comments last night, and seeing it overflowing, decided to do my bit and empty it. I couldn't be bothered to mess about with bin bags and the like, instead just carrying the bin downstairs, out of the back door and tipping the contents loose into the dustbin.

It caught my eye immediately. At first I thought it was a vibrator, and then on closer inspection it looked like an electric toothbrush, but on reaching it out, I realised exactly what it was. A pregnancy test. Used. And I was holding the business end.

I dropped it hurriedly and ducked back indoors, piling washing up liquid onto my hands in order to wash off God knows what. I had to have another peek, though. It had two red lines on it: positive.

Shit.

I could think of nothing else as I chugged down the M4.
I was going to be a granddad at forty-four. But whose test
was it? Both girls were active. Both girls in (relatively) serious
relationships. Perhaps it wasn't an accident? After all, Lucy had
suddenly decided to take a year out, having always previously
been driven by academia. Maybe she wasn't saving money –
at least, not for university, but to have a family. Even Emma
Kenton had commented on how serious Josh and Lucy were
getting. Maybe she knew more than she was letting on. She was
always in contact with Lucy on Facebook, and she hadn't been
shocked to hear that Lu wouldn't be joining her at York this
autumn.

And then there was Nicola, who liked a drink – nothing
wrong with that – but could she have overdone it one night? Had
a bit too much, and then got frisky with Jake and gone without
a condom? Those two were walking hormones at the moment; I
was almost surprised she hadn't already immaculately conceived
just from holding hands.

But then I thought of the real Nic. My little girl, who lied
about her promiscuity only to get attention from her mother.
The girl who waited for the right time. I thought back to Nicola's
birthday in the summer, and her face as I handed over all that
cash for a hotel room. There was too much thought in that face.
Too much care and responsibility.

Could it be one of her friends who might not have been so
careful? Of course – Matt Carter's little conquest, Bryony. So
drunk that she wrecked the lounge carpet. The more I thought
about it, the more likely that scenario seemed. It would make
sense that Bryony, no doubt ashamed of what happened, would
return to her friend's house – the scene of her irresponsibility
– in order to see whether she was going to pay a heavy price.
Surely no teenager was going to pee on a pregnancy test without
a friend around to hold their hand? Not actually when they
were pissing on the test, obviously, but I mean for moral and
emotional support. It could make sense, but I wasn't convinced
enough to rule either of my daughters out of the frame.

Emma Kenton might know, I've just realised sitting here, if it's Lucy or Nicola. She does seem to know a lot about them both. I'll grab another pint and maybe see if I have her number.

Twenty-three missed calls. Twenty-two of which are from Mick. I completely forgot to turn my phone back on after landing. To be honest, the flight had been a bit bouncy, so I was just relieved to make it in one piece, and then once here on St Mary's I was so intent on tracking down the American purple gallinule that's got everyone so excited that I forgot all about my mobile. I bagged the gallinule (a moorhen on acid, basically) having simply found the crowd – there must have been a hundred watching it – and then booked into my lodgings and came to the pub.

I thought Mick must have been calling about a mega-sighting, but on checking my board phone (which I'd also left off) I found no word of any new sightings, just more missed calls from Mick. I phoned him back, and his voice was a peculiar mixture of nervous excitement and melancholy.

'You heard about Keith?' he asked.

I sat up straight.

'Has he died?' It was the only natural progression of his previous situation.

'No. He's hanging on …' I relaxed in my chair again. '… but they reckon he was poisoned.'

'Really?' I was very slightly anxious.

'Yeah. His kidneys are shot. Both completely failed. If he survives he'll need a transplant and dialysis for the rest of his life.'

'So who poisoned him?'

'Not who, *what*!' Mick was sounding ever more jittery. 'They reckon it was those mushrooms we ate. The ones we *all* ate. He must have picked a bad one and accidentally eaten it.'

'But that was weeks ago.'

'It can take that long for the poison to kick in. I spoke to Cherry earlier, and she says that night we were with him was the last time he ate anything he picked. Think about it, Ted. It could have been one of us who ate it!'

Technically true, Mick, but actually, it could *only* have been one of us – and in this instance, you. As it is, though, my efforts, and the hopes for them, have paid dividends. Keith's out of the running for the rest of the race.

The field narrows.

October 7th 2007

377 species

I should, tonight, be anticipating the third quarter results, which would – and should – have been published in the morning. I can't believe that I wouldn't have been the main player – 365 species at the end of September is most likely a record, and my current total is only a dozen shy of the all-time twelve-month record. Emu won't be far off, though he's been unusually quiet over the last week at a time when my pagers and board mobile haven't stopped buzzing.

Of the remaining challengers, Cyril 'Terry' Nutkin will most likely have lost a bit of impetus. His age certainly won't suit the mad, crash-bang-charging-around that the current race has become, though what he lacks in mobility, he makes up for with considered, meticulous planning. Emma Kenton will have surely lost too much ground getting pissed and shagging around at university. Andrew 'Cyclops' Johnson, though, is certainly still in with a shout. A serious shout. I've spent a fair bit of time with him this weekend, and while he's keeping his cards close to his chest, he certainly has a confident air about him.

I'd hazard a guess that it's a three-horse race: Emu, Cyclops and myself – though the concern is that if someone left-field's charged ahead, I simply won't know about it without the results. I need to keep up; not waste a moment, and, as it is, I've spent most of today in bed – hungover, admittedly, but also recovering from an exhausting few days which culminated yesterday in the emotional turmoil of a seagull hunt.

Last week's storm worked its magic, dropping rarities all over the country in none too convenient a pattern. Scilly was productive – and ridiculously busy. Tom and the rest of the

Cornish boys were out in force, and Friday was a day of constant island-hopping; chasing shadows for much of the time but picking up some clonkers as well, blackpoll warbler and white-rumped sandpiper included. Then, on Friday afternoon, news filtered through from Shetland. Among a mass of arrivals, a Thayer's gull and a High Arctic gull had been spotted among a flock of three hundred or so mixed gulls near Brae.

This was my worst nightmare. Two big, big ticks that I couldn't afford to miss, but they were bloody *seagulls*. I rang Mick, who was heading south-west for the weekend.

'Screw the gulls, Ted, I want me a blackpoll warbler.'

Selfish shit. He knows my phobia. Then the board phone buzzed with a text. It was Cyclops. **Solid word on the Shetland gulls. Heading north in the morning.**

That made my decision easier (though the adrenaline also helped), but I had little time to waste. I'd packed my bag that morning, so was ready to go. Now I just needed to find a flight to Scotland. There was plenty of room on the plane leaving Scilly – most people were heading the other way – but on arrival at Bristol I discovered a major problem. There was no service between Bristol and Lerwick. I could head to Edinburgh, but not in time for a connecting flight, and Saturday's flights from Edinburgh to Lerwick were fully booked. There was, however, a flight from Exeter to Lerwick, leaving early on Saturday morning. This was my best and only option, so I jumped in the car and headed down the M5.

Exeter Airport isn't the biggest and isn't served by a whole heap of hotels, but by the time I'd got there, texted Cyclops with my plans and slumped down in the waiting area, I didn't need a bed. I slept solidly for about four hours and then dozed through the rest of the night, desperately aware that I couldn't miss the flight. And I didn't. By mid-morning I had hooked up with Cyclops, dumped my luggage in the room we would share in Lerwick and begun heading north across Mainland and towards Brae.

I didn't know Cyclops well enough to share with him my dislike of gulls, and instead had opted for liquid assistance to help me get through the day. Our driver (some local chap that Cyclops regularly uses as a chauffeur) flashed me a disdainful glance as I unscrewed the top of my whisky bottle and necked a seriously large measure.

'It's alright,' I grimaced, 'I don't normally drink during the day – but I don't travel well and it settles my nerves.'

The driver acknowledged me with a slight nod.

'I care not aboot yae drinking habits, sir – just the *quality* of whit yae drink …' I glanced down at my bottle. I'd grabbed it from a service station on the M5. It wasn't even branded as such – just a supermarket's own. I laughed.

'I'm not drinking for pleasure,' I explained, 'it's for purpose – and then any old blended shite will do.' The three of us laughed, I passed the bottle round, and though Cyclops and our driver only took the smallest of sips ('aye, shite it is …'), I was able to tuck in with less self-awareness, and by the time we reached Brae I was trollied.

I cannot abide seagulls. The memories of my childhood and the death of my brother are too vivid and too painful for me to think about, let alone write about. Suffice to say that, thanks largely to Cyclops, I bagged both the Thayer's and the High Arctic, along with a ring-billed gull for good measure.

Cyclops's driver hung around while we got our ticks and brought us back to Lerwick. I slept most of the way, and Cyclops thought I was still sleeping when he handed over £100 for the taxi rides. No wonder he's always available. I had a ripping headache by this time and needed food, but with the whisky wearing off and leaving only negative effects, I realised I had to make a decision on the drinking front, too. I plumped for the less sensible option and got the beers in. We drank steadily, and were joined by other birders as the evening progressed. Cyclops is well known in the twitching community, being a double champion – though he is, perhaps, more recognisable for his eye patch than his birding endeavours these days.

I got a second wind at around nine, as my dinner digested and the alcohol kicked back in. Saturday night in The Pony in Lerwick promised to be a late and lairy affair, and I ducked into our room to freshen up. While in the shower, I started troubling myself with that pregnancy test again: it was becoming an itch that I couldn't scratch. I pondered texting Abi and getting her opinion, but figured that she would see it as me dumping the problem onto her while I lived it up several hundred miles away. I would be better off waiting until I returned home and then calling another family meeting where I could broach the subject calmly with a glass of wine to hand. It would gnaw away at me in the meantime, though, and I thought back to Emma, and whether she might be able to shed any light. I grabbed a towel and my phone and scrolled through the contact list. I did have her number. I sent her a distinctly indirect text. **Hi Emma. How is uni? Ted.**

Minutes later I got a reply. **Hey Chip! How ru? Not at uni tonite. On Scilly. Where ru?**

I seriously hate 'text speak'. It takes me longer to work out what's actually been written than it would have taken for the sender to spell it out properly. **Shetland. With Cyclops. Have you seen Mick?**

No, thank God ... have seen chestnut sided tho – chestnut sided? A chestnut-sided warbler? Fuck it! That was a mega to miss.

Who else has seen the warbler? I was back in the bar with a pint by this point. Our table was full of birders talking birds, so I was missing little by texting.

Cornish & Emu & maybe 100 others.

Double fuck it! Emu had shown his face and sunk an advantage.

Contacting Emma had been a mistake. I hadn't even broached the pregnancy issue and now I was panicking about what I'd missed by leaving Scilly so soon. I tucked into my pint and followed it with another. A couple of guys were setting up instruments in the far corner of the bar, and more and more people were piling in. I remember the music starting, and I've got a vague recollection of dancing. While I know I was outside at some point, and may have been sick at another, I don't remember calling Emma – though I must have, judging by the message she left me this morning.

'Morning, Chip,' she chirruped, 'how's your head? Thanks for your message, or what I could understand of it. Don't worry about the pregnancy test. Lu's on the pill and Nic is too headstrong – it must be a friend's. I'll let you know if the chestnut-sided is about today. Have a good one. See ya!'

Okay, so Lucy's on the pill? Is this not something her father should know about? I'm always the guy kept in the dark. At least, though, it would seem that the test was someone else's. And Emma mentioned it being a friend's – perhaps she knew more than she let on.

I did make it downstairs for breakfast this morning, though it was nearly eleven and only the rubber eggs and plastic bacon were left. Food had a negative effect, unfortunately, and merely sped up the arrival of my hangover, which has been brutal.

Cyclops made it out this afternoon but with little reward, and he's headed home this evening. I can't decide what to do. I feel seriously rough. It's getting dark already, and I haven't eaten (or even left the room) since that grim breakfast. I can't face going anywhere this evening – it would destroy me – so thank God I booked the extra night. I need to shape up, get some supper and get to bed. I'm in Shetland. My car is in Exeter. And the birds seem to be showing up in Scilly. I need a plan.

At least the house was clean and tidy when I arrived home today. I've called a family meeting for Saturday, which has pissed Nicola off because she's supposed to be going out on Saturday evening.

'It won't be all evening,' I reasoned, 'just half an hour or so, to catch up and chat about anything that needs discussing, whether negative or *positive* ...?' My emphasis on my final word didn't appear to stir Nicola in any way, though it was most likely too subtle.

'Are we gonna have wine and Chinese again then, Dad?'

Was her desire for wine significant? If she were pregnant it probably wouldn't be the first thought on her mind. Food for thought, and certainly a factor worth exploiting. In fact, with it being a Saturday, there'll be no excuses for anyone *not* to enjoy a drink at our family meeting. If I pick up a couple of bottles of Prosecco (all the girls love fizz) I can see who turns their noses up.

I made it back to Scilly on Monday afternoon, but I was too late for the chestnut-sided warbler. It had shown, briefly, on Sunday morning, but got spooked by the sheer number of birders gawping at it and took flight – last seen heading north from St Martin's – which means that if it makes land again, it'll be in Wales or more likely the south coast of Ireland. Either way, it's unlikely to be picked up.

Scilly did produce a Richardson's Canada goose at least, which unfortunately Emu was still around to bag, but the real action by then was coming over on the mainland in Cornwall itself.

I hopped back to Exeter on Tuesday morning and then drove most of the way back down the peninsula, where south-west

Cornwall was alive with birds and birders alike. I hooked up with Cornish Tom (*sans* Emu, thankfully, though it wouldn't surprise me if I was just following in his footsteps) and we tracked down a zitting cisticola, a lifer for us both.

I resisted the temptation to go and stay in the Porthcove Guest House, though I'm sure Mrs Bellchambers would have been delighted to see me, and instead found a Travel Inn. Cornish Tom had also offered me a bed for the night, but I was concerned about the tales of his *persuasion*, and worried that even if he shouldn't make any advances towards me, I might end up staying in the bed where he'd played Emu like a puppet.

I did, of course, ensure that I was in his company yesterday – I may have been utterly opposed to his appointment, but hanging out with a fellow board member meant that anything we saw was as good as ratified, and having ticked a Swainson's thrush, our joint presence proved invaluable at a site near Sennen Cove. One of the Cornish boys had picked up a funny-looking sparrow, and by the time we'd reached him, he was practically doing cartwheels.

'Spanish sparrow! Spanish sparrow!' he was all but shouting.

Tom fixed his scope, and gave the thumbs up: another lifer and another bird that Emu and Cyclops have yet to see, though I don't doubt that they're both camped in Cornwall as I write.

For the second Sunday running I've woken upstairs in a pub with a brutal hangover. This week, though, I'm in The Adder, down in the New Forest, and I didn't come here to look for birds: I came here to see Donna and get laid. I can be candid, as I achieved neither, though I did succeed in driving here while probably over the limit (not something I'm proud of), having a pathetic effort at chatting up the girl who was working behind the bar (who was barely twenty, not particularly attractive, and applied her make-up with a trowel), and consequently getting so pissed that I had to be helped upstairs and into my bedroom at about nine thirty.

I didn't go down for my breakfast this morning – not due to my excesses, but due to my embarrassment. But wouldn't you guess, Donna (who I told the pub I was crazy about last night) is actually working today, and knocked on the door half an hour ago with a tray of food.

'You paid for breakfast,' she'd called nervously, after enduring for several minutes my attempts to ignore her knocking. I didn't recognise her voice, but opened the door out of curiosity, and wished I hadn't. I'd come down here to see that face. Donna's face. But not when I was in a state of semi-nudity, hair sticking out sideways, with the stench of alcohol tainted vomit on my breath.

It took a couple of seconds for her to recognise me, at which point the penny dropped: I was the drunken nutjob who turned up on a Saturday night, desperate to see her – my love, my saviour.

'Oh, it's you …' she said, darting her eyes up and down my wrecked body and attempting a weak smile. She thrust the tray forward, and I took it – noticing, as I did, the diamond on the ring finger of her left hand. It just got better and better.

'Thanks …' I mumbled, actually close to tears. She smiled again and trotted off downstairs. I stood for a moment, slightly shell-shocked, before a whiff of bacon hit my nostrils. Christ, I was hungry.

I hadn't eaten since the mouthful of sweet and sour prawn that I nearly choked on last evening. It was a tasty prawn as well … and a decent takeaway. Nicola had certainly tucked in, and didn't object when I cracked the cork on the Prosecco.

'Nice one, Dad! I'll be well on the way for tonight's party after a few glasses of this!' I filled all four glasses and Lucy didn't flinch at the prospect of a drink either, even if she wasn't quite as keen as her younger sister.

I took a deep breath. I'd been pensive all day, but now, seeing both girls acting completely normally, I realised that the pregnancy test belonged to neither of them. It had to be a friend's – it had to be Bryony's. At least Matt Carter was going to leave a legacy.

'So, Nic, how's your friend, Bryony?' I felt happy to be fairly direct.

Nicola raised her eyebrows in an exaggerated a look of confusion.

'Er, fine, Dad – thanks for asking …'

'She's in good health, then?'

'Well, yes, as far as I know. At least she was yesterday, and she is today. I daresay she'll be feeling pretty shit in the morning though; tonight is going to be mass-eeeve.'

Maybe I was wrong after all.

'She'll be drinking tonight, then?'

Nicola put down her fork and raised her glass, eyeing it dramatically before draining it in one and letting out a rasping belch. I glanced at Abi expecting a rebuke, but she was oblivious, poking her food around amid her own thoughts. Nicola laughed.

'We're sixteen, Dad – in fact, Bryony's only a week away from seventeen. We do drink, and we do get drunk. I'm sorry if that alarms you.'

I should really have pulled Nicola up on her flippancy, but, in truth, I find it rather endearing and often quite funny. I think I was smiling at her then, and I was certainly looking at her as she pulled a funny face to break my gaze.

'Have a drink, Dad.' Nicola grabbed the bottle and topped up my glass and I automatically took a sip. I was confused, and could beat around the bush no longer.

'Right.' I sounded more authoritative than I had meant to, though it grabbed everyone's attention. I decided to continue with the bold approach. 'Last Thursday, before I went away, I emptied the bathroom bin.'

Nicola clapped her hands and nodded sagely.

'Good effort, Dad, good effort.' I gave her a stern look and continued.

'When I emptied the bin, I found a pregnancy test. A positive pregnancy test. Now. Would either of you girls care to shed any light on it?'

Nicola shrugged.

'Certainly not mine.' She returned to her plate.

'Could it, perhaps be one of your friends? Either of you?' I looked at Lucy, who'd been quiet all through the meal, though that wasn't unusual – especially with a sister as trappy as Nicola. Lucy shook her head slowly, but she looked distracted. Her gaze drifted away from me and then stopped. She frowned a little, a crease of concern in her expression. She was looking at Abi.

I turned to my wife. She was desperately trying to stifle a sob. I looked at her glass: it was untouched. At her plate: she had been poking around at a small pile of rice, but there was nothing else on there. No sweet and sour prawns. Her favourite. No *seafood*. As the grim reality swept through me, she looked up.

'Oh, Ted,' she half covered her mouth, 'I'm sorry …'

That's when I nearly choked.

We had the delayed board meeting last night, held over from last Tuesday due to the extraordinary amount of birds dropping after the storms. There would have been a lot of absentees last week, myself included, though I may as well have not gone last night, such was my lack of input.

It was all a bit sombre. Claypole had invited a policeman in (some Community Support bloke) to discuss the dangers of picking wild mushrooms. I think that with Keith Atkins still lying in intensive care we were all well aware of the dangers of mushroom picking, but Claypole wanted a message to go out in the next newsletter and felt it would carry more weight with a uniformed presence in the accompanying photos.

With such a stack of sightings over the last month, the bulk of the meeting consisted of accepting, rejecting or deferring – a dull process at the best of times, but with such a weight of claims, it just became mechanic. Species? Location? Photographic evidence? Board witnesses? Other witnesses? Detailed description? – a never ending circle. Emu's name seemed to pop up more than most when the question of 'board witnesses?' was posed. I wish I'd been in a better frame of mind in order to jot down some details. I swear he was in two places at once on more than one occasion.

No one wanted to hang around for post-meeting pints last night. I certainly didn't. I'd tried to sound upbeat on the journey there – not too hard with Mick's motor mouth in the driving seat – but even he was aware that my mind was elsewhere.

'Come on then, Chip, spill the beans. What's troubling you?' Mick's never been a good listener, but at that moment, I realised

I had to talk to someone.

'I found a pregnancy test at home, Mick. In the bin. A positive test.'

'Whoa … gotta be Nicola's … you're going to be a granddad, Ted!'

'No. I thought it might have been her, or one of her friends, but, no, it's actually Abigail who's pregnant.'

Mick was initially silent. I looked across at him – his eyebrows were somewhere up near his hairline.

'Holy shit, Ted! You're gonna be a daddy! Again! But I thought Abi was on the pill?'

'She's not. But I've had the snip, Mick, remember?'

'Oh, yeah – I forgot you'd had the chop. But that means …'

'Exactly.'

'So whose is it?' Mick actually sounded a little concerned.

'I don't know, Mick.'

And I wasn't going to know until I confronted Abi, and that I'd so far put off. I'd got home mid-afternoon on Sunday, and Abi kept her distance. The girls were lovely, though. Big hugs and lots of concern. I felt guilty for having just taken off, and then for not phoning to let them know I was safe, but under the circumstances I think my silence was excusable. Despite the girls' good intent, I was too tired for company, so made my excuses and tucked myself away in the conservatory with a bottle of Jura under my arm. I spent the night downstairs on the sofa, and was then woken at six on Monday morning with a simultaneous buzz of pagers.

A bufflehead had been spotted on a reservoir in mid-Wales, picked up late the evening before. The board phone was soon alive. No one had any concrete details, but the general consensus was that this was too good a bird to potentially miss. I jumped in the shower, cleaned my teeth and hit the road.

I shouldn't have bothered. A sprinkle of people (Emu, Cyclops and Cyril Nutkin included) wasted a day driving circuits around Penygarreg Reservoir in the vain hope of spotting a small and solitary American duck. I'd never before seen a bufflehead, and I still haven't.

By the time I got home on Tuesday I had barely enough opportunity to shower and change before heading off to the board meeting, so, with Abi working today, our paths have not yet (properly) crossed since Saturday's bombshell. And to be honest, though my pride's taken a bit of a blow (the thought of my wife sleeping with someone else isn't exactly a pleasant one) the fact that Abi's treading on eggshells and entirely at fault for this situation means that I can just get on and focus on winning this competition.

It's certainly easier while I don't know the identity of the father, though I do have my suspicions – Abi's been going out regularly with Lucy's circle of friends, and I can imagine an eighteen-year-old lad being rather taken by the attentions of an older woman. Hmm. That thought actually doesn't help. Abi lost her virginity to me, and I firmly believe that she's shared a bed with no other man until now. But a hormone-filled teenager would have blown her away, especially compared to my own recent efforts. He would have been lean and lithe and well-endowed. He would have smelled and tasted clean and masculine. He would have been ready to go again, minutes after finishing the previous bout. Abi would have experienced new levels of sex. Multiple-orgasms-amid-swinging-from-the-chandelier sex.

Or maybe it was a drunken fuck in a pub car park. A one-off. All hazy and sordid, over in seconds. I remember my early sexual encounters – sometimes I'd burst before I even got my pants off. Perhaps that's what happened to Abi; she risked her marriage for the sake of a minute's worth of intercourse with a spotty little prick. That's a much better thought – an entirely unsatisfactory encounter. Abi had always been curious about what sex would be like with another man, and now she knew: it was crap. And she would be beating herself up for ever wanting to know; for ever having believed that her husband was anything other than a supreme lover ... a love god. She would never stray again, and would do anything to turn back the clock – after all, she'd been so drunk and the whole thing over so quickly that she'd barely even felt aroused. *Oh Ted*, she would say. *How could I ever have been so stupid?* But now she couldn't just brush it aside, could she? She was carrying a reminder of her infidelity in her womb. A reminder that was going to become harder and harder to ignore. And then what? Single motherhood?

Abi couldn't expect her husband, the idiot who'd supported her for her whole adult life, to stick around and play happy families with another man's child.

The bufflehead reappeared on Wednesday morning, and yesterday I finally ticked it, along with half a million other people. I kept a low, low profile, not socialising at all. Time alone was good. Really good. I pretty much regained my focus, and realised that I'm not going to let my wife's behaviour ruin my chance of glory.

I got home on Friday night and told Abi to pack her bags. It's my house, my home, and for the next ten weeks I need it as such. I don't want to come home after an exhausting twitch only to have Abi's swelling belly reminding me of her indiscretion. She can go and stay with her brother, or her parents (she's initially opted for the latter) and when I'm ready – when I have time to give it my attention – I'll decide on a further course of action.

It would have been so sweet to have beaten the record with two full months to spare or equalled it even, but I'm still two ticks shy. What an effort. I don't doubt that Cyclops and Emu will be sitting in a state of similar confidence, but neither of them'll be expecting the challenge from me. I'm Rook of the Year, yes – but surely not a title challenger so soon. Not in this record-breaking year.

Mick could do himself a few favours if he wanted – he'd definitely be in with a shout of finishing in the top ten – but he's really going off the boil. He just hasn't got the commitment; tonight is a perfect example.

A tufted puffin was sighted this afternoon in the English Channel, just off Lyme Regis – a potential first for Britain. A single (distant) photo was taken at dusk and sent, in confidence, to Mike Phelps, who forwarded it on to the rest of the board. We decided to suppress it until we'd had a chance to bag it ourselves.

I headed straight down the M3, finding a room in a pub in Lyme Regis itself, where I now sit. Emu, Cyclops, Cyril Nutkin, Mike Phelps – even Cornish Tom – are all in or around town. Mick 'has a meeting in the morning' and will try and make it mid-afternoon tomorrow. Silly sod. This could be the bird of the decade, and it could fly by lunchtime.

NOVEMBER

Well, I'm going to add the tufted puffin to my tally for now, but I won't know for sure until the board meeting next Tuesday, and it looks like that's going to be another sombre affair.

Six of us gathered on the Cobb at Lyme Regis this morning. It was pre-dawn, but we wanted to be on the water before it got light. Mike 'Penguin' Phelps, being the most local, had chartered us a fishing boat for the day, but we weren't going to be doing any fishing. The skipper had been charged with finding us a small raft of puffins, the hope being that the tufted bird would still be among them. The guy who got the photo the day before from the shore was a mate of Penguin's and had given him specific coordinates towards which he should head. Penguin's mate – his name was Andy – wouldn't be joining us due to work commitments (another bloke with no dedication), but would be about later in the afternoon on the shore.

I had queried the validity of an offshore sighting, but was quickly appeased. Should we find it, Emu said, we would try and spot the bird again from the shore; but if we were only able to see it from the boat, we would discuss the issue at next week's meeting – in other words we would gloss over the contention.

We left harbour just as it was starting to get light, and as the rising sun began to reveal the coastline, I realised the main reason why Penguin had got us all on a boat. The coast around Lyme is made up of towering cliffs, and Andy had spotted the puffin from a spot near Golden Cap which looked tricky for an able-bodied person to access, let alone Penguin with a ton of steel in his foot. This way, Penguin had a good chance of spotting it – he could just sit tight and wait until we chugged up to it.

We didn't. After four hours at sea there was nothing except the endless fucking seagulls that flapped around the boat. I was terrified, spending as much time as I could up front and undercover with the skipper. Of course, he wanted to make small talk, and had a typically thick West Country seaside accent which was all but impossible to discern amidst the noise of the engine and constant threat of the gulls. I don't know what I actually confirmed to him, but at one point, he asked me a question of which I didn't catch a word, so I just nodded vigorously. He rolled his eyes, looked at the heavens and stopped the conversation dead. No bad thing, but as we walked away from the boat back in Lyme I saw him say something to the ship's mate, point in my direction, and the two of them fell about laughing. I didn't worry too much, such was my relief to be back on dry land and away from the gulls. There were plenty lurking around the town, though, and I quickly persuaded the rest of the party that a pub lunch was in order, along with a plan of action for the afternoon.

I necked a couple of sneaky whiskies en route to and from the toilet, which settled the nerves nicely, and, having followed them down with a couple of pints of local ale, I was in a floaty state of mind by the time we ventured back outside.

We'd devised a plan, which involved splitting up. Penguin and Cyril Nutkin, being the least agile, would stay in Lyme keeping a lookout from the Cobb. Emu and Cornish Tom, being bum chums, would make for Charmouth, a couple of miles east. Cyclops and I would head even further east, to Golden Cap. It was all a bit Scooby-Doo, but I was certainly happy with my lot. We were heading to the area where the bird had been spotted, and though our search from the boat had been unsuccessful, if we could take a position on top of the cliffs we'd have a much better aerial view of the water.

Cyclops offered to drive – fortunate, given my tipsy state – and we were soon heading down a single-track road and onto National Trust land. There were regular signs stating 'No cars beyond this point', but Cyclops ignored them. I thought for a moment that his limited eyesight may have blocked them from view, but on passing yet another 'No vehicles except for access' sign, he felt compelled to comment.

'It's alright, Chip – I know this area. I've holidayed in a cottage down at the end of this track. There's room for a couple of cars.'

And there was. Cyclops certainly did know the area, and he soon had us hiking up the steepest slope I've ever tackled.

'It's the most direct route,' he muttered, in response to my huffing, 'straight to the top of Golden Cap – we'll have most of the Channel in view.'

I had to stop halfway. I was gasping for breath and close to puking, though Cyclops was reluctant. He did at least pass me his water bottle – I'd forgotten to bring one – and I took grateful gulps. My phone buzzed as we rested – it was Mick. **On my way – where ru?**

I texted back as detailed a description as I could and the phone buzzed again. **Know it – cu in an hour or 2.**

We stomped on up the slope, the wind freshening the higher we climbed. A couple of spots of rain bit into my face. This was not fun. We veered off as we neared the top and headed seaward, direct to the cliff edge. I was at least grateful for the lack of seagulls in the vicinity.

'That's down to the peregrines,' Cyclops explained, 'they keep the gulls quiet. We should see them if nothing else.' A peregrine? Great, I ticked that back in January, and seeing one today would be little compensation for the near heart attack I was suffering.

Finally, Cyclops stopped walking, unshouldered his scope and knelt down, scanning the sea below through his binoculars. I collapsed into the grass breathing hard, my head spinning as the lunchtime alcohol pulsed through my veins. I needed more water, and turned to Cyclops to ask for another glug. He was in the zone, though. And agitated. He mouthed something and leant forward slightly, as though the extra inches would give him a better view.

It puzzled me for a moment why he bothered with binoculars. Surely a piece of kit designed for two-eyed sight would be something of a hindrance. You can get monoculars – they look like miniature telescopes – but I suppose the weight of binoculars makes them easier to hold, giving a more stable image.

'I have auks – definitely auks …'

Cyclops's voice broke into my thoughts with these words. 'Auks' could mean anything – guillemot, razorbill, even little auks – but his tone suggested he was looking at puffins, and that meant, possibly …

I shuffled alongside him, wary of my mild drunkenness and the drop below. I couldn't help but grin as Cyclops first put his eye patch against the eyepiece of the telescope. Old habits. I was briefly concerned that my mirth may have offended him, but of course, he couldn't see me – I was on his blind side. I certainly saw his smile, though. Just the slightest hint of one.

'I think we're in business …' he whispered. Cyclops sat back and gestured for me to have a look. I obliged. They were distant – very distant – but sitting amidst the waves was definitely a small raft of maybe a dozen puffins. Their bright beaks had faded with the onset of winter, but one of their number was distinctly different. Bulkier, dark all over – the normal puffins had white breasts – this one was surely a tufted, a long way from its normal Pacific home. I turned back to Cyclops and nodded.

'Looks good, doesn't it?' he said, looking again down the lens. Then he grimaced. 'I've left my bloody camera in the car, though. With that attached, I can zoom in and get a better view and a photo.' So what? I thought. There were two of us – two board members. We needed no photographic evidence. But Cyclops seemed intent, and was on his feet, checking his pockets for his car keys. 'Don't let it out of your sight, Ted – I'll be as quick as I can.'

'What about the others?' I was surprised that Cyclops had forgotten them. 'Should I put the word out?'

'No need to be hasty …' I think he winked as he spoke, but without seeing the other eye, it could have been a long blink. 'We can get a couple of snaps first, and then call the others. Be a shame if Emu should miss it, but …'

I liked his thinking. We weren't being selfish, just making sure of our identification. And yes, if it flew in the meantime and Emu and the rest missed it, well … that's birding.

As Cyclops jogged off down the slope, I turned back to the scope. The puffins had almost moved out of view, but there it was again. It was definitely a tufted puffin; it could be nothing else. It was the first one ever seen in Britain and it was mine to tick. It wasn't doing a great deal, though. Just sitting tight, riding the waves.

Then something flashed across the lens – a blur of white – *seagull!* I jumped back in panic and scanned the sky around me. Nothing – just a pair of crows over the top of the Cap. I gathered my breath, taking a couple of big lungfuls, and turned my attention back to the puffins.

They were gone. I eased the telescope left, in the direction that they'd been bobbing. Nothing. A wider scan with the binoculars also brought nothing – but though they'd disappeared from view, I could also see no birds out there in flight. They could have dived, or been hidden by a big swell; either way, I kept a half-hearted look out as I waited for Cyclops to return.

'Gone? What, flown?' Cyclops was back, and his demeanour was none too friendly.

'Disappeared behind a wave,' I was staying calm, 'and there was nothing in the air, so they either went under or are still out there.'

Cyclops flopped on the grass next to me.

'Sorry, Ted – just frustrated, that's all. It's such a massive, massive mega; I really wanted a decent photo and a definite ID.'

'Well the IDs alright. The views I had – and you had – were pretty damn good … it was definitely a tufted puffin.'

Cyclops grimaced slightly and shrugged.

'It definitely wasn't a regular puffin – *Fratercula arctica* – but we can't call the species for certain.' I may not know the latin names, but I'd done my homework on puffins last night, and I'd learnt a thing or two.

'Look, Cyclops, – sorry, *Andrew* – we agree that we've been watching a puffin that isn't an Atlantic puffin, yes?'

'Well, yes …'

'And that leaves two other species that it could have been – horned or tufted, yes?

'Yes, of course – *Fratercula corniculata* or *Fratercula cirrhata*.'
Pretentious twat.

'Well, the bird we saw was dark all over – no white breast – so it could only have been a tufted.'

'It may have been a juvenile horned though, Ted. You can never discount the variations of plumage in a young bird.'

I shook my head. An hour ago, Cyclops had stood there giving me the wink, wanting to keep word of our sighting quiet for as long as possible, but now he was disputing the bloody ID!

He could clearly sense my frustration.

'Look, Ted, whatever we saw – and I'm ninety five per cent sure it was a tufted puffin – was here, at this spot, yesterday and today. It'll reappear, if not today, then tomorrow. We'll release details of the sighting this afternoon, and after that there'll be hundreds of cameras pointing out to sea. *Someone* will snap it. Someone will get undeniable proof.' I said nothing, so Cyclops continued. 'Let's give it another hour now, Ted, then let the others know. Let's just make sure of it ...' He turned back to his scope, checked the focus, and resumed his sea-scanning through the binoculars.

What a knob. There was no value to his argument. If there was sufficient doubt I wouldn't give myself the tick. I have integrity. But there *is no doubt*. Alright – maybe, as Cyclops says himself, the tiniest fraction of doubt. But he might as well argue that it could be a species never before discovered. There's a fine line between scrupulous identification and pure pedantry.

But here *we* were. Two board members equalled automatic validity as long as both parties were singing from the same hymn sheet. We had a chance to get one up on Emu. If the bird had flown, it might not stop flying. It was a long way from home, after all, and Emu wasn't going to get another chance to see a tufted puffin before the New Year, if ever.

I looked across at Cyclops. I was on his blind side once again, so I gave him the finger and mouthed 'wanker' in his direction. Still he kept scanning. I looked around. No one else was within eye- or earshot. It would be a terrible shame, I thought, if he slipped off the cliff.

I raised my hands, and then feigned a stretch and a yawn. He didn't notice my movement; or certainly didn't seem to. But pushing him would be risky. I would be falling forward too, and it was a long, long way down. There was also the possibility that he might grab me as he went, either taking us both down or forcing me to pull him back to safety, whereupon I would struggle to explain my actions. I shifted my legs from under me, crossing them so I was sitting on my backside. Then I slowly shuffled sideways, just behind Cyclops's main bulk. Still he didn't move. I had another glance around me. No one. Then above me. Nothing – but it was wise to check. A hot-air balloon or paraglider could have crept up on us in near silence.

I slowly lifted both feet off the ground, leaning back to maximise the angle of trajectory, and then thrust my legs forward. Wham! Straight into the base of his back. I had expected a scream or shout, but I must have kicked the wind straight out of him, because the only sound was a peculiar *gulp*. I heard no crash as he landed … *if* he landed.

I turned onto my belly and inched over to the edge of the cliff. There was nothing but a sheer drop. No lower ledge, no branches or tree trunks to break his fall. He'd gone. I inched backward and sat up, glancing around the area – still no one. Cyclops's telescope still stood on its tripod, but there was no other trace of him, save his water bottle. What next? I suppose to support the 'he slipped' argument I was inevitably going to offer, it was best that I leave the scope and water exactly where they were. Then I'd drive back, raise the alarm, and … oh, shit. Cyclops was driving. The keys would be in his pocket. Bollocks; I had a long walk – if I could remember the way. It was a maze of tracks that we'd driven down earlier, and I wasn't paying much attention at the time. Still, I had to do something, so I started down the slope, watching my feet, deep in thought.

I nearly collided with Mick.

'Whoa, *shit!*' I practically jumped out of my skin.

'Easy Ted! You alright? What's going on?'

Think on your feet, Ted.

'Desperate for a shit, Mick – desperate …' I nodded towards

the small coppice some fifty yards or so away. 'I need a bit of privacy though.' Mick laughed, and I felt it best to continue the charade. 'Can't stop, but I won't be long – Cyclops is up on the top, you'll find him – tufted's showing well.' With that I stumbled my way across to the trees and into the shadow of an oak. I glanced behind me. Mick was striding on up towards the cliff top.

Okay. This was okay. I thought of the chaps down the coast. They were still in the dark. I grabbed my personal phone and fired a text to Emu and Penguin. Then, and by now I wasn't acting, I found a suitable hollow and dropped my trousers.

By the time I made it back to the cliff top, Mick was peering through Cyclops's telescope. He turned quickly as I approached.

'So where's this puffin then, Ted? And where's Cyclops?'

Suddenly, Mick's arrival was perfect.

'Well, the puffin was pretty much where that scope is pointing. And Cyclops was right here – though he was getting obsessed about getting a photo, so maybe he's gone to find a better vantage point.'

'He likes his photos, does Cyclops,' said Mick, returning his eye to the telescope, 'but I can't see any tufted puffins …'

I spied a big bottle of water poking out of Mick's bag and helped myself, taking huge welcome gulps. My phone buzzed. It was Emu. **On the way. Why not on board phone?**

Will explain later, I replied.

Emu and Cornish arrived within forty minutes, with Cyril Nutkin trailing along another half an hour later (he had left Penguin back in Lyme with his club foot). I'd built the anxiety at a sensible rate in the interim; my initial disregard for Cyclops's absence growing slowly and steadily as time passed. Phone calls to him went straight to voicemail (of course) and Mick and I had searched the immediate area for signs. Concern grew, and by the time Cyril arrived, I had called the coastguard.

There was no further sign of the tufted puffin.

Three hundred and ninety species. A new record, though it's possible that Emu's reached or might be near the same landmark. For the record, the 390th bird was a Siberian rubythroat, ticked this afternoon at Flamborough Head. Another lifer, except this time round there was no privilege of exclusivity due to board membership. Some local chap picked it up yesterday, spent the afternoon taking endless photos and then published them on his blog last night. Word soon spread, the internet forums went into meltdown, and as a result there were over two hundred people there this morning, Emma Kenton included. She had some new fella in tow; he looked about twelve and was clearly disinterested, but I guess you'd put up with a lot if you were on a promise from Emma.

She invited me out for a drink in York tonight – just a few quiet ones. Hanging out with students isn't something I find particularly inviting, but as my home currently resembles a student lair (Lucy's doing her bit, but it's become a bit of a doss-house) I thought sod it, booked a room in York itself and am meeting up with Emma and friends in about half an hour. I won't get too pissed; I have a doctor's appointment tomorrow afternoon – time for another sick note – but I do have a new record to (silently) toast after all.

November 14th 2007

393 species

I was pretty tired after three days chasing a king eider on
the Moray Firth, but it was definitely Mick that I passed this
afternoon, two streets away from home. I flashed him but he just
drifted by, staring dead ahead.

I haven't actually seen him since the fall of Cyclops. He
missed last week's board meeting, letting me down at the last
minute. I had to drive myself, and he knew I couldn't miss it – I
had to present my case for the ratification of the tufted puffin.
Though I'd had text conversations with him since, he'd been
oddly quiet, even missing a couple of decent twitches during the
last fortnight. Even so, I still felt it strange that he should call
round to see me without ringing first. Then, on arriving home, I
found Abi getting into her Ka. I hadn't seen her for nearly four
weeks, and as soon as she saw me, she put her hand on her belly
and flushed red.

'Ted …' She lifted her hand again: she was showing.

'What did Mick want?'

'Mick? I, er, haven't seen him – I just popped round to do
some cleaning. Thought you might appreciate it while you were
away.'

She talks regularly to the girls – would probably have known
I was away – and so at the time I bought her story. I didn't hang
around for pleasantries, though, and unlocked the door, pausing
as Abi drove off. Her exhaust needed looking at. It struck me
that she hadn't exactly made a good job of the cleaning; there
was dirty crockery in the sink and the dishwasher had finished a
cycle but was still loaded.

Now it seems clear, when I think about it, that she'd only

come round to meet with Mick. She knew I wasn't home. The girls were both out. It makes sense. Looking back, lots of things make sense. Even Emma Kenton knew something was going on.

'I wouldn't look beyond Mick,' she'd said dismissively upon my revelation that my wife was pregnant by someone else.

'No, not Mick …'

I couldn't believe that I was sharing such intimate issues with her. We'd had a fair few drinks in a quiet little pub in York. Her boyfriend (can't remember his name) was playing darts with a couple of other spotty student mates, so Emma and I wound up putting the world to rights. She didn't mince her words, either.

'You got your tufted puffin ratified, then?' she said as we had first sat down. She couldn't have known for sure that I had. The board meeting had been held just the evening before, but word was obviously out that Cyclops and I had seen it and that he'd got greedy and wanted to suppress it from the rest of the board. I'd disagreed with him, though, and snuck off to secretly let them know, leaving Cyclops desperately trying to catch the perfect photo of the bird – which was when he must have slipped to his death.

But it was Emma's dislike of Mick that most sticks in my mind from that evening.

'Mick Starr is a dirty old pervert,' she'd stated firmly.

'He's a bit of a player …' I'd reasoned. Emma had chewed her lip at that point, her eyes narrowed.

'I'll tell you something about Mick,' she said, putting her glass down and leaning across the corner of the table. 'Nic's party. At your house. Matt was there, crashed on your sofa. He'd been getting pissed with Nic's mates, and looked after one of them when she was sick …'

'Bryony,' I added.

'Yeah. Well, Matt found her a blanket and made her a makeshift bed in the conservatory as close to the downstairs toilet as possible.'

'She still puked on the floor, though.' Emma flashed me a look. I disguised my grin with a swig of beer.

'Matt was nearly asleep on the sofa, when he heard someone

come in the room. He thought nothing of it at first, but then he heard whispers and giggles, and then some serious noises …'

Emma had a sip of her wine and continued. 'He crept out and peeked through the conservatory door. There was Mick, on top of Bryony. Naked. Having *sex* with her. Matt said that Bryony couldn't have known what was going on, she was so pissed. It was practically rape, Ted.'

Emma had a tear in her eye. I squeezed her arm, and she wiped her face with the back of her hand.

'Why didn't Matt say anything?'

'He *did*, Ted. The next day. He sent a text saying Mick'd better have used a condom, or words to that effect. Then a couple of days later, Mick turned up at his house. Went ballistic. Told him to forget anything he thought he saw, or else he knew people who would make him forget. Matt was terrified, really terrified …'

I was pretty stunned; I'd been convinced it was Matt I heard that night.

'The thing is, Ted,' – Emma was crying again – 'Matt texted me the night before he died, making a semi-serious joke that Mick was getting him on his own in the middle of nowhere to bump him off … and maybe he *did* …' Emma was looking straight at me, looking for my reaction.

'No, Em – Mick's a twat, but he wouldn't have. Besides, the police said it was just a terrible accident.'

'Maybe …' Emma was far from convinced. Not surprising. That was one hell of a motive …

Wednesday's bin day, so I began today by taking a stroll past Mick's house in the very early hours of this morning. A quick sneaky peek in his wheelie bin and there was what I was after – a plastic bag. I had gloves on, of course.

Last night I swung by Mick's mid-evening and asked to borrow a garden fork. Mick was surprised to see me; in fact, he looked a little pale, but couldn't have been more helpful.

'Of course, Ted, of course,' he jabbered.

I opened the boot, let him put the fork in, and then headed home.

I didn't worry about taking my car back down the track on the heath at Bisley. If the police did make further searches, they wouldn't waste their time looking at tyre tracks. I left Mick's fork, with plastic bag around the handle, just off the little path near the burnt-out car, which was rusting well.

Next stop was home, for a snooze, then back out to Homebase, where I picked up a new fork. I didn't worry about the appearance – Mick wouldn't notice; his old one was barely used. I popped the new fork round to Mick's. He was out at work, but Kerry thanked me for it and put it in the shed.

Then, tonight, I called Emma.

'Chip! How are you?'

'I'm okay, thank you … given the circumstances.' My tone was downbeat.

'Oh, Chip. Have you found out … the father …?'

'No. I haven't. Though that won't really change the situation.'

'No, no – of course not …'

'I've been thinking about something you said though, Em.

The thing about Mick and Matt.'

'Right?' Emma's sounded anxious.

'I was thinking back to the morning that Matt was … discovered, and the way Mick was acting.'

I left a pause for dramatic effect.

'Go on, Ted – what was he doing? Do you think he might have done it?' The pause did the trick; Emma was taking the bait.

'I don't know, Emma. I really don't know. But I think that you should maybe tell the police about the threat. I mean, it's probably nothing, but …' I didn't need to finish the sentence. Emma had heard all she needed to hear. To be honest, I'm surprised she hadn't mentioned Mick threatening Matt to the police back at the time, but I suppose she might have been scared – scared that he would then come after *her*.

It was the funeral of Andrew 'Cyclops' Johnson yesterday afternoon, and with nothing moving on the bird front, I made a late decision to go along. My motive was politically driven, as well. Not only would it further strengthen the credibility of my version of events surrounding his death, but I also had a seed or two to sow. The service was in Oxford – home, apparently, to generations of Johnsons. Though it would have been a relatively short drive home, I decided to make a night of it.

There was a solid board turnout, the only absentees being Keith Atkins and dear old Mick Starr. I made the right noises to Cyclops's family, and then coerced the board to go for a post-wake beer. There were too many nice pubs in Oxford for us not to, I argued, and we should hold our own toast to Cyclops.

Emma Kenton came along too, which was perfect luck, because she made no hesitation before bringing up Mick's name.

'You heard from him, Ted?'

'Not since his arrest, no.' I had my downbeat voice on again. 'I did briefly speak to his wife Kerrie this morning. She said the police have applied to hold him for another twenty-four hours …'

Claypole cleared his throat.

'A dreadful business. It really is. What do you think, Ted – did he do it?'

I breathed deeply and took a thoughtful sip of beer.

'I really don't know. I mean, he's my oldest friend. We went to school together. And yes, he's been a bit of a rogue … but *murder*?' I enjoyed uttering that sentence, and emphasising the final word of it. It felt as though I was in an episode of *Midsomer Murders*.

'They've found evidence.' Emma was sitting forward to speak;

the wine had loosened her tongue. 'They found his garden fork at the scene.'

There was an audible gasp around the table.

'But that could have been put there by anyone,' I said, playing dumb.

'He wrapped a plastic bag around the handle!' Emma laughed. 'He was trying to stay anonymous, but all the silly sod did was protect his fingerprints underneath!'

Bingo!

'And they're Mick Starr's fingerprints?' Claypole was riveted.

'They're not saying. At least, they aren't telling me. But it seems a bit of a coincidence that he is being detained for this long; they *must* have something on him.' Emma sat back and drained her glass. She had a real edge about her tonight, but stopped short of telling everyone about the night of Nicola's party.

I fetched another round. Mick's potential guilt was still the hot topic of conversation as I passed the drinks round the table.

'Sorry, Chip.' Terry Holden was speaking. 'We should change the subject.'

'No, no, it's fine …' I trailed off and then grimaced, shaking my head.

'What's up, Chip?' The Guv'nor sounded concerned.

'It's just … well, I hate to think the worst, especially of Mick, who's my friend – but something's been troubling me about Cycl– er, Andrew's passing.'

'Go on, Ted, go on …' Claypole was loving the drama.

'Well, I left Andrew on the cliff, watching the tufted puffin. Yes, he was getting pretty desperate to nail the perfect photograph –'

'And keep the tick to himself!' Emu butted in, clearly resentful. He waved his hand in apology and I continued.

'Well, Mick was potentially alone with him while I answered nature's call and texted you guys – and we've presumed until now that Cyclops slipped before Mick found his abandoned telescope, but what if –'

'Mick *pushed* him!' Claypole clapped his hands to his mouth in horror.

This was fast becoming my favourite funeral ever.

DECEMBER

Got the police call round this morning around half eight,
wanting to take a statement. First, the death of Matt Carter.

Was I aware of any dispute or disagreement between Mick
and Matt?

What was Mick's mood like in the days before Matt's death?

What were my movements around that time?

What did I know about the appearance of a 'masked shriek'?

'It's pronounced *"shrike"* ...' I had pointed out.

So many questions. Next it was Cyclops, meaning Claypole
must have done his bit. Then, less expectedly, questions about
Smoker Joe, John Perry (wasn't Mick quick to jump into his
board seat?) and even Keith Atkins and Mike Phelps. Phelps, it
seemed, suddenly remembered being pushed – and Mick was
standing right beside him as the tractor approached.

This was fantastic. The police were looking at pinning
everything on Mick. I said nothing of Abi's pregnancy or my
suspicions that Mick and she had been conducting an affair. As it
stood, the good lady circumstance seemed to be pointing every
finger in Mick's direction, and I couldn't risk there being any
distraction.

The officers were with me for nearly three hours, and would
be calling again for further questions. They would also need to
speak to Nicola at some point.

'Nic?' I'd said, with a shocked gasp. 'What's she got to do with
any of this?'

'It is nothing to worry about, Mr Banger –'

'*Bayn-ger.*'

'Sorry. We have a line of enquiry that Nicola may be able to help us with. We may also have to conduct some forensic tests within your property, though as yet that line of enquiry is still ongoing.'

Half an hour after the police left, Kerrie Starr turned up in tears.

'Oh Ted, I don't know who else to talk to …' I ushered her in. 'Mick's been charged with murder, Ted. Murder! He's no killer …'

The *Midsomer Murders* theme began to echo inside my head.

'What's he said to you, Kerrie?'

'Nothing, Ted. He just keeps saying that he's done some silly things and he's sorry. But when I push him – ask exactly what he's done – he just closes up and cries. I'm his *wife*, Ted, and he's completely shutting me out …'

Kerrie began to bawl: proper, big yelps of pain as she let out a flood of emotion. I moved around the table to offer her a cuddle and she stood at once, sinking into my chest, tears streaming. She was clutching me tightly. Really tightly. For a brief moment, I considered taking advantage of the situation. She was certainly vulnerable enough, and her distress had nudged open a small door in my mind; the door closing out all of the feelings of rejection, the pain of Abi's infidelity, the spectre of my own sexual inadequacies. Perhaps this was destiny. Kerrie and I pushed together by the indiscretions of our spouses.

Or maybe not. I slammed the door shut. *Focus, Ted, focus*, I told myself. *You're so close to the finish line. Don't lose it now.* Kerrie seemed to sense my rigidity and pulled away, wiping away her tears and sitting back down.

'Will you go and see him, Ted? Talk to him? Find out what he's hiding from me? I don't know who else to ask …'

I could hardly say no, though a visit would have to fit around the birding, especially at this late stage.

'I'll see him this week, Kerrie.'

It was three o'clock before I finally had time to sit down, check through my phone and pager messages and fire up the computer to check out the birding websites. Fortunately, it had been a quiet day, the only message of note being from Claypole, indicating that tomorrow's board meeting had been postponed until the New Year due to current 'extraordinary circumstances'.

The New Year meeting's going to be the big one. Thursday 3rd January. It'll be a long evening, as every outstanding claim will be resolved before the final totals are totted up. And I'll know, come the end of that night, whether or not I've done it.

December 6th 2007

399 species

Little has moved on the birding front this week and the four hundred-bird barrier is proving to be a difficult one to cross, but at least it means I had the time and inclination to go and visit Mick today. He's being held in Brixton prison; a bit of an awkward drive, though it gave me plenty of time to consider what I was going to say.

'Has Abi been to see you?' I thought I'd open on the front foot. Put Mick straight on the defensive.

'She's told you, then …' He already looked anxious.

'Nope. But you just have.' I folded my arms and Mick bowed his head.

'I'm sorry, Ted. I really am. It just got out of hand.'

'Getting my wife pregnant is a little 'out of hand', yes. I take it Kerrie doesn't know?' Mick shook his head. He really did look pathetic: pale-faced, gaunt, his lips permanently quivering as if he was on the verge of tears.

'They'll kill me, Ted. Kill me. Kerrie's brothers. If they find out. And it won't be nice …'

He was crying now. I gave him a moment and looked around me. I'd hoped to have this conversation through thick glass using those phones that they have in the movies, but we were in a small square room with a guard just outside the door, sitting on chairs that looked as though they'd been donated by the local primary school. My arse was getting seriously uncomfortable, though Mick's, I mused, was probably one hell of a lot sorer.

'Seems as though you're in the safest place, Mick.' I wasn't going to show him sympathy.

'Maybe, Ted, maybe … but it could get worse …' He looked

at me. I raised my eyebrows as a prompt for him to continue.

'I didn't do it. Matt, I mean. I didn't kill him. They think I did, though – found a fork with my fingerprints on and reckon I set a trap for him.'

'And did you?'

'Of course not, Ted, but they *planted* that fork.' He looked at me. 'I thought you might have planted it for a time, Ted, because of Abi ...'

'What, you mean when I borrowed your garden fork the other week?' I leant forward, hand on my chest, aghast and taking the moral high ground.

'I know, I know, Ted ... and you gave it back the next day. It's just that your head goes mad in a place like this.'

'Why would anyone plant evidence, Mick? I don't get it.'

Mick shuffled awkwardly.

'There's a motive, Ted. Sort of.' He looked up at me beseechingly, a shamed look on his face. 'At Nicola's party ... one of her friends had been a bit flirty early on.'

'And?'

'Kerrie went to sleep. I needed a drink of water. I went downstairs and there she was. Half-naked under a blanket. She was well pissed, Ted, but so was I and I couldn't resist ...'

'Poor you, Mick – must have been tough with your wife *and* your lover both asleep upstairs. You were lucky not to be caught.'

'I was caught, Ted. Matt saw us. He sent me a text the next day, and I shat myself. If that had got out ... whoa ... so I paid him a visit. Put the fear into him. Told him to keep his mouth shut.'

'Shagging a schoolgirl, Mick? That's dangerous ground. Very dangerous.' Mick nodded in earnest.

'And they're digging, Ted. Digging everywhere. They're saying I forced her. I don't know what she's telling them. And now they're playing mind games with me. Did I kill Cyclops. Did I poison Orville. Even the whole Smoker Joe thing's been dragged up; I don't know what the fuck I'm going to do.' Mick looked at me. He was a broken man. A desperate man. Perfect. 'If Kerrie finds out, Ted. If her brothers find out ... about the girl ... and

Abi … they'll see me dead. But not until they've broken every bone in my body and cut my balls off …'

I pressed the palms of my hands together and brought my fingertips up to my mouth, nodding slowly as I did so. Then I took a sharp breath and looked directly into Mick's eyes.

'You have a choice, Mick. One choice.' I lowered my voice. 'Take the rap for one of the other deaths. Cyclops, for example. You had a bit of an argument with him on top of the cliff. Then you scuffled and he fell. It was an accident. But you'll admit manslaughter. The police are happy; they've got their man for no further effort. Job done. They'll let the Matt Carter case slide, because they've got you for something else. You do five, maybe six years, and you're out.'

Mick was motionless. Mulling carefully over my words. He nodded his head, but then wrinkled his nose in doubt.

'It'll still come out, Ted, all of it. And they know people inside – they'll still get me.'

'But this way there's at least a chance that they won't, and it buys you time. Safe time. For whatever reason, Abi's not told Kerrie yet, so she probably won't –'

'And you, Ted?' Mick interrupted. 'Will you tell Kerrie?'

I sat back in my chair and rolled my eyes dramatically.

'No, Mick. Not if you do this. It's down to you and Abigail what you do about the baby, but at the end of the day – and despite her betrayal – I don't want Abi's name smeared in the dirt, for the girls' sake if not her own.'

Mick exhaled long and slow, and began to nod vigorously.

'I'll do it. Thank you, Ted. Thank you. You're a truer friend than I'll ever be.' He offered me his hand, but I shook my head and rose from my chair.

'So long, Mick.'

I gave a weak smile and left the room.

December 8th 2007

400 Species

Well, the four hundred is up. Quite a landmark. Many people strive to tick that many British boxes in a lifetime, so to do so in little over eleven months is quite extraordinary. For the record, the clincher was a Central Asian lesser whitethroat. *Sylvia curruca halimodendri*, as Cyclops would have said. What a shame he missed it.

Emu didn't, though. We ended up side by side this morning, telescopes lined up on a small area of scrub where the bird had shown yesterday. It wasn't my favourite twitch of the year, stood as we were on the side of a main road, just south of Lewes in Sussex. The whitethroat had taken up residence right next to a tidal river (the Ouse, I believe), which had obviously burst its banks in the last few weeks, because the whole area stank of stagnant sea water. I did get a chance to tap up Emu for a bit of chat, though.

'So, Rod, do you think the record will be broken this year?'

'Possibly. A couple of months ago I would have said definitely, but I've missed a few this autumn, and a lot of the biggies are ticks I made earlier in the year.'

Typical Emu. Arrogant prick. It's not only him who's in with a shout.

'I reckon I might threaten it,' I said, coyly. 'The record, I mean. Got a few to get in the next few weeks, though.' Emu raised an eyebrow in a blatant display of contempt. He didn't believe me, though rather brilliantly, it was because he didn't think it possible. I squeezed him some more. 'So, Emu – how many have you got so far?'

Emu smiled.

'Now that would be telling, Chip – but, like I said, I have an outside chance of breaking the record, so if you're there or thereabouts, you may just pip me.' He put his binoculars to his eyes and crumpled his lips together. He was stifling a laugh – his flaring nostrils gave him away.

At that moment I felt like ramming his scope up his arse, but now, with time to reflect, I'm glad I kept my cool. He was telling the truth about his total, I'm certain of it. He implied that he was a little way off the record, whereas I'm already eleven ticks past it. And his arrogance will be his downfall. He's certain that I'm no threat to him or the record, and that can't help but count against him. In Emu's world, the result is academic – and now he's simply easing his way to the finish line, picking up the easy ticks that remain. He may have felt threatened by Matt Carter or Mike Phelps, and certainly Cyclops, but now they're out of the running, he's overlooked the Rook of the Year. The guy who's going to take his crown.

I got home to a letter from Whitcombe today, requesting a home visit. He wants to come here with an HR woman to discuss how they might be able to help with my ongoing illness. He can screw himself if he thinks that's going to happen before the New Year, and frankly, I'd rather he brought one of the office cleaners round rather than a pompous Human Resources woman; the house is an absolute state. I'm going to have to get the girls into line and pulling their weight. I sat down on the sofa last night, moved a cushion, and found a pair of boxer shorts. They weren't mine. Christ knows how long they've been there, but it isn't hard to imagine the reason they were there: both Josh and Jake seem to spend more nights here than they do in their own homes, and one of them's clearly got frisky with one of my daughters on my couch. Thank God neither of the policemen chose that seat yesterday.

Three more hours of questions; this time, though, all about Cyclops. They were clearly buoyed by Mick's confession, but wanted to upgrade his slant from manslaughter to murder. Did I think it was premeditated, they kept asking, in a thousand different guises and I certainly didn't suggest it hadn't been.

No sooner had they left than Kerrie arrived in tears again.

'Oh, Ted. He's *killed* a man!'

'So I hear, Kerrie …'

Again, as I hugged Kerrie in support, my thoughts began to wander toward the most basic of male urges, but I shrugged it off and sat her down.

'I'm afraid it gets even worse, Kerrie.' I swallowed hard. 'Abi's pregnant. And Mick's the father. They've been carrying on behind our backs.' I really did use a cheesy turn of phrase to deliver such brutal news, but it was at the moment when I actually said the words out loud and made it real that it really hit me. My wife and my best friend. The ultimate betrayal. Kerrie went into shock, her face draining of all colour. For a moment I thought she was going to faint, but instead she just sat stock still with one hand to her mouth, her eyes unblinking.

After five minutes or so I got fed up with her expression and reached for a couple of glasses and an unopened bottle of malt. I needed a drink, though it took Kerrie to have a couple before she finally spoke.

'How, Ted? And when?'

'Erm, I'm not su–'

'And when's Abi due?'

'Not sure, to be ho–'

'Where did they *do it*?'

Kerrie had leapt from blank stupefaction to amphetamine-fuelled mania in a matter of seconds. The questions kept coming, and perhaps it was no bad thing that they did, because I had no real answers. Since putting two and two together, I hadn't considered the logistical aspect of Abi's affair; it had been irrelevant to me when I was so close to the big prize. But should I have cared? Should I have demanded the (not literal) ins and outs – the dates; the motives; the feelings; the guilt? Perhaps I'd been in shock. Or denial. Perhaps I didn't care because I didn't love Abi.

Kerrie and I must have talked for a good hour and a half. It was only Lucy, arriving home from work, who stopped us opening a second bottle. She surveyed the scene, clocked the all-but-empty bottle of scotch on the table and realised that Kerrie probably needed to go home.

'I'll drive you,' she'd said to Kerrie. Lucy can drive? I don't even remember her taking a test.

I must have been asleep on the sofa before Lucy returned, because that's where I woke up in the early hours of this morning. Lucy, presumably, had laid a blanket over me and put a glass of water on the coffee table. I was grateful for both, and drained the water before reaching for my phones. It had been the text from Emu about the Central Asian lesser whitethroat; news which had certainly straightened my head.

A good, solid week: three more ticks, yet another trip to Scilly
(for a lesser scaup) and word from Cornish Tom, who I saw
in Scilly, that Emu's been laid up with flu (sadly not the avian
variety) and has missed both the scaup this week and the Eastern
black redstart that I ticked in Suffolk on Tuesday. I feel bloody
great. The girls went out to buy a Christmas tree and then spent
the afternoon decorating it, Lucy turned her hand to making
mulled wine, which we sipped, warm, this evening, and thanks to
Kerrie, who turned up on Monday with a box of cleaning stuff
and *insisted* I let her in, the house is looking neat and tidy. We
even managed to persuade Nicola to have a takeaway other than
Chinese. It's late evening now and I'm full of curry and spicy
wine, though I should just about have room for the whisky in my
hand.

I think my favourite part of today came this morning, though
it was possibly due to relief as much as anything. The doorbell
went at about ten. I was still in my dressing gown, having
ascertained first thing that nothing much was showing today. I
thought it was most likely the postman, but on swinging the door
open, I came face to face with two man-mountains. It was two-
thirds of the Bowers Boys.

'Ted?' The nearer one asked. I nodded.

'We're Kerrie's brothers – dunno if you remember. Can we,
er, come in? Just for a quick chat?' I nodded again, without really
thinking straight, and before I knew it they were in my hallway
taking off their boots, which was very polite of them.

'Er … can I get you guys a drink?' I closed the front door as
I spoke, surreptitiously flicking up the latch as I did so – I might

need to make a run for it, and undoing the lock would speed up my escape.

'We're fine, Ted, thank you – we just want a couple of minutes of your time.'

I was shitting myself. What did they want? I thought back to last Friday, when Kerrie was here. Perhaps she felt me getting slightly aroused as I comforted her. Perhaps they hadn't taken kindly to me getting their sister smashed on whisky. I'd only been trying to help.

I ushered them into the lounge where they shared a sofa, their combined width easily filling it. I sat down opposite them and smiled awkwardly.

'How can I help you, gentlemen?' I asked. I'd met them before. I'd met all three brothers before. But I could never remember their names, let alone who was who. I hoped to God that I wouldn't offend them; call them something stupid, or disrespect them by only calling them 'mate'.

The one nearest me, who looked to be the elder of the two, spoke again.

'Ted. Kerrie's told us about Mick. And about him carrying on with your wife –'

'And getting her up the duff,' the other brother interjected.

'And getting her *pregnant*, yes.' The elder one was definitely the more eloquent. He continued, 'Now, Ted. Mick's our brother-in-law, and, therefore, he's family. *Our* family.'

'Okay …' I didn't know what else to say.

'We have strong family ethics, Ted. Very strong.'

I nodded. The situation was still very much in the balance. I wondered if either of the girls were in, or either boyfriend. If Jake and Josh were both here, they might be able to make a charge, take both Bowers brothers by surprise, and I could make a dash for the door and call the police.

I worried needlessly, it turned out.

'Mick Starr has besmirched our family name.' That elder brother really was eloquent. 'He's caused offence and distress to you and your family. For that, we want to apologise. We are in your debt.'

Wow. For a moment I wielded a mighty weapon. The Bowers Boys, there to do my bidding. They could drive me to every twitch. Clear the prime spot. Stand in a small semicircle five feet from me, shades on, arms relaxed but not folded – they might need to move at any given moment. Coiled springs. Then in the evening they would escort me on a night out. We'd be in York, and Emma would be there with her spotty boyfriend and his mates. They would be disrespecting her; making a fool of her. I would walk up to them, and simply say, 'Out. Now.' And they would pause and then laugh and say, 'You and whose army, mate?' and I would step to one side, and the three Bowers Boys would step out of the shadows and I'd give a half-smile as Emma clung gratefully to my arm. Blimey, I can see how Mick used to get so power-hungry, though I'm not sure why Emma cropped up in my daydream of danger.

I glanced at both brothers.

'Thank you,' I said, 'but it's no problem, really …' They looked at one another, and then the younger one spoke.

'But don't you want us to do 'im?' – he looked puzzled – 'rough him up a bit? Maybe snip off his –' The elder brother held his hand up toward his sibling and then turned to me, offering a quizzical look. It was up to me. Did I want Mick to take a pasting, or worse?

'He's in prison, though …?' I asked the question as I considered.

'Not an issue,' the elder brother said dismissively.

I felt a pang of guilt. Mick may well have violated our friendship in the most unforgivable manner, but I'd already stitched him up. Plus, I'd promised that I'd keep my mouth shut about his misdemeanours with absolutely no intention of doing so. On the flip side, though, if he was silenced, none of the events of the last twelve months could come back and bite me on the arse.

No, I couldn't do it.

'It's okay, gentlemen. Thank you, but I wouldn't like anything to happen to Mick on my account.'

The two brothers looked at each other with puzzled

expressions. The elder one rose to his feet and offered me his hand, which I shook.

'Very well, Ted. Not a bother.'

'Thanks. Maybe see you guys for a beer sometime?' I'm not sure why I made the suggestion, but it was well received.

'I'd like that – we'd all like that.' The elder brother smiled, and headed for the door. The younger Bowers also shook my hand, but after he had made his way into the hall and put his boots back on, he turned and cocked his head in thought.

'You won't mind if we do 'im anyway, will ya?' he asked.

The house looked like Santa's grotto when I got home this evening. Kerrie'd been round again to give the place a proper clean, and Lucy seemed to have spent most of her wages on tinsel and baubles. I can't deny that it looks nice – cosy, even – and thankfully Lucy's kept her expansive ornament collection limited to indoors, unlike the house on the corner of our close. Their place gets more garish every year, and they now have a ten-foot illuminated Santa Claus crawling across their roof. Where do you buy this stuff? They justify the light pollution and visual offence by sitting a little money box on their picket fencing with a note attached: 'This is for charity', they claim, and invite donations. Bollocks. This is just a blatant plea for attention.

The girls have invited Kerrie round for Christmas day. I don't mind. In fact, to be honest, I don't know where I'll *be* on Christmas Day – I certainly can't risk missing a tick for the sake of a glorified Sunday roast and *Finding Nemo*. The girls seem happy to carry on as if my presence is optional; they blame my indifference on the treachery of Abi and Mick, and I'm more than happy to let them think that. I know Abi was hoping to come home for Christmas Day, but instead, the girls will go over to see her at their grandparents' on Boxing Day. My mother will be here, as usual, as will, I presume, both Nic and Lucy's boyfriends. It'll be quite a houseful. I rather hope something rare turns up in Scotland on Christmas Eve …

Well, I might not be in Scotland, but I almost got my wish. A slender-billed curlew was reported last night among a small flock of mixed waders in a flooded meadow near Morpeth, Northumberland. My first reaction was utter scepticism: this was one of the rarest birds in the world and hadn't been reported in Europe for nearly ten years – surely someone had found a rogue whimbrel, or a standard curlew with light plumage, and got their ID wrong. More likely was that someone had thought it might cheer up their Christmas to ruin hundreds of other people's, and would laugh from a distance as desperate birders waded through the floodwaters of the river Wansbeck.

But then the board phone began to stir into life with a surprisingly positive bent. Tim Rettard-Smith, a seasoned birder, had witnessed the bird and sent a photo direct to Claypole. He was convinced enough not just to pack his overnight bag and dust off his telescope, but to make noises in the President's direction and, according to Terry Holden (via Mike Phelps), the President was considering making the trip him- or herself. No sooner than I picked up the first really promising report, I was checking room availability in Morpeth. There weren't many vacancies, so I had to book a three-night package (including Christmas dinner) at what's turned out to be quite a charming old coaching inn. I could have made it back home tonight, but having booked in and noticed the smiling barmaids and open fire, I decided that slender-billed or not, I would be spending Christmas here.

I struggled to find the twitch. Normally it's simply a case of looking for the rake of parked cars, but I couldn't find any, instead driving aimlessly around country lanes for at least an hour. Then I spotted Emu's Saab parked down a little wooded track and tucked the Focus in behind him – if anyone had stumbled on the curlew, it would be Emu.

He took a bit of finding. Not because he had walked far, but because he was dressed in green, and blended well into the undergrowth. I spotted movement in the binoculars, though, and clocked him squatting near the riverbank just behind a barbed wire fence, telescope pointing across the adjacent flood meadow. I worked my way around a tangle of brambles and began picking a route toward him, through the trees. He hadn't heard or seen me – or at least, he hadn't acknowledged me – and as I got to within fifty yards or so I paused, breathing slowly and silently through my mouth. A flicker of possibility had presented itself.

It was specking with rain. Large, cold, sleety drops that slapped hard as they touched down – not as loud as hail, but still cracking like broken twigs. Perfect cover for my footfalls. About fifteen feet behind Emu was a pile of wood; not logs, as such, but the remnants of some tree surgery or clearance. There were a couple of weighty looking lumps right on the top – if I could make it that far without alerting him, I could definitely take two further strides and crack him over the back of the head before he had any chance to argue.

I slipped closer, watching my feet and rolling them into the ground, keeping noise to a minimum. I worked my way directly behind him, where the tree trunks all but merged together, creating a perfect shield. Still he scanned; methodical, long sweeps of the water meadow. Still I moved forward; gently, gently. And then I was there, beside the wood pile. The very top stick was a brute – long, solid, as thick as my arm – but it felt balanced in my hand as I gently gripped and lifted. It would do some serious damage. I stopped all movement for a moment, and counted three slow breaths.

Three long quick strides and I would be upon him, slamming the club down onto his crown. One blow might do it, and two or three certainly would, before I dragged him over to the riverbank and cast him away …

I paused. For what purpose, though? To what end? I must, surely, be ahead of him, leading the competition. There would be little chance of him catching up with just a week left. If he was, somehow, beating me, I would be unlikely to catch him up – and then I risked losing to a dead man. Besides, I wasn't going to get away with *this*. There were too many points of evidence. And then what? All the fingers of guilt currently pointing in Mick's direction would start to waver and come swinging around to me. And then, finally, I realised what the clincher was, and as I loosened my grip on the stick and let it back on the pile, I almost laughed.

On January 3rd when the final totals are verified and the winner announced, I want to be looking at Emu's face. I want to see that smug, arrogant expression dissolve into shock as he realises that I, Edward Banger, haven't just royally kicked his arse, but smeared his record and all other records into insignificance.

We saw the slender billed curlew just before tea time. There were a few of us gathered by that point, and camera shutters clattered as if at a film premiere. Claypole cried. Unashamedly. Even I too felt myself fill, briefly, with emotion: here was a bird on the brink of extinction. Yes, it was far from spectacular; it was smaller and duller than the other curlews that probed the mud around it. But it was living history.

It was definitely the first twitch where I hadn't felt the urge to dash as soon as it was in the bag. I stayed with everyone until the light had almost gone, when the flock in front of us took flight and headed across river – off to roost – and we all headed back here to the St Cuthbert's Arms, to raise a glass and warm our hands by the fire.

December 31st 2007

408 species

Just one more tick, but a good one: the chestnut-sided warbler
Emu gripped back in October.

Four hundred and eight species. Ridiculous.

JANUARY 2008

Results

1st	Edward Banger	408	
2nd	Rod Smyth	389	
3rd	Cyril Nutkin	381	
4th	Andrew Johnson (deceased)	379	
5th	Leighton Stewart	378	
6th	Michael Phelps	377	
6th	Zachery Bader	377	
8th	Emma-Erin Kenton	375	*Rook of the Year*
9th	Thomas Spargo	373	
10th	Oliver Mills	372	
10th	Anthony Rufus Adamson	372	

Subscribers

Unbound is a new kind of publishing house. Our books are funded directly by readers. This was a very popular idea during the late eighteenth and early nineteenth centuries. Now we have revived it for the internet age. It allows authors to write the books they really want to write and readers to support the writing they would most like to see published.

The names listed below are of readers who have pledged their support and made this book happen. If you'd like to join them, visit: www.unbound.co.uk.

Edward Allen
Justin Allen
Saira Amin
Debbie Apted
Helen Arnold
Caroline Bainbridge
Derren Ball
Damon Barker
Tanina Baronello
Emma Bayliss
Jessie Baynes
Jon Berry
Victoria Berry
Sue & Phil Bird
Mary Brazier
Catherine Bridge

Naomi Browne
Alison Burns
Laura Burt
Sarah Butterworth
Bill Buzzard
Beccy Byrne
Fay Cameron-Clarke
George Campari
Xander Cansell
Andrew Carless
Lyn Carless
Allan Chard
Ian Clark
Steve Clark
Andrew Clist
Stevyn Colgan

Laura Cook
Brian Crowe
Emma Cullen
Rachel Dance
Steve Dance
Les & Cheryl Darlington
Gavin Davis
Mel Dean
Simon Difford
Stephanie Downes
Jan Doyle
Lawrence T Doyle
Katrina Ellis
Rob Ellis
Carlien Els
Tanya Fell
Gregory Fenby Taylor
Jeannie Ferguson
Charles Fernyhough
Bader Fitch
Ben Fitch
Bertie Fitch
Cath Fitch
Cerelia Fitch
Ilana Fox
Helen Frankish
Isobel Frankish
Paul Fuller
Stewart Fuller
Hilary Gallo
Suzanne Gander
Jules Gibson
Gerald Gittens
Dave Goodman
Katherine Green
Mandy Halsall

Edward Hancox
Craig Harper
Nick & Lynne Harris
Caitlin Harvey
George Hay
E O Higgins
Robin Humphreys
David Hutchinson
Jeannine James
Melanie James
Karine Jegard
David Jones
Rachael Kerr
Jan Kewley
Dan Kieran
Kevin Kieran
Andreas Lammers
Jimmy Leach
Mike Lewis
Henry Littlechild
Denise Littlejohns
Rebecca Lynn
Evan Mac Cann
Oisín Mac Cann
Sadie Mac Cann
Sarah Mac Cann
Andy Macrae
Stuart McKears
Andy Maple
Michael Maw
Dede Millar
Janis Milne
Margo Milne
John Mitchinson
Richard Montagu
Bobby Moore

Geoff Morgan
Heather Muddiman
John Muddiman
Benjamin Munday
Andy Munnings
Mr & Mrs Newington
Val Newington
John Oakshott
Cath O'Brien
Cath & Mark O'Brien
Mark O'Brien
Paul Omeara
Hugh Ortega Breton
Guy Osborne
Greg O'Toole
Torquill Pagdin
Rosie Palmer
Geoff Parr
Geoffrey Parr
Jill Parr
JP Parr
Kevin Parr
Richard Parr
Sue Parr
Sukey Parr
Bob Parrish
Kirk Parsons
Hili Pate
Dan Perry
Vivienne Plewes
Lawrence Pointer
Ann Pointing
Justin Pollard
Rachel Poulton
Heather Price
Stan Pugh

Sheila Rees
Chris Revett
Josie Rhisiart
Philip Riches
James Robbins
Chris Rocker
Christoph Sander
Chris Semple
Louisa Semple
Anna Simmonds
Richard Smedley
Pete Smith
Therese Smith
Nat Snell
Karen Speechley
Matt Spence
Janette Staton
Liisa Steele
David Stelling
Adam Stevens
Martin Stevens
Phil Stevens
Tina Stevens
Ash Stewart
Colin Stokes
Camilla Stoppani
Michael Storey
John Stubbs
Blake Stubley
Sarah Sutton
Harriet Swift-Marshall
Jenny Tanner
Philip Tatham
Adam Topping
Ewan Topping
Jan Topping

Kieran Topping
Sally-Ann Vesey-Thompson
Ian Vince
Lisa Wallis
Peter Watkins
Helen Watts

Ian Williams
Alex Yates
Camilla Yates
Chris Yates
Heather York
Mary Young

Acknowledgements

Foremost, my thanks to everyone who pledged money to the cause and whose names are listed in the back pages of this book. It simply wouldn't have happened without you.

Joining the Unbound adventure has been a privilege and the camaraderie between authors something quite unique. I have had huge support from my fellow scribes – thank you.

As for the Unbounders themselves, well, they have been magnificent – though special thanks must go to Isobel Frankish, Caitlin Harvey and Cathy Hurren.

Thanks to Ian Robins for his camera work, Hugh Ortega Breton for dying so well so many times and Will Yates for letting Memotone put sound to it.

My ma and pa Jill and Geoff, brother Richard, sister Cath, in-laws, aunts, uncles, cousins and those more distantly related have been immense in their support – as have so many friends, new and old.

Special mention for those who took it upon themselves to champion the cause: Cath Fitch, Ben Fitch, Martin Stevens, Jon Berry, Colin Stokes, Kieran Topping, Mel James, Lawrence Pointer, Matt Spence, Matt Merritt, Kirk Parsons, all at Bird Watching magazine, and a multitude of others.

Without the Twitchers of Britain I wouldn't have had a plot – no one does obsession quite like us – thank you.

I wouldn't have made it past page one but for the encouragement of Chris Yates, wonderful support from my wife Sue, and the unwavering belief and friendship of Dan Kieran. Thank you.

A NOTE ABOUT THE TYPEFACE

The serif Garamond typeface is named after punch-cutter
Claude Garamont (1480–1561), who came from a family of
French printers, and is widely acknowledged for its grace and
fluidity, though Garamont himself is said to have claimed 'the art
I practice is but a small thing'. Among its most definitive features
are the small bowl of the a and narrow eye of the e, along with
the crossed w. It is one of the most popular 'early' typefaces
in the readily available catalogue of fonts in standard word-
processing programmes, and is also one of the most eco-friendly
typefaces for printing in terms of ink consumption. Garamont's
career began in 1540 with the commission to punch-cut the
grecs du roi, a series of Greek letters which were used by Robert
Estienne on behalf of the French king Francis I. In a more
recent century, the iconic children's picture books of Dr. Seuss
were set in a version of Garamond.

Garamont died in 1561 shortly after drawing up his will in
which, after providing for his second wife, he instructed 'the
surplus of all his goods' to be sold by a friend in order to pay for
his elderly mother's care.

With the rise in popularity of the Garamond typeface
has come an ongoing debate over the contentious issue of
the spelling of Claude Garamont's name; we have taken the
lead of Jeanne Veyrin-Forrer, whose comprehensive research
concluded that since Garamont signed his own name with a t,
perhaps the rest of the world should follow suit.

Chapter and running heads are set in Amatic SC, which was
created by Vernon Adams.